A Web

"I did not destroy ⟨...⟩ soothingly. "Nor did ⟨...⟩

Samidar backed a⟨...⟩ step. Her senses reeled. "They attacked and killed that woman," she challenged. "Tried to take a little girl."

The soft weblight and Eetha's voice had a mesmeric quality. "Yes," Eetha whispered. "A sweet child. As I said, I must eat."

With a shock, Samidar snapped her head up. Eetha had worked her magic well. She found herself already ensnared by coils of fine webbing, lying nearly cocooned, suspended high in the air in the great web itself.

Eetha straddled her on eight horrible legs, and she bent her face near to Samidar's. "The villagers are bound to me by spells and cannot flee. I know their flavor too well. You, an outsider, I shall savor."

From "The Woman Who Loved Death"
by Robin Wayne Bailey

SPELL FANTASTIC

Edited by
Martin H. Greenberg
and Larry Segriff

DAW BOOKS, INC.
DONALD A. WOLLHEIM, FOUNDER
375 Hudson Street, New York, NY 10014

ELIZABETH R. WOLLHEIM
SHEILA E. GILBERT
PUBLISHERS

ACKNOWLEDGMENTS

Introduction © 2000 by Larry Segriff.

Saving Face © 2000 by Kristine Kathryn Rusch.

A Spatter of Later Stars © 2000 by Nina Kiriki Hoffman.

The Woman Who Loved Death © 2000
  by Robin Wayne Bailey.

Sacrifice © 2000 by Michelle West.

Spellsword © 2000 by Jane Lindskold.

Curse of the Dellingrs © 2000
  by Mickey Zucker Reichert.

For the Life of Sheila Morgan © 2000
  by Dennis L. McKiernan.

The Sagebrush Brujo *Meets the Last of The Platters or
  Why Do We Live in LA?* © 2000 by John DeChancie.

To Catch a Thief © 2000 by Lisanne Norman.

The Thronespell © 2000 by Diana L. Paxson.

And King Hereafter © 2000 by Rosemary Edghill.

The Midas Spell © 2000 by Julie E. Czerneda.

Embracing the Mystery © 2000 by Charles de Lint.

CONTENTS

INTRODUCTION
by Larry Segriff

I've always been in love with the idea of magic. To cast a spell and rid myself of the schoolyard bully. To win the heart of the pretty blonde in the fourth row of my Language Arts class. To ride the wind on wings of magic, flying like a dragon through space and time. These were the dreams I had, first as a child, then as a teenager riddled with acne and angst, and then as a young adult with less acne but even more angst.

These days, my dreams are somewhat smaller. I have found my own forms of magic, both in the life my family is building and in the illusions I strive to weave at the keyboard. Because of this, or because of the way I've grown and changed through the years, given a chance at magic today I would set my sights lower and closer to home. If my magic were strong enough, if it were real enough, I would cast a spell to protect my daughters from much of what I see lying in wait for them: boys, drugs, learning to drive, leaving home.

Given a choice, given the power, I would put more hours in a day, and more days in a life. I would change things to give me more time to treasure this day, and the one tomorrow, and the one after that. I would slow each moment's passing so that I could have more time with my family, more time with my books, more time to live, to think, to dream, to be.

Those are the magics I wish for: protection for those I love, and time to spend with them. Small magics, perhaps, but important, at least to me and mine.

This book is about bigger dreams, bigger magics, bigger spells. We've asked thirteen of today's top authors to let us peek inside their own personal grimoires, their private collection of spells. And unlike my own small versions, these magics are real, these spells work—if sometimes in unexpected ways—and these dreams can come true, if one is willing to pay the price.

SAVING FACE
by *Kristine Kathryn Rusch*

Kristine Kathryn Rusch has worked as an editor at such places as Pulphouse publishing and most recently *The Magazine of Fantasy & Science Fiction.* Her recent novels include the Star Trek novel *Double Helix: Vectors* and the stand-alone novel *The Tenth Planet,* both cowritten with her husband, fellow author Dean Wesley Smith. Her short fiction appears in many anthologies and magazines, among them *Once Upon A Crime, First Contact, Alien Abductions,* and *Wizard Fantastic.* A winner of the World Fantasy Award, she lives in Oregon.

The bell above the shop door tinkled. Winston looked up in surprise. It was February, it was Tuesday, and it was raining—the hard cold downpour that made all but the hardiest locals complain. Tourists rarely came to Seavy Village in February, and if they did, they spent most of their time holed up in a hotel room staring at the ocean. They certainly didn't come to a run-down magic store in a run-down part of town.

"Hey, big guy." Ruby, his familiar, stood underneath the beaded curtain that hid the back lab from the storefront. She was still a kitten, although she didn't talk like one. She never had, really. But she was healthier than she had been when he found her. Her black coat shone now, and she had the lanky swagger most normal six-month-olds had. "You got a customer."

3

"Thanks, Ruby," he said softly and got up from his stool. His back hurt. He'd been mixing potions all morning, filling mail orders that would go out in the afternoon's UPS. The summertime tourist trade supplemented his income. He kept the store for them, but with the advent of the Internet, he really didn't need the extra advertising. The store just gave him and Ruby a place to spend their days.

He walked through the beaded curtain and stopped as he entered the narrow storefront. A woman stood near the dirty display window, studying a shelf of cut glass potion bottles. All were empty and most were antiques, things he had acquired in trade or found in the junk shops that ran along this stretch of Highway 101.

She looked up when she saw him. She was slight, with oval-shaped brown eyes hidden by large glasses. Her dark hair was pulled away from her face, in a style too severe for her round features. Still, he could see, no matter how hard she tried to hide it, she was very beautiful.

"Are you Winston?" she asked.

He nodded, his heart in his throat. People never came to the store looking for him. They came to find baubles, silly souvenirs from their vacations.

Ruby had come up beside him. She leaped on the counter and lay across it. She knew his history, knew that he had run from San Francisco twenty years before with the police on his heels. He'd always tried to convince himself that no one cared about him, no one would come to the Oregon Coast looking for him. He had changed his name, and he was twenty years older.

He hadn't made a mistake since.

"I've come from Ohio," the woman said. "I've been looking for you."

It was the tiny movement, the double clasp of her hands over her purse strap, the tension in her shoulders that made him realize she was afraid of him.

No one had ever been afraid of him, even after they had found out what he was. He was a small wizard with even smaller magics, not like his mentor who could have destroyed an entire town with the snap of a finger, or the crazed woman he'd met at a Nevada roadside twenty years before, who had burned up her entire family—even the scattered members all over the country—simply by cursing them.

"Looking for me?" he repeated, rather stupidly. He felt a flush build in his cheeks. Would the police still be interested, all these years later?

"Yes. Looking for you." She glanced around, her gaze stopping on the mass market items he kept for the tourists—the cheap magic kits, the books on magic tricks, the pinwheels and the silly jewelry. "Are we alone here?"

"Except for Ruby," he said, putting his hand on the cat's silken back. "But she knows all my secrets."

The woman looked at Ruby as if she were seeing the cat for the first time. "I was told by a man in New Orleans that you could help me."

Winston felt a bit of relief then. Many of his referrals came from New Orleans, from the voodoo shops and the tourist traps, places his shop had been modeled on. Many of his kind found a refuge on Bourbon Street, where no one questioned oddity of any kind.

"Then he should have told you that you didn't have to come here," Winston said gently. "I do most of my business by mail."

Her gaze met his. The glasses distorted her eyes slightly, making the lashes larger than they should have been, the eyes bigger and more vulnerable.

She shook her head. "He said this was the one time I would have to come."

Winston moved closer. "What do you need?"

"I don't know," she said. "I thought you would."

His smile was small. This was why he hated having customers come in person. They expected more from him. They expected him to be like Gandalf the Great or like the wizards they'd seen on television. All knowing, all powerful, charismatic and forceful and strong.

"I'm afraid I'm not psychic," he said.

She sighed and loosened her grip slightly on her purse. "I know," she said. "I guess I was looking more for a solution, one I haven't been able to come up with."

He was silent. He didn't diagnose. He was like a pharmacist. Someone else diagnosed and prescribed. He fulfilled the order.

"The man in New Orleans said you were the most creative wizard he'd ever met. He said you'd know what to do."

The compliment didn't move him. "I have a small talent," he said. "Nothing that would warrant a trip from Ohio."

He turned his back on her and parted the beaded curtain. Ruby jumped off the counter and loped toward the back.

"Please," the woman said. "Just listen to me?"

Perhaps it was the plaintive note in her voice. Perhaps it was her beauty, hidden behind the inappropriate hairstyle and her severe clothing. Perhaps it was the way she moved, like a person who expected rejection from every place she turned.

He bowed his head. Ruby cursed softly, something about dogs and men and stupidity.

"All right," he said. "But I guess you'd best come back here."

He never let anyone inside his inner sanctum. For the nineteen years he'd owned the shop, ever since he'd arrived in Seavy Village, he'd been alone except for his familiars. First Buster, who arrived with the cliff house that Winston rented and finally bought, and now Ruby, who'd appeared the day after Buster died.

The woman held the beaded curtains apart and stared at the filled bottles, the careful labels, the cluttered worktable. It seemed to Winston that her skin had paled considerably.

"I don't think this is such a good idea after all," she said.

He waited. This was new for him as well.

After a moment, she let the curtains drop. They clicked against each other. He started to follow her, but Ruby moved in his path.

"That's trouble," Ruby said.

The bell over the door jangled, and then he heard the door click shut.

"She came all the way from Ohio," he said.

"Yeah," Ruby said, sarcasm in her tone. "By way of New Orleans."

He concentrated on his cat. Her yellow eyes filled her black face. "Do you even know where Ohio is?"

She bristled. "I watch TV, same as you."

He nodded, not quite sure how to take that, and let himself out of the beaded curtains. The front of the shop felt emptier and colder than usual, and he couldn't shake the feeling that he'd made some kind of mistake.

When the bell above his door jangled the next afternoon, Winston got off his stool and headed for the beaded curtain. Ruby watched him from her basket, her golden eyes hooded. She had said nothing the night before, and her silence showed her disapproval of the woman visitor. Ruby usually commented on everything.

Winston drew the beaded curtain back, an apology on his lips, when he stopped. A policeman stood there, looking uncomfortable.

His rumpled uniform proclaimed him a member of the small Seavy Village police force, but Winston had never seen him before. The man was red-headed, freckled, and young enough to be his son.

"Mr. Karpathian?" The young man stood in the center of the store, his cap beneath his arm like a recruit at graduation.

"Yes." Winston let the beaded curtain close behind him.

"Mind if I talk to you, sir?"

This was it, then. He had thought the statute of limitations was up, thought, perhaps, times had changed just enough. In his first days on his own, he had believed he didn't need a familiar to keep his magic from curdling. He had mixed potions and fulfilled orders, but they had spoiled. A young woman who had special ordered an aphrodisiac nearly died. Fortunately her boyfriend hadn't tried it, and he had gotten her to the emergency room. The cops thought it a drug overdose, and thought Winston the supplier. He had left San Francisco on a dead run, stopping only when he saw Seavy Village and its gothic landscape.

"Sir?"

He realized he hadn't answered, hadn't done anything except stare into space like a man numbed by time.

"I'm sorry," he said. "You had a question?"

"Yes, sir." The policeman glanced at the glistening glass bottles, and then took a step forward. "Yesterday, did a woman come to see you? From Ohio?"

Winston felt his shoulders relax slightly. Ruby leaned against his lower leg. He hadn't even realized she had come out of the back room.

"Yes."

He still couldn't bring himself to offer information to the police. Perhaps it was his natural caution, perhaps it was his generation, or perhaps it was that experience in San Francisco, which taught him he would always be misjudged.

"Is this her?" The officer held what looked to be a blow-up of a driver's license photo. The woman in it didn't wear glasses, and her hair flowed about her shoulders, but she had that stricken look most people got before the flash at the DMV.

"Yes," Winston said, still not sure what this was about.

"Trouble," Ruby whispered from the floor.

The officer frowned, just a bit, as if he had heard something, but didn't know what. "She was found dead in her hotel room this morning, sir."

Winston drew in his breath, and gripped the edge of the counter. *I didn't do it,* he wanted to say. *I didn't sell her anything. I only spoke to her for a few minutes.*

"What happened?" he managed to ask.

"It was murder," the officer said. "But we're not releasing any of the details."

Winston nodded, as if he understood that when, in truth, he didn't. "I'm sorry."

"Did you know her well?"

Winston shook his head. He felt slightly sluggish. He didn't want to leave Seavy Village. He'd lived here too long. But he didn't want to be associated with a murder. He couldn't afford to have attention drawn to himself.

"She came into my shop for the first time yesterday," he said. "I didn't even know her name."

"Her name was Gwen Winnick," the officer said, as if that should jog Winston's memory. It did not. All it did was make him think, sadly, that her name didn't suit her. "She had your name in a notebook. She had circled it."

He nodded. As much truth as possible, then. It was the only thing he could do. "She said she had come all the way from Ohio to see me."

"Why would she do that?"

Winston shrugged. "She never told me. She said a man in New Orleans gave her my name."

"A Boyce Theriot?"

Boyce. Of course. They had exchanged a lot of business over the years. "I don't know," Winston said. "She didn't tell me that either."

"What did she tell you?"

"That she had come from Ohio, looking for me." Ruby was leaning hard against him now. A warning? Or support? "That she needed some sort of advice. I told her I didn't give advice, and that I did most of my work by mail order. She said she'd still like to ask me something, so I invited her into my workroom in the back. She opened the beaded curtains and stopped, said she couldn't do this after all, and left."

"That was it?"

Winston nodded.

"She came all the way from Ohio and then turned away at the last moment?"

"To be honest," Winston said, "I kinda thought you were her. I expected her to come back."

"Why?"

"For that very reason. Because she had come so far."

The officer nodded. "You never saw her before?"

"No."

"Ever been to Ohio?"

"No."

"Did she tell you someone was following her?"

"No." Winston frowned. "Was someone?"

"Apparently. That's what she told the desk clerk. Under no circumstances was he to let anyone in her room." The officer flushed slightly as if he'd said too much. He stared at the pinwheels, then looked at Winston. "What kind of store is this anyway?"

"A magic shop," Winston said. "It's for the tourists, mostly."

That was what he told all the locals. Most of them bought it.

"Then what do you do mail order?"

Winston smiled. His smile was the soft, practiced one he gave to people who wouldn't understand, people he didn't want to ask any more questions. "I send out spells."

"Spells?"

Winston nodded. "You know," he said. "Specialized tricks." He could say that without lying because he did send out a few, usually to a tourist who had stopped in during the summer, and wanted to learn a few special moves to impress the neighborhood children or the bar crowd.

"Oh," the officer said. "There's money in that?"

"Enough to take care of me and Ruby."

"Ruby?"

"My cat," Winston said.

The officer looked down. "She's got marvelous

eyes," he said, crouching and holding out his hand. "I've never seen eyes like that on a cat before."

Ruby sat up and stared at him. Winston knew the posture. It was the one she always used when humans treated her like an animal instead of a person.

"She's not a friendly one, is she?" The officer stood. "I would have thought she was, being a store cat."

"She's only six months old," Winston said.

The officer nodded as if that explained everything. The tip of Ruby's tail twitched.

"You've been here a long time," the officer said.

"Almost twenty years."

"Most people have no idea what you do."

Winston looked at him, trying to see if the young man was probing or just making a statement. "I keep to myself."

"Any reason for that?"

Half a dozen, none of which you would believe, Winston thought. But he said, "Habit."

"Hmm." The officer turned, started for the door.

"I didn't catch your name, Officer."

The officer stopped, picked up a bottle and turned it over in his fingers. "Park. Scott Park."

"Should I be hiring a lawyer, Officer Scott Park?"

Park turned. There was something in his green eyes. Something cold and a little wary. Something that made him seem older. "Not yet."

And then he let himself out.

Winston waited until Park walked past the dirty display windows, then leaned against the counter.

"Not yet?" Ruby said, her voice rising with indignation. "Not yet? That means yes in police talk, doesn't it?"

"It means maybe," Winston said.

"I watch television. It means I'm looking for evidence."

"Television isn't real life, Ruby."

"And your rules are silly ones. Hire someone, will you?"

Winston shook his head. He wasn't ready to hire anyone. In a world filled with fingerprints, hair fibers, and DNA testing, it was a long way from suspicion to arrest.

I don't think this is such a good idea after all, she said to him.

Sure it is, he said in his imagination. *Come sit with me. We'll figure it out.*

But he hadn't said that. He hadn't reassured her, hadn't taken care of her. He had let her leave, and she had died.

He had small magics. What had she thought he could do?

There was only one way to find out.

He placed the call from his store. Ruby already had him thinking of covering himself, of a future trial that might or might not happen. He could say on the stand in his own defense—honestly and rightly—that he called Boyce Theriot to gossip, and to place a long overdue order for some ingredients for his love potions, ingredients Theriot sold cheaper than anyone else, thanks to the large voodoo culture in New Orleans.

Boyce answered the phone, his customary "Good afternoon," spoken with its combination of Southern warmth mixed with Bourbon street disinterest. Winston introduced himself, and Boyce said, "I spoke to a police officer about you this mornin'. He asked me if you had a history of assaultin' young women. Do you have a history, Winston?"

Winston couldn't tell if Boyce was teasing or not. They'd only met briefly, in San Francisco, twenty-five years before. Both had been apprentices, and both had been very, very different. Even at twenty, Boyce had a sophisticated and charming mixture of cold disinterest and sudden warmth.

"Who was she?" Winston asked.

"Why, you should know that by now."

"I just spoke to the police. She was Gwen Winnick from Ohio. And that's all I know."

"Not all," Boyce said. "If that was all, you wouldn't be callin' me, now would you?"

"She told me that a man in New Orleans had sent her to me. The cop was the one who gave me your name."

"And did you help her?"

"She ran away before I even found out what the trouble was."

Boyce let out a small breath. "Little brown wren, right to the very end."

She had dressed like a brown wren. But she had been beautiful. For some reason, the comment irritated Winston. "Why'd you send her to me?"

"She'd been doin' lots of research on lots of things. It brought her to me. I sent her to you."

"No games, Boyce," Winston said. "She came to me, and I didn't help her, and now she's dead. What did she want?"

"Do you know anyone in Ohio?"

Winston sighed. "No."

"Neither do I, but someone there did somethin' awful to that poor girl. Seems she was in a car accident, and it left a long pucker on her cheek that she thought kept other people from her. Happened when she was just a little thing. She tried conventional methods, you know, surgeries and all, and they made it better but didn't make it go away."

"You saw it?" Winston asked.

"This here's just what she told me." Boyce spoke in a tone that said he didn't really believe her. He would have done as any good white magician would have done, helped her realize her problem was more a lack of confidence than a single scar alongside her face.

"So she went to see someone."

"She went to see someone in Ohio," Boyce said. "Wouldn't tell me his name. Said it was best all 'round if she never spoke it again."

"I don't like the sound of that," Winston said.

"Neither did I, but it was too late, even then, wasn't it?"

"I don't know," Winston said. Ruby jumped on his desk and pawed at the phone cord. Winston put a finger to his lips. She gave him a look that showed her displeasure—she clearly wanted him to share the call *now*—but she sat down and waited. "What did she ask for? An illusion spell?"

"Somethin' to cover the scar—make her normal, she said. Maybe even pretty, she said."

Probably wistfully, Winston thought.

"And he did, and when she left, people were staring at her, just like they always had, so she thought it hadn't worked."

"Until she looked in the mirror."

Boyce said, "But it wasn't an illusion spell. It was a beauty spell, and he mixed it with some kind of attraction potion. Suddenly the girl who couldn't get anyone to be with her couldn't get anyone to leave her alone."

Winston shuddered. Nothing seemed worse to him than unwanted attention.

"Why didn't she get him to reverse it?" he asked.

"She tried. He called her ungrateful, and cursed her, saying she would suffer it for the rest of her life."

And she had.

"You have no idea who he was."

"None."

Winston sighed. "So she came to you."

"After maybe fifty others. No one could reverse it. Includin' me."

"So why'd you send her to me? I don't have half your magic."

"All I could think of was a potion," Boyce said. "A sort of antidote. Something she could take every day to nullify the effects. I certainly couldn't do that, but you could."

Winston's stomach clenched. "I don't know."

"Well, that was the point of havin' her see you. I figured you'd keep trying till you came up with somethin' that worked."

Winston was silent for a moment. Ruby tilted her head slightly. He would have. Yes. He would have.

"She stopped at the door to my lab," Winston said. "Does that mean anything to you?"

"She wouldn't come into my lab either," Boyce said. "Maybe she'd been in one too many."

"I don't know," Winston said. "It seemed like she was scared."

"She's dead, ain't she?" Boyce's voice was soft, full of regret. "Maybe she had her reasons."

*   *   *

Her reasons. Winston couldn't get that phrase out of his mind. He went through the next few days with a sort of watchful numbness: filling his orders, taking care of Ruby, following his routine. In his spare time, though, he found himself tinkering with a potion that would neutralize both a beauty and an attraction spell, a potion he would never ever sell, never ever use.

Ruby watched him with a sort of sadness in her eyes.

On the fourth day, she sprawled across his worktable, her hind feet pushing against some of his more expensive potion bottles. He caught the bottles and put them on a shelf behind her.

She had his attention now. "What do you know about beauty spells, Big Boy?"

He shrugged. "The basics. And enough to know I can't do them."

She nodded, her golden eyes narrowing. She knew something, something she expected him to understand. "Aren't they incredibly nasty spells?"

He frowned. "It depends."

"On?"

He felt as if he were back in his mentor's lab, listening to lectures on magic. He hated quizzes. He'd always done so poorly at them. "I guess it depends on who writes the spell and how long it lasts."

She blinked at him. Her sphinx look.

"You have no proof that Gwen's spell was black magic," he said, "or nasty in any way."

"Proof." Ruby rumbled the word. "I have enough. For me."

"For you," he said, leaving off, but implying the last: *You're a cat.*

She heard it anyway, and stood, licking her shoulder

as she often did when she was offended. Then she sat
down and wrapped her tail around her front paws.

"Think it through, Big Boy. A curse that the spell
will last all her life. A mage who refuses to reverse
his own spell. A mage who adds another spell, and
gets angry when the client says it goes awry. That
doesn't make for good business, does it?"

"We only have Boyce's word for this, a story he
got secondhand."

"And her fear." Ruby's tail twitched. "What would
make a woman afraid of a simple lab in the back of
a store? Not you. And not me. Maybe the bottles of
potion? The jars of ingredients? The smell?"

"She'd clearly been in a lab before," Winston said.

"Yes," Ruby said, "and look where it got her."

In the end, he decided, as he always had, that it was
none of his business. His business was simple, it was
small, it had only to do with him and Ruby and the
clients he never met. He did his work in peace, and
he never bothered anyone. He went to his stone house
on the cliffside, built fires against the cold, rainy
nights, and listened to the ocean pound the beach
below.

He tried not to think of Gwen, just like he tried
not to think of that girl in San Francisco, the one who
had almost died.

It was nearly March when the bell above the door
tinkled again. That day's rain was a light mist, slanted
sideways, annoying only because it made a man wet
in the space of five minutes. People didn't shop in that
kind of weather; they didn't browse either, and Winston knew, with that subtle certainty he sometimes
got, that his visitor had come because of Gwen
Winnick.

He wiped his hands on his work towel and hung it over the small sink. Then he pulled back the beaded curtain.

Officer Scott Park stood there, his uniform beaded with moisture, his red hair curly with damp. "You have an interesting Internet site."

Winston froze. Only Ruby moved forward, her tail held high, as if she really were a store cat who wanted to greet a customer.

Park hadn't removed his hat this time. And he had lost his deferential manner. He tilted his head slightly. "Do you think a person's lying when he answers someone's questions and leaves things out? Or do you simply believe that it's the job of the questioner to ask the right question?"

Winston's heart was pounding. He had to keep himself from speaking. If he opened his mouth, he would say that he had never seen her before, that he hadn't given her a potion. He had a familiar this time, so it wouldn't have mattered if he sold her something or not. This time, he would say, he was innocent.

"Mr. Karpathian?"

Winston blinked. He had to think. Ruby sat down and looked at him over her shoulder.

"Do I need a lawyer, Officer Scott Park?" Winston asked softly.

Ruby's tail twitched, ever so slightly.

Park's eyes narrowed. He hadn't expected Winston to say that. "No," Park said at last. "We know who killed Gwen Winnick."

"Then why have you come to me?"

"Because I looked at your Web site. I think you might be able to explain some things to me, things that don't make sense." Park shifted from one foot to the other, showing his discomfort. Perhaps that was why he had been so forceful a moment before. To hide the fact that he was asking a wizard to consult on a case. "Would you come to the station?"

"No." Even within that short word, Winston's voice shook.

"It's easier," Park said. "Everything's there."

Winston sighed. "All right," he said. "But Ruby comes, too."

Park glanced at her. "It's a strange place. You sure it won't frighten her?"

"She's used to strange places," Winston said. "She'll be fine."

Winston drove the Gremlin to the police station in the center of town. The car was now belching blue smoke, and he knew it wouldn't last much longer. He wanted a car with a magical name, but he doubted he would find one, not in the bright new century with its focus on the future.

Ruby hid beneath the dash. She didn't like the idea of Winston going to the station, she didn't like Officer Park, and she hadn't liked Gwen. Ruby hadn't voiced her opinions, but she didn't need to. She thought Winston was taking an unnecessary risk.

The station was a new fake brick construct near the Factory Outlet mall. There was a spacious parking lot near a grove of trees, and that lent the place a certain privacy Winston had never seen in a police station before.

He went inside, Ruby at his heels, to find Park waiting for him near what looked like a reception area. There were plants and double-paned windows which he had read in the local paper were bulletproof. The only thing that made it look like a police station at all was the double-reinforced steel door leading to the back.

"This sure ain't *Hill Street Blues*," Ruby said under her breath. Only Winston heard her. But that was enough. He had to choke back a smile, and then he vowed to stop watching so much television in the evening.

"I think you better carry her," Park said, looking at Ruby. "There's a lot of coming and going around here. It might spook her."

Winston's gaze met Ruby's, and hers had warning in it. But he picked her up anyway, not because he was afraid she'd be spooked but because he worried that she would go exploring on her own.

They walked through the double doors into a maze-like corridor. Park led him to an office toward the back. It had a view of the trees, although the glass seemed to let in almost no light at all. The desk was covered with files, and toasters flew across the screen of the old computer sitting atop the credenza.

Park closed the door and sat behind the desk. Winston took the only chair in front of it. Ruby jumped out of his arms and began pacing the room as if she were under arrest.

"Okay," Park said. "First, I've got to ask, more for me than anyone else, those folks who order your love potions and aphrodisiacs and 'perfect day' spells, do they actually believe that stuff will work or are they doing it as a gag?"

Ruby stopped pacing. Winston felt his shoulders tense. He could lie, he supposed, but what good would it do? "I think they believe."

"Do you?" Park asked.

"I guess I do," Winston said.

Park frowned, as if that wasn't the answer he expected. "Do you think Gwen Winnick believed?"

Winston nodded. "Enough to frighten her from my lab, I think."

"Why? Would you have hurt her?"

"No." Winston's denial was soft. "But she might have gotten hurt in someone else's lab. It seemed like it."

"So the stuff I read in books, about white magic and black magic, that's true?"

"In its way," Winston said. "There are those of us who do small things, favors almost, always pleasant, and then there are those who do bigger things, rarely favorable, almost always unpleasant."

"How do I tell the difference?"

Winston shrugged. "By feel I guess. If you're not comfortable, you don't do business with someone."

"People can tell that on the Internet?"

"No." He threaded his fingers together. It still felt like he needed a lawyer.

Park sighed and walked to the window. Ruby followed him and jumped on the sill. She sat down in front of him, and let him pet her. She rarely did real cat things like that. Maybe she was afraid he'd arrest Winston, too.

"Okay," Park said after a moment. "I'm going to ask you to consult on this case. We can pay you a token amount. But you have to swear you won't discuss the details of the case unless you're before a court of law."

"I can promise that." Relief made him slightly dizzy. He must have been forgetting to breathe. "Why do you need me?"

"Because you understand this world, and I don't. I probably never will." Park scratched Ruby's back, and she arched in pleasure. She shot Winston a glance to see if he was watching. He was, and he felt vaguely jealous.

Then Park patted Ruby's back and returned to his desk. "The police in Astoria arrested a man for starting an illegal bonfire on the beach, and found that he matched the description we'd released of Gwen's killer. They also found some things that they thought might be hers and, they said, he seemed to be performing a ritual of some sort with them."

Ruby sat down and stared out the window as if the news didn't concern her at all, but her ears went flat back. Winston frowned. No rituals should be performed around the first of March. Any sensible mage would wait until solstice, and then not do it on the beach.

"He was quite upset when they arrested him, saying someone else would suffer if he didn't finish. They thought he was threatening someone and put him in isolation until we could get there." Park ran a hand through his hair. "It wasn't until we got him that we realized he thought his failure to finish the ritual meant someone else would live in pain forever."

"Did he say pain?" Winston asked.

Park shook his head slightly. "He said suffer."

Winston nodded.

"What does this mean to you?" Park asked.

"What exactly was he doing?" Winston asked.

Park gathered some photos from the top drawer of his desk. "He had a blazing fire going at twilight, and he had some powders we can't identify. He also had two dolls, one with the victim's photograph taped to it, and another with another woman's. He had placed them in boiling water, and he was carefully mixing two vials of what later turned out to be blood, one from the victim, and one from someone we can't identify."

"This isn't enough to convict?" Winston asked.

"It's not your garden variety murder," Park said. "It looks like an act of passion, until you factor in the blood. It looks premeditated, until you look at the opportunities he must have had earlier, since we can document that he followed her from Ohio. She was running from him in particular. If we made this sound random, the defense would prove us wrong. If we made it sound premeditated without any motive—and we can't find one—he'll plead insanity, and it'll stick."

"I didn't know police worried about motives and proving court cases," Winston said.

Ruby huffed. Apparently she knew, from her vast television watching experience.

"I think this guy is a real danger. I want him put away." There was fervor in his voice, a certain hunching about his shoulders. Something that made this case mean more to Park than solving Gwen Winnick's murder.

"You've had a case like this before," Winston said. "And lost."

Park looked down. He no longer looked young. There were lines around his eyes. "In Seattle," he said. "When I worked at a real police force."

That was the joke, of course. Seavy Village's force was small and rarely did more than vandalism, drug possession cases, and traffic stops. Seattle handled everything from vice to murder.

"It was something similar, same kind of creepy behavior, only he walked. We set up a murder one case, no motive, and the jury came back with reasonable doubt. I figure there are some people out there who died because we—I—fucked up the case."

"And that's why you're in Seavy Village," Winston said.

Park's eyes were old. How had Winston not noticed that before? The age in them was the result of guilt, not of years.

Winston considered for a moment. He could walk, even now. But he wouldn't. Each man had his own reasons for solving this case. They needed each other.

He decided, then he said, "Ruby. Explain to Officer Park what the man was doing."

Park looked at Winston as if he were insane. Ruby's entire body went still. Then she jumped from the sill to the desk, and looked in Park's face. "Do you believe in magic, Big Boy?"

"No," Park said, frowning at Winston as if he were doing a ventriloquist act.

"Well, you will," Ruby said. "Believe me. You will."

"He didn't believe me," Ruby said, from her spot under the dashboard.

"He believed *in* you," Winston said. "That's more than I would expect."

"Yes, and now the whole town will come to see your talking cat."

He couldn't tell if she sounded excited or disappointed. Probably neither.

"I don't think so," he said. "No police officer would want a town as small as this one to think he's seeing talking cats."

"Good point," Ruby said. "But he still didn't believe me."

"We gave him an argument, a motive."

"I won't testify in court." She said that as if someone was going to ask her, as if she was turning them down.

Winston smiled, and flicked on the windshield wipers. The mist was continuing, steady, heavier than expected. "I'm sure I can take care of that part."

"Then why did you have me talk to him in the first place?"

"So he wouldn't question the magic."

"Other people will."

"Other people need to know that the *suspect* believes in magic, that's all."

Ruby sighed and laid down. "Human justice is so complicated. Just beat the crap out of the guy and throw him out of society. Or kill him. It's so much easier."

"And so much less civilized."

"Oh, I forgot. We must keep up the pretense to civility at all times." She said that last with a fake British accent. "Now what? Old Park isn't going to want to talk to us again."

"No," Winston said. "He's solved his problem."

He could feel Ruby's scrutiny.

"And?" she asked.

"We're not even close to solving ours."

"I didn't know we had one."

He pulled the car into its spot behind his shop, and opened his door. Ruby zoomed out of it, dashing so quickly across puddles that he doubted she touched them at all. She huddled against the back door of the shop and he unlocked it, letting her in.

It seemed so unfamiliar, and so warm. His place. He had risked it, by letting Ruby talk to Park. Fortunately he hadn't misjudged the man, a man with enough curiosity to save them all. Winston had given

Park a motive, and Park had given Winston a headache.

Winston closed the door, and leaned on it. He would have explained what happened to Park, except that it sounded too unbelievable, too crazy. And Winston placed value on sounding sane.

So he had let Ruby speak. After a few sentences, when Winston had excused himself and gone to the men's room, Park started to believe. By the time Winston came back, Park believed entirely and seemed at a complete loss as to what to do—about Ruby, not the case. Winston helped him with that last part.

It was so simple and so sad. The suspect—the murderer—was named Eugene Grimsrud. His fiancée was one of the most beautiful women in Columbus, and she had had a run-in with "a crazy man" at one of the local art fairs. Apparently, the crazy man had decided to get back at her. One morning, she woke up, her face shriveled and misshapen, her eyes too big, her nose so small as to be nonexistent, her teeth crooked and yellow. Doctor after doctor couldn't explain it.

At least, that was what Grimsrud had said. It wasn't until the crazy man had shown up at their door to see his "handiwork" that they began to understand that the force they dealt with had nothing to do with modern medicine and everything to do with one of the darker forms of magic.

That was the suspect's story, which Park told them after he heard Ruby talk. All Ruby had said was this: it was clear Grimsrud was trying to reverse a beauty spell. Beauty spells, done by dark practitioners, take the essence of one person's beauty and give it to someone else. Such a spell is reversed by mixing the blood of the two, and boiling it over a real fire at twilight. Dolls placed in the water had to have pictures of each person—as they originally were—and those pictures would guide the spirits to put things right.

Grimsrud had taken no chances. He even had a magic charm to help. But it hadn't. For Grimsrud had no magic of his own, and didn't know there were rules other than the ones he'd been told.

All magic gained more power on the solstice.

And a successful spell reversal was impossible whenever one of the parties to the original spell was dead.

Grimsrud's fiancée was doomed to wear her new face forever.

Unless Winston could come up with something that even he, with his small magics, could perform.

For that, Winston needed the answers to a few questions.

For that, Winston needed to speak to Grimsrud.

Park arranged it, against his will. But, Winston said, it might help with the consult. It also, Winston said, would help if he knew the details of the murder.

The papers had been vague about it. Woman found dead in her hotel room, attacked by a stalker. People in nearby rooms heard screaming, shouting, and by the time the police arrived, she was dead and he was gone.

Dead. Beaten about the face and shoulders with a blunt object. Skull crushed. Murdered, it seemed, in a rage.

And Grimsrud looked like a man who could kill that way. He sat in one of the fancy new cells in the back of the new police station, waiting to be sent somewhere else to await trial. He was large and bony in a rangy sort of way. His eyes had an edge to them, the look of a man no longer quite sane.

Winston was glad he hadn't brought Ruby with him. He was glad she wouldn't have a chance to worm her way into the cell, and let that man touch her.

"So you're one of them," Grimsrud said. "Like Hubble."

"Hubble?"

"The man who ruined my Kelly's face."

"Does Hubble have a last name?" Winston asked. He couldn't do much: just report the unorthodox methods to his colleagues, and see if someone stronger, someone with more magic, decided to pursue punishment.

"Pierce."

Winston nodded, took note, and then folded his hands behind his back.

"You're like him, aren't you?"

"No," Winston said. "I don't hurt people."

Grimsrud winced. The expression seemed off somehow, as if it weren't natural.

"Tell me about your fiancée," Winston said.

"Why?" Grimsrud asked.

"So that I can see if I can help her."

"Why would you do that for me?"

It was a strange question, more self-absorbed than Winston expected. "I wouldn't," he said. "But by killing Gwen, you've stranded your girlfriend, you know, made it impossible for anyone to reverse the spell."

Something flickered in Grimsrud's eyes. Hatred? Remorse? It was impossible to tell. "I didn't plan that."

The murder? The impossibility of reversal? Winston didn't know, wasn't sure he wanted to. "You didn't plan to strand your fiancée?"

"She's not my fiancée any more. She couldn't stand it, to have someone see her like that, especially me."

A shiver ran through Winston. "Is she dead, too?"

Grimsrud shook his head and lowered his gaze. "I think she might want to be," he said.

Winston stiffened. Something in Grimsrud's tone, something in his manner, made him pause. Black magic was so beyond him. He almost wished Ruby were here, to listen to this. To figure out what lurked.

"Would she come here?" Winston asked. "Maybe stand by you in trial?"

Grimsrud shook his head. "She says I'm no longer the man she loved."

Winston understood that. "At least give me her name, so that I can help her."

Grimsrud frowned. "What can you do, now that I— that Gwen's dead?"

Winston thought of the potion, sitting on his desk. A few tweaks and it might work the other way, it might make a woman who lost her looks regain them. "Probably nothing," he said. "But it is worth a try."

He left with fiancée Kelly's last name, and a headache so fierce he doubted any spell could cure it. His stomach was in knots. The drive home was longer than usual, and by the time he got in the house, he was almost physically ill.

"I wouldn't have gone in the cell," Ruby said. She was sitting on the rug in front of the fireplace, waiting, he knew, for a real fire. No little snap of the fingers and magical sparks for her.

She would have to wait a moment. He was feeling faint.

"So he killed her, huh?" Ruby asked, studying his face.

Winston nodded.

"Why?"

Winston swallowed. "We didn't get to that."

"But you suspect something."

If he remembered his spellcasting correctly. "Tell me, Ruby," he said. "What happens if a reversal spell succeeds and one of the parties is dead?"

Ruby twitched one ear, a sign of annoyance. She hated it when he didn't remember the details of spells. "The other one dies, too."

"I thought so," he whispered. He bowed his head, felt the tension in his neck muscles.

"He wasn't getting revenge for his girlfriend's disfigurement," Ruby said.

"No." Winston raised his head. "He was getting a different kind of revenge."

Ruby was standing now, concern on her feline face, concern that vanished when she realized he was looking at her. "For her rejection of him."

Winston nodded. "I'll bet he used Gwen, convinced her that magic would change her life, and then he killed her."

"He didn't expect to get caught?" Ruby asked.

"Oh, he did," Winston said, "but not until after he succeeded. He just hadn't counted on how much of a difference magical ability makes."

"And how badly he needed the solstice." Ruby approached him cautiously, her tail up, her face gentle. "What are you going to do?"

"Help Park nail this bastard."

"And what else?" Ruby asked.

Winston shook his head. "The mage was Hubble Pierce. He probably did the spell for money. He wouldn't reverse it for Gwen. He won't reverse it for me."

Ruby was silent. Winston thought there was judgment in that silence.

"What else can I do?" he asked. "If I fly to Ohio, she won't see me because I'm from here where Grimsrud killed Gwen. She won't see me because I have magic. If I contact her, she won't trust me for the same reasons. And if I tried to help her, I'd fail."

"No," Ruby said. "You wouldn't fail."

Winston looked at her. She seemed less like a cat now. More like a familiar. Like she was tapping into an area he didn't quite understand.

"What do you suggest?" he asked. "I can't leave this woman, this Kelly, a victim of Grimsrud's revenge."

"What do I suggest?" Ruby asked. She tilted her head as if listening to a voice inside her. Then her whiskers twitched. If she were human, Winston would have thought he saw the trace of a smile.

"I suggest," she said slowly, "the subtle approach."

"And that is?"

"Temptation," Ruby said. "Something no sane woman can ever resist."

At first Winston thought it wouldn't work. He thought any woman—any person—who'd been injured by magic would reject magic out of hand. But he sent Kelly flyers advertising his Web site, and then he sent offers for free samples. He got testimonials from a few clients, and built a small newsletter—which he liked so much he sent it to other clients, and found that they passed it on.

For months, he tried, and for months, he did not hear. A year went by. Grimsrud had his day in court, and was presented as a psychopath who dabbled in black magic. Winston did not have to testify, but he read his words in the prosecutor's case, saw how his insights—minus the fact that magic really did exist—

created the motive that brought Grimsrud down. There was no mention of a beauty spell, no mention of reversal, no mention of Kelly at all. Just of craziness and witchcraft and destruction.

It was enough to put Grimsrud away for life.

And to make Park, who occasionally bought Winston lunch along with salmon for Ruby, lose some of the sadness around his eyes.

But the true victim, the one Winston had never seen, the one he had only imagined, remained out of reach.

Until one afternoon in late February. It was Tuesday, and it was raining—the hard cold downpour that made all but the hardiest locals complain. Winston was working in the back of his shop when he heard the bell above the door tinkle. He looked at Ruby; she looked at him, and he knew they were remembering a February Tuesday one year ago, a day they both hadn't yet put behind them.

This time, he stood and opened the beaded curtain. A woman stood near the dirty display window, studying a shelf of cut glass potion bottles. She looked up when she saw him. She was slight, with mismatched blue eyes. Her dark hair fell in waves about her face. She wore a lot of makeup, but it didn't hide the fact that she was one of the homeliest women he'd ever seen.

"Are you Winston?" she asked.

He nodded, his heart in his throat.

"I've done some checking up on you."

He waited.

"Everyone seems to like you."

He smiled a little and almost made a self-deprecating remark, then remembered how fragile trust could be. "I'm glad to hear it."

"They say you have never harmed anyone in your life."

He wished that were true.

She raised her chin. "You know who I am."

"Kelly," he said.

She nodded. Her movements were graceful, where Gwen's had been awkward. "You think you can help me?"

"Yes," he said.

"I hear you have only a small magic."

She had checked on him. Of course. She would be very, very cautious.

Ruby came out of the back. She leaped onto the counter and sprawled across it, the picture of relaxation.

"It's very small," Winston said. "And I won't pretend to try to reverse your enchantment. But I can block it, for a day."

"A day."

He could hear the disappointment in her voice. She shook her head slightly. "To gain my face back for a day—" Her voice broke a little. "I know you mean well, Mr. Karpathian. But I'm finally getting used to this."

"Not *one* day," he said. "*A* day. Every day. One day at a time."

He was making no sense, as usual.

"I make potions. You'd take a potion every twenty-four hours, and no one would need to know that you once looked like this."

Her smile was small, almost invisible. "They already know, Mr. Karpathian."

"In Ohio."

A frown formed on her face. He had her attention now. He could see the temptation, and the unwillingness to believe. "What do I get? Someone else's face? Would I be forced to pass the misery along?"

"No," he said. "The potion simply blocks the enchantment for a few hours. During that time, you'll have your own face again."

She put a hand on the edge of the counter, and it took him a moment to realize she was holding herself up.

"I want to say no to you, Mr. Karpathian." Her voice was soft. "How I look, it shouldn't matter that much. If I've learned anything these last few years, it's that."

"I won't make you beautiful," he said. "And you'll age, as you would have before. I'm just giving you, for a day at a time, what's rightfully yours. What was stolen from you."

A wealth of emotions crossed her face. Temptation. Joy. And then a sadness that she couldn't seem to shake.

"The face I used to hurt Gene Grimsrud," she said softly. "The face I thought made me better than everyone else."

"Did it?" Winston asked.

She shook her head.

"Would you believe it again?"

"It's not that simple," she said. "Perhaps now I wear the face I deserve."

He didn't argue the point because he didn't know her. Ruby was watching him and he wondered if he were missing another opportunity, if he were making another mistake.

"It's not something you have to decide today," he said. "I'll keep some on hand. You can come to me whenever you like."

Kelly stared at him for a moment. "Why?" she whispered. "Why me?"

He wasn't thinking of her. Instead, he was thinking of a woman so beautiful she felt she had to hide it, a woman who only wanted the face she'd been born with, not the one that had been stolen for her at such great cost.

"Because I have only a little magic," he said. "And very rarely does it give me the chance to do things right."

This time she really smiled. It didn't make her pretty, but it brought her features together into something better than they had been before.

"You're a good man, Mr. Karpathian," she said. "With a beautiful cat."

Ruby preened, but Kelly made no move toward her.

"I'll think about your gift," she said, in a tone that let him know she already had. She started for the door, and stopped with her hand on the knob. Her gaze met his. In it, he saw something soft and grateful and sad.

"Thank you," she said.

And then she slipped out, into the rain.

The shop seemed emptier without her. Ruby rolled over on her back. "I thought she'd go for it."

Winston took one step forward. "Maybe she would have—once."

Ruby sighed and rolled again. "She doesn't know what she's missing."

"Oh," Winston said. "I think she does."

Ruby gave him a small feline frown and closed her eyes. His familiar was too young to realize that Kelly needed the chance to regain her beauty, not the beauty itself.

Just like he had needed this day. He'd needed her

to come, if only for a brief moment in the space of a rainy afternoon.

He stared at the door, the small bell on top, eloquent in its silence. Then he turned away from the rain, from the gloomy February afternoon, and went through the beaded curtains into his lab. Into the place where he spent most of his life, practicing his very small magic, for people he never met—and never would.

A SPATTER OF LATER STARS
by *Nina Kiriki Hoffman*

Nina Kiriki Hoffman has been pursuing a writing career for
fifteen years and has sold more than 150 stories, two short
story collections, and several novels, including *The Thread
that Binds the Bones,* winner of the Bram Stoker award for
best first novel, and *The Silent Strength of Stones.* She has
also written one novella, *Unmasking,* and one collaborative
young adult novel with Tad Williams, *Child of an Ancient
City.* Currently she almost makes a living writing scary
books for kids. Her most recent novel is *The Red Heart
of Memories.*

"The blue wig, I think," said my father.
Sweat bloomed on my upper lip. I wiped it
off with a tissue and watched the customer think about
the blue punk wig. Her gaze shifted toward the multi-
colored tinsel wig, which would be too much. She already wore big red rhinestone-studded glasses, bright
red lipstick, and enough rouge to coat a person's
palms. Only her hair failed her, brown, thin, damp
and flat with sweat. The blue wig would make her
look patriotic, which would work: it was the Fourth
of July.

It was my fourteenth birthday.

Beyond Big Red, sun-bleached people walked up
and down the board pedestrian bridge over the river,
checking out the booths along the rail. The hot air
smelled of creosote from the bridge, swampy plants

from the river below. Cicadas sang a song of summer
heat in bright metallic notes.

"Chemical fireworks, safe, legal," yelled the guy in
the booth next door. He held up plastic neon-looking
tubes that glowed when you broke something inside.
"Sno-cones," yelled somebody else. A kid walked by
licking from a cotton candy cloud, and I shuddered.
It must be like licking fire in this heat. Below us, water
gurgled over small falls.

"Trust me," said my father. "The blue wig will be
best."

Red glanced at me. I sat at my makeup table next
to the prop table. I smiled and nodded. "You'll look
like the Fourth of July," I said. "I could put some
white stripes across your face to make you look like
the flag. Maybe some white stars?"

Sometimes it's hardest to convince the ones who
look wildest. Like they have so much invested in how
they look already they don't want anybody else mess-
ing with them.

"All that's included in the price?" Red asked.

"Sure," said my father. "All we want is to make a
good picture, give you a fun memory that'll last.
Cammie?"

I sat Red down at my makeup table, helped her
settle the blue wig on her head, brushed it to spruce
it up, patted the sweat off her face with a purple bandana, and painted three white greasepaint stars across
the rouge on her left cheek. My hand prickled while
I applied the makeup. "Check it out," I said, holding
up a hand mirror.

"Oh!" she cried. "I look—" She blinked three
times, then stared at me. "I—" She smiled.

"You look great." My voice came out with a silvery
edge. I felt strange. Something had happened while I

touched her. It had all come together: she looked larger than life, perfect, like someone playing a part.

"I do." She smiled wider.

"Do you want the Marilyn Monroe body, the Princess Leia body, or the pink kimono?" my father said.

"Which do you think would be best, dear?" the customer asked me.

"The kimono, the butterfly wings, and the liberty torch," I said.

"Oh." She looked at our prop table. We had a sword, a rubber skull, a big teddy bear, an assortment of snazzy sunglasses, a magic wand with tinsel ribbons, a silk rose, all sorts of things people liked to pose with, and to the side, cardboard cutouts of male and female celebrity bodies, their heads folded down. You could pose with a celebrity, or just have your head on one of their bodies. Full-service manufactured memories. "Are you sure?"

"I'm sure," I said, tasting silver in the edge of my voice. Pinpricks studded my throat. Maybe I was coming down with something.

"Then let's do that."

I helped her into the pink kimono and slipped the butterfly wing straps over her shoulders, then handed her the liberty torch.

"You want the star background," Dad said.

Red checked out our three standard backgrounds: glittering holograph-sticker five-pointed stars against a dark blue background, huge pink tea-rose wallpaper, and a sepia-toned Wild West town background. She nodded. She stepped in front of the stars.

"Hand like this," I said, showing her how to pose so the torch would show in the picture and she would look cute. "Cross one foot over the other." I bent the wire frames of the wings so they showed to best advantage. She looked like a big cotton-candy fairy on a mission from the U.S. government. I brushed a strand of blue polyester hair out of her face, felt more prickles in my hand. What? I stepped away. "Smile," I said.

"Hold it!" said Dad, and snapped two pictures, one with his little stealth camera, and the second with the Polaroid.

Big Red kept smiling even though the flash had already gone off twice. She lowered the torch and grinned at me.

"We have to wait a minute for it to set," Dad said, waving the Polaroid around. "Five dollars, please."

Red retrieved her green purse from my makeup table and dug out a bright blue wallet. She handed me a ten. "I don't know how to get out of these wings," she said.

I set the ten on my makeup table and helped her ease out of the wings. I lifted the wig off her head. Her hair looked even more flat and dull now. "Okay if I brush you out?" I asked.

She dug in her purse some more and produced a purple comb, handed it to me. I combed through her hair. My hand tingled and prickled. Her hair lifted up and curled, thickened, its dishwater brown color lightening to honey. I combed some more. "What are you doing?" she asked, peering into the mirror.

"I don't know." I put down the comb. I glanced at my father.

He smiled. "It's a gift," he said. He slipped the Polaroid picture into a cardstock photomount and gave it to Red.

She stared and stared at her picture.

After a moment, she murmured, "It's wonderful!"

I peeked over her shoulder. "You look terrific."

"I do." She sounded surprised and happy.

"Do you want to keep the stars?" I patted her cheek with my bandana. Despite the heat, she wasn't sweating.

"Sure," she said. She rose and slipped out of the pink kimono.

"Your change," I said. I headed for the cash box to get change for her ten dollar bill.

"Keep it. This is a great picture!" She smiled as she left our booth.

I looked at my father.

"A gift, Cammie," he said. "You've got a gift." He parted the curtain that separated our booth from the one next door, where my mother sat at her green felt-topped table with her deck of tarot cards, her velvet bag of rune stones, and her crystal ball on a bronze dragon stand. "Reya! Cammie's got a gift!"

My mother jumped up and came through the curtains to hug me. She smelled like amber. The coins stitched to the hem of her skirt jingled, and the bugle beads on her embroidered peasant blouse pressed into my cheek. "Which one?" she asked.

"The one that makes people feel beautiful."

Mother kissed my forehead. "That's a wonderful gift," she murmured. "Congratulations, and happy birthday, my heart."

This was my gift? Most of the people from my mother's side of the family had a gift of some sort, and a few from my father's side. My mother could read the present and the future. She had practiced until she knew how much truth she should use when telling fortunes at the fairs and powwows and celebrations we traveled to—not much—and she never looked at our own futures.

Father had no obvious gift, but he was creative in coming up with ideas that would make enough money to keep us going. He was doing something with cameras now that I didn't understand; it seemed different from what most people used cameras for. He hadn't explained it to us yet; he was still experimenting.

On my mother's side of the family, I knew people who could make things float through the air—how I'd longed for that gift!—or start fires with their fingertips, or see through walls, or cast love spells. Cousin Carlos could gentle any animal; Cousin Meriel could summon money, sometimes right out of people's wallets without their knowing.

Making people feel beautiful. What kind of gift was that?

"I feel so thirsty," I said.

"Of course. Using your gift tires you," my father said. He popped the ice chest we had under the cash-box table and got me a bottle of Gatorade.

I had always thought Gatorade was awful, and I couldn't understand why my mother and father drank it. This time my first sip tasted like heaven, and the rest of the bottle went down easy. I glanced at the label, wondering if it was a new flavor, but no, it was Iced Tea Cooler, a flavor I'd tasted and hated before.

"It only tastes good when you need it," my father said.

"Hello?" A couple stood at the entrance to our booth. "This where Roberta got that great picture took of her?" asked the man. He was tall, skinny, and tanned to leather, with his hair white wisps around his head, and large-lensed glasses shrinking his eyes. The

woman was short and squat as a fire hydrant, with a
face like a Pekingese dog.

"Yes," said my father. "We do take lovely pictures
of people. Take a look at our prop table. Do you see
anything you'd like to pose with? Or ask my daughter
for advice. She'll make you look fine."

"That's what we heard," said the little woman. She
smiled at me, and I saw something in her that made
my palms tingle and itch. "She said you painted those
stars on her, and I wondered if you could do me something like that." Her dark eyes sparkled.

"Do you know what you want?" I asked.

Her gaze shifted away, fixed on the ground. "No,"
she said.

"Have a seat." I patted her face dry, then opened
my box of colored greasepaint pencils. They were soft
with the heat, their tips broad and melty. I thought of
makeup I'd put on people before: cat, dog, skull, half-
blue face, tiger stripes. Rough clown faces. Anything
like that would probably insult this woman and make
her mad. Maybe all her life she'd wished for the perfect face and knew she'd never see it on her head.
Maybe today I could change that.

My hands buzzed and tingled. I smoothed my palms
over her cheeks, touched her forehead, the hollows
under her eyes, her pug nose, her lips, the pouching
below her jaw. I reached for the black greasepaint
pencil, and then the red. My father showed the man
the props while I worked. Color came off the pencils
one hue and flowed onto her face another, so I didn't
have to switch pencils at all. I didn't know what I was
doing, had no plan, but I let the tingles in my hands
take over.

After a little while I sat back and looked. Painted

flames rose from her eyebrows across her forehead.
Her lips were full and red, and lines of red glitter
spots curved below her eyes. She looked like someone
who should live in a volcano and come out to curse
people who mistreated it.

I wiped my forehead with the back of my hand. My
father handed me another bottle of Gatorade.

"Ruby," said the man, who now wore a black-and-
white-striped swallow-tailed jacket and a tri-cornered
hat. "You look like a goddess!"

She stared at me, her eyes bright and powerful
below the flames. I handed her the mirror. "Oh," she
said softly. Her eyes met mine again, and I felt her
delight and awe, and then her power. "You got anything red I could wear?"

My father gave her a black cape with red satin lin-
ing. She turned it inside out and flung it over her
shoulders.

"Can you do anything for me?" the man asked.

I smiled at him. He traded places with the woman
and took off his heavy glasses, and I patted his face,
my hands tickling. Something . . . something . . . I
picked up the black pencil, put an X below one eye,
an O below the other. I outlined his eyes with thin
black lines and touched his forehead with the red
grease pencil. A single flame formed just above the
bridge of his nose. I was finished.

"Why, Thaddeus," Ruby said, her voice soft and
wondering. To me, "How did you know he loves tic-
tac-toe?"

I shook my head, smiled, handed him the mirror.
He had to put his glasses back on to take a look at
himself, but then he nodded.

I felt too tired to pose them. My father did it, taking

off the man's glasses, gently talking them into just the right pose, then snapping their picture with both his cameras. I watched, thinking long thoughts.

What kind of gift was this?

Dad returned the glasses to the man and handed the couple the Polaroid as the colors came up on it. They stared and stared at the picture, not moving. Finally, Dad slipped it out of their hands and put it in a photomount, then coaxed them out of their borrowed clothes. They gave us five dollars for the picture and another five for the face painting. "What you do is too special not to pay for," Ruby told me. "You ought to charge much more than this."

When they left, they walked differently. They looked stronger.

"She's right," my father said. "This is not the best way to use your gift."

My mother came through the curtain. I hadn't heard her murmuring fortunes to anyone in a while. "It's not the best way to use it, but for now it's good to use it at all. You want it to know you like it and welcome it. The first day, you have to dance with it. Use it until you're too tired to go on. Otherwise it might leave you."

"What am I going to do with a gift like this?" I felt strange. I loved what I had done to Ruby and Thaddeus, and knowing that they loved it also gave me a peculiar delight, as though I had bubbles in my stomach and might laugh a color or burp an orchestra if I didn't take care. My hands had stopped tingling and just felt smooth and cool and right.

"I'll think of something," said my father.

"You the picture people?" A large man in a panama hat, gaudy Hawaiian shirt, and khaki shorts stood in our doorway. He wore sunglasses and had lots of dark hair on his arms and legs. "I heard you do good work. Who's this?" He stared at me. "What a good-looking babe," he said. "You pose with me, little lady? I'll pay extra."

"Sir, we are not that kind of outfit," said my father.

"What do you mean? It's just a picture," said the man. He smiled wide. "Not like I'm asking for anything bad."

We'd had offers like this before. I'd posed with people in the past, if my father said it was all right. Usually I was dressed as a sprite, and they just wanted a little extra magic in their picture. Today, thanks to the heat, I was wearing a yellow sleeveless cotton dress that only came down to midthigh. I hadn't put on the crown of dried flowers or the dragonfly wings, and I hadn't painted my eyebrows into crooks to look elvish or put latex points on my ears with spirit gum. I was just my newly fourteen-year-old self.

This request felt different from the usual. Creepy.

We'd had a slow day in the photo booth, and my mother hadn't been reading many fortunes either.

"How much?" I asked.

"Hey, my kind of people." Hawaiian shirt smiled, showing lots of nice white teeth. "How much you want?"

"Fifty dollars," I said.

"You charge me that, I'm gonna want a kiss."

"Sir!" my father cried. "How old does she look to you? Leave at once!"

"Just a peck on the cheek. A little peck on the cheek. I want something nice to show my buddies at work tomorrow."

"Not a chance—" said my father.

"Pay first," I said. "Five dollars for the photo and fifty for the kiss."

"Quite the little businesswoman, aren't you? I like a girl who knows what she's worth." He chuckled and handed my father some money.

My father's face was grim. His hand trembled as he took the money.

"Which background do you want?" I asked.

Hawaiian shirt checked out the three options. "Let's go with the roses. It's romantic." He strode over and stood behind the yellow taped line on the ground in front of the roses, fists on his hips and elbows out. I went to him and he leaned over so that his cheek was low enough for me to kiss if I stood on tiptoe. "Plant it right here, sweetheart," he whispered, pointing to his cheek.

"Not yet," said my father, shifting his cameras to aim at the roses. "All right."

I stood on my toes and touched my lips to Hawaiian shirt's cheek. "No, that isn't quite right," he said. He whipped his arm around me and gripped my buttock, hauling me closer. "Now."

My lips tingled and buzzed as I pressed them against his cheek. My father's cameras flashed.

"Ouch!" Hawaiian shirt let go of me, shaking his hand, then touched his cheek. "What did you—"

I jumped away from him, rubbing my butt. I had felt some kind of sizzle there.

"What—" my father said, his voice a puff of air. He stared at Hawaiian shirt's face.

I studied him, too, stepping farther from him. It wasn't obvious, what I had done to him. Perhaps his nose hooked a little more. Perhaps his lips drew up more so his many fine teeth were more visible. There was a suggestion of vulture in his features now, but you had to look hard to see it. His features were the same: pleasant. Yet there was something in his face that made you want to look away.

Hawaiian shirt took the Polaroid from my father's fingers and looked at it. "Mmm, baby," he said. Then he frowned. "Hey, there's something not quite right here. We have to do it over."

"You have what you paid for," said my father. He took the picture from Hawaiian shirt, put it in its photomount, and handed it back. "And now, good day."

"But this—hey!" Hawaiian shirt was out of our booth without being able to figure out what hit him. Sometimes my father can tell people what to do. Hawaiian shirt glanced back at us once, shook his head, and walked on.

"Cammie," said my father.

I sagged in my makeup chair. I was sweating again.

"When I say no, I mean no."

I hung my head. "I'm sorry," I whispered.

"Are you happy with what you did to him?"

"I don't know. He grabbed me, Dad. I don't know what I did."

"He was not a nice person. We are never so poor that we have to work with people who aren't nice, Cammie. We don't open the door to them at all, because they will push past and come farther into the house than we want." He came and kissed my forehead. "You'll be more careful from now on, won't you?"

"Yes."

"We're done for the day." He took down our sign and pulled a curtain across the front of the booth. "Stay here. I'm going to get you a sno-cone. Blue raspberry, right?"

I nodded. He left, and I sat in my chair and shivered despite the heat. What kind of gift was this?

I heard my mother murmuring on the other side of the curtain. "The man you trust with your heart, he is not good for you. I know this is hard for you to hear. Perhaps you will want to forget what I say. You can do that. Leave, laugh, say it was nothing, only a fake gypsy at a summer carnival. This is your choice. The one you look to for love right now, he is not faithful to you. Please watch and listen. Take care of yourself. You are precious."

Soft crying.

My mother spoke soothing words. I was sure she was patting the woman's hand, perhaps stroking her hair. Too much truth? Necessary truth. You could give people truth, Mother said, and they would throw it away. Many people were happier without it.

The Hawaiian shirt man now had the look of a vulture, hungry for unclean food. How long would that last? Who would even notice it?

How long would any of my changes last? What if Ruby could not get the flames and glitter spots off her face? What had I done?

My father came back and handed me a blue sno-cone.

"Daddy. What kind of gift is it? When I do something to someone, do they stay like that forever?"

His eyebrows rose. "What did you think while you were using your gift?"

"The first ones were just for the pictures," I said. "But then they were so happy. I wished they could stay like that as long as they liked."

My father smiled. "You answer your own question. When they want to, they can change back."

"But the last one? He scared me, and I was fighting back. I don't know about that one."

"His actions brought consequences. He will live with them."

I sucked flavor from my sno-cone, cooling my hands on its white paper cup. My tongue froze from the ice. Hawaiian shirt was a big jerk. Maybe he *should* look a little like a vulture.

I touched my cheek with my ice-cold index finger, and felt an answering buzz in my fingertip and then in my face. I picked up the hand mirror and saw a Pierrot diamond teardrop on my face.

My father touched it, too, and smiled sadly at me.

I didn't know how long it would last.

My father unloaded the film from his stealth camera, developed it in a formula he had designed. He snipped off the last negative and threw it away. He used the rest of the pictures to brew soul tea. We each drank a tiny cup.

I could taste their joy: Big Red, Ruby, Thaddeus. Stronger and brighter than any soul tea my father had made before.

After supper, we loaded our props and tents and tools on our truck, everything stacking and folding in just its own way and leaving enough room for our beds under a roof, and a small space to stand up in.

Long after dark had fallen, we sat on grass by the river and watched the fireworks. We were so close to where they were being set off that each percussive boom pressed my dress against my skin. I had to lie on my back to see all the purple, red, gold, green firebursts, galaxy rains of stars, rocket trails of light. Each display flashed so bright we could see the medusa-heads of smoke left behind by the last one.

I lay with my arms wide, my hands open, light powdering my skin, pooling in my palms. I had a gift. It was my birthday, and everybody was celebrating with me. Whistling stars sang me a song all across the sky, and I danced.

THE WOMAN WHO LOVED DEATH
by *Robin Wayne Bailey*

Robin Wayne Bailey is the author of a dozen novels, including the *Brothers of the Dragon* series, *Shadowdance,* and the new Fafhrd and the Grey Mouser novel *Swords Against the Shadowland.* His short fiction has appeared in numerous science fiction and fantasy anthologies and magazines. An avid book collector and old-time radio enthusiast, he lives in Kansas City, Missouri.

She was beautiful beyond all measure. The Lord of Death had given her this beauty, and he made love to her now on his black silken sheets, as he had too many times, with a gentleness that astonished him. When it was over, as too many times before, he felt confused and troubled as a god should not have been.

He cradled her head in his elbow. With one careful finger, he brushed a stray lock of raven hair from her eyes, those sleepy emerald eyes that struck fire in him, but also regret, and perhaps even a little unseemly fear. Her feathery breath tickled his neck as she sighed. *I must not allow myself these feelings,* he thought.

In all his domain he owned no greater treasure than her lips.

He rose from the bed. Around the chamber candles came to life with small unnatural violet flames. He paced, and she leaned up on one elbow. A look of worry creased her brow. It stabbed him through the heart he had forgotten he had.

He spoke her name. "Samidar," he said, and though his throat was dry as ash, he put power into his voice. A void yawned in his very being, grew wider as he looked at her, threatened to draw him in. He knew he had to close that void while he could. "There is no longer a place for you here."

She answered with tender heat that threatened to melt his resolve. "My lord," she said. For an instant he thought he heard, *my love,* but that could not have been. He was Death. "I would not, for my soul, have you think ill of me by giving plea or argument." She showed no fear as she spoke, but slipped from between the sheets to stand in a manner both meek and proud. "What use to gainsay such a will as yours? You have shown me kindness I never knew in life, and for that I am grateful. Do with me what you will."

Her acquiescence pierced him like arrows, and he almost found it within himself to hate her. She was a dark flower, subtly poisoning him with a perfume of unwise emotion. He barked a short laugh at that. How easy it would be to blame her for his weakness.

He caught her in his arms, forcing himself to feel nothing even as he pulled her close. "In Esgaria, your birth-land, a great and arrogant enemy has destroyed my temple." He drew one hand along the delicate line of her right cheek, memorizing its shape and the softness of her skin.

"Esgaria," she repeated. "A curious resonance in that word."

He lifted her chin. Already, he told himself, her mouth held less allure. "You will discover the offender and bring me his name."

She recoiled. Then, as if ashamed of the horror on her face, she turned away. "You would send me back," she whispered, "to the world of the living?"

Death hardened his features. The dangerous void she had caused within him began slowly to close, and he looked upon her through narrowed eyes, feeling less and less, or so he assured himself. "I dare not keep you close," he answered, "nor can I set you free. You will be my agent, then. My minister and my scourge. I cannot make you, once mortal, my queen, so I will make you my right hand."

She trembled, so naked and small, as she turned once more toward him and bowed. Her hair cascaded forward, hiding her face. "Do with me as you will," she repeated. "I have never been more than your servant."

Was that bitterness he heard? Or did he imagine more than she meant? He tasted his own anguish. If he did not send her away quickly, he would never send her away at all.

He backed away from her and gestured. In a corner, the candle flames flared. "There is my armor," Death said. "While you wear it, no harm can come to you."

Samidar lifted her head, then rose slowly to her feet. "Give me nothing that was not mine when I came to you," she said quietly, taking his hand. "Except this garnet ring so like a drop of blood upon your finger. And put no magic on it."

What might he read into such a request, he wondered? What should he read into it? It was not right that a god should know such trepidation and doubt. Like love, those, too, should be denied him. Yet he slipped off the ring and placed it upon her finger, and the only magic he put on it was to make it fit.

"I have set you a task," he said, making himself

stern. "All that you once had you shall have again, even the Demonfang, the better to serve me."

She tilted her head, her brow furrowing. "The dagger?" she said.

Ignoring her questioning look, he bore her down on the bed. Her mouth, so close, became too much for even a god to resist. He kissed her, then he made love to her, though with deliberate roughness this time, eschewing gentleness. "Now sleep," he whispered in her ear when he was done. "And in a while some little dreams may come."

She woke to the warmth of sunlight on her face. It streamed down through a shattered roof. She luxuriated in the sensation, but at the same time it frightened and aggrieved her. There was no sun in Hell, and she knew she was once more in the land of the living, apart from her Lord.

Eyeing the gaping rent above, she remembered her purpose. The floor where she lay was strewn with broken stone, mortar, splintered beams, crumbled tile. She smelled the dust, and more acutely, the green and fragrant world beyond the temple walls. Slowly, testing unfamiliar flesh, she sat up, and finally, with a fluid, catlike grace, rose to her feet.

Her gaze fell first upon the temple altar, which lay cracked, as if with a great hammer, and overturned. Beyond that, a length of broken rope revealed how great columns had been pulled down and the roof made to collapse. Sacrilege! She turned, breathless with shock, to stare at Death's obsidian fountain. It lay in large pieces. And the Pool of Welcome Relief, from which any man or woman may drink, had been fouled.

Her hand went instinctively, not to the sword on her right hip, but to the dagger on her left. It surprised and troubled her to find it there, to curl her fingers around its silver hilt, to feel it shiver against her palm with long-unsated hunger. She whispered, *"Demonfang,"* and the weapon trembled to hear its name.

The sword was good steel, well-balanced and razor-edged, but unlike the dagger, there was nothing special about it, nothing—*evil.* She tasted that word in her mouth, nibbled it again, wondered if it still meant the same to her after her stay in Hell.

Seeking distraction from such thoughts, she checked the armor she found herself wearing—black lacquered breast plates inlaid with gold geometries over black leather, lacquered greaves, and arm bracers. So like the armor of Death, she realized, but made feminine. It gleamed in the slightest ray of light.

A round shield, black and highly polished, leaned against the broken fountain, and beside that, a helm inlaid with gold tracings. She went to collect them, but paused as she passed the Pool of Welcome Relief. Her reflection regarded her, and she bent, mesmerized, to touch the watery shape of her cheek, her lips. The face looked strange. Her own, yes, but too young, idealized, almost inhuman in its perfection.

After a while, she rose. Taking up the shield and helm, she walked from the ruined temple, fighting confusion, haunted by her own image, by memories long forgotten that came trickling slowly back upon her.

Anticipating the blue-green expanses of Esgaria, she lingered outside. Esgaria—her homeland! The rolling steppes stretched before her, and in the far west she spied the purple peaks of the Suncradle Mountains. She smiled as the name came back to her. She drew a breath, tasting sweet air, inhaling the delicate fragrance of white starflowers that dotted the ground.

Then, with an anguished cry, dropping shield and helm, she sank to her knees. "Patricide!" she cried. As if a dam had broken, all her memories surged back. "Fratricide!" Father and brother, she killed them both again in her mind, and yet again, just as she had done in life. The memories—black deeds!—tore at her, rent her to her very soul.

Do I have a soul? she wondered, wiping away her tears. For these crimes and more had she suffered torment until Death, in his mercy, took notice of her. She looked at her hands, studied them, squeezed her fists and opened them, strove to reconcile them with the hands of a murderess. The white flesh flushed pink. *Blood I have, then. But do I have a soul?*

"Oh, my father!" she whispered, plucking one of the small white starflowers from among the grass. "My brother!" She picked another and cast them both to the wind. "Forgive me!"

A crash sounded from within the temple. Another beam fell; another section of the roof slithered inward.

Her lips drew into a thin, taut line. Reminded of her purpose, she got to her feet. She was not here to seek forgiveness, but to serve her master.

The ground was churned with hoofprints and footprints. The tracks were old, but clear. A dusty road ran along one side of the temple. Another coil of rotted rope lay to one side of it, and nearly concealed in the grass nearby, something else—an arrow. Retrieving it, she noted three red bands circling the shaft just beneath three white goosefeather fletchings. The marauders had left a clue. A loud snap. She cast aside most of the shaft and shoved the marked piece into her greave.

Her gaze settled once more on the sunlit mountain peaks, and another memory stole unbidden across her thoughts. Her father, she remembered, once had hunted there, and she had dined on a bear he had killed. Again, regret and grief threatened to overwhelm her, but she steeled herself against old emotions, reminding herself that it was, after all, so long ago. Another lifetime, literally.

Embracing that truth, she started down the road.

It was a small village, just a scattering of shops and dwellings on either side of the road. Sunset had turned the sky blood red, and her black shadow stretched far before her as she passed the first cottage. From within came the odors of cooked venison and warm bread. A mother with an infant nursing at one breast watched from an open window. The lullaby she hummed abruptly ceased, and she closed the shutters.

A smith was just closing his smithy. With hostile eyes, he watched her advance, his hammer gripped tightly in one hand. She passed him by, not because he intimidated her, but because an old woman at a cottage down the road caught her attention with a beckoning hand.

The cottage needed repair, but the roses growing around it poured sweet perfume into the evening air. The old one sat in her doorway where she could see the road, a small table before her. With gnarled hands she idly shuffled a deck of cards; her pale eyes took in everything. She began to rock back and forth, and her head began to nod. "I know you," she said.

Curious, Samidar left the road and approached her. "Do you, grandmother?"

The old woman continued to nod, but the cards became still. "Dare you match your magic against mine?" She placed one palm on her table. The scarred wooden surface transformed, became water upon which waves danced and surf foamed. Yet it remained smooth, a table.

Samidar gazed into ancient eyes, measured the knowledge in them, the wisdom, before she leaned down and touched the table. The old woman's spell dissolved. The tabletop became night sky, pure and deep and black and full of tiny stars, a hole into infinity. Yet it remained a table. Then it became a mirror that reflected both their faces, and though one was old and the other young, they were not such different faces.

Wordlessly, the old woman rose and went inside, only to return with a ladle full of cool water, which Samidar accepted. Setting aside her shield, she drank. It was not as sweet as Death's wine, yet it pleased. She returned the empty ladle, then extracted the piece of feathered shaft from her greave and placed it on the table.

The old woman needed no explanation. "The Blood Spiders," she answered in a somber voice. "Their red marking is well-known." She hesitated and looked unflinchingly into the younger woman's eyes. "Are they your business—or am I?"

It was Samidar's turn to hesitate. "You do know me, don't you?"

"I am old, and Death has been creeping up on me a long time," she answered. "I know the sound of his footsteps. You walk with his tread."

The wind blew, and the roses' fragrance wafted in the air. A long strand of hair whipped across Samidar's face. She brushed it back, but in the fading whisper of the breeze, she thought she heard her master's voice. "Sleep at peace tonight," she answered the old woman. "My Lord has no interest in you yet. Tell me of these Blood Spiders."

"Brutal servants of the Faceless Lady." She pointed up the road. "Walk on. If they are your business, you will surely meet them."

Samidar regarded the old woman with a strange unease. "I regret that I have no coin to give for this information," she said.

A weak smile turned up the corners of the old woman's mouth. "You have granted me a night of peace," she answered. "That is worth more than treasure." She glanced up the street again, and the smile faded. "But have a care, Chooser," she added. "Our village is cursed, and danger lurks for even such as you."

The wind gusted, raising a swirl of dust that wound up the dry street. Already the first stars appeared in the darkening sky. Samidar walked at a cautious pace. She looked at homes and shops, noted the tight shutters, the stout doors.

A palpable fear hung in the air. It brushed her skin like a chill draft; she tasted it like salt on her tongue. Somewhere a door slammed, and wood scraped on wood as a heavy bar dropped into place. Pausing, she turned. Even the old woman had retreated with her cards and table into her cottage.

How swiftly night came on. In Hell there was no night, no day, no dusk, no dawn. She listened to the rising insect songs. Just beyond the village, a pheasant lifted suddenly on frantic wings from its grassy nest.

A scream sounded from the last house on the street. Not a window opened, not a face looked out from the other houses. The scream came again. The door of that last house wrenched back. A mother rushed out with her child in her arms.

Behind her came a pair of red-masked warriors, and

from around the house came four more. They chased
the woman down, beat and kicked her. The child, a
little girl, scrambled loose. Shrieking, she tried to flee.
A red-gloved hand caught her arm and yanked her
cruelly into the air like a prize.

"Kill the sow," one of the men said. "We have
the piglet."

A sword flashed above the woman. Another raw-
throated scream tore from her, and she raised a hand
as if her flesh could ward off the blow.

A piece of an arrow fell suddenly in the dust, like
a challenge, at the feet of the sword's wielder. He
hesitated, his blow undelivered. Four more drew
swords. The one with the child fell back.

"Who are you?" one called nervously, squinting at
the dark shape that had crept upon them unnoticed.

Anger prevented Samidar from speech. She waded
into them, taking one across the chest with her drawing stroke, smashing another with her shield, clearing
space around the mother. "Run," she urged. But the
mother sprang, instead, for her daughter, and a cursing red-mask cut her down. Samidar's next stroke
repaid him.

The one with the girl released his struggling captive,
turned, and ran. His two standing companions followed. Weeping, the little girl threw herself upon
her mother.

Samidar looked around, her rage unabated. No
other villager ventured out; none offered help. She
wiped her blade on one of the red-masks, sheathed it,
and returned her shield to her back. Next, she gathered the child in her arms.

A strange feeling overcame her. The small bundle
radiated such warmth. Its hands clutched at her, and
it buried its face against her shoulder. Helplessly, she

rocked the child, wondered what else she should do. She glared with hatred at the dead men on the ground.

"Let me care for her."

Samidar turned. The old woman held out her arms and took the child, her expression sadly tender. She cooed to the weeping girl, brushed back a tear-damped lock of black hair, wiped a small pale cheek with a gnarled finger.

"Of all your people, only you dared come out," Samidar said bitterly.

The old woman's eyes were full of their own mist. She hugged the child to her withered breasts. "I remembered that you said Death had no interest in me tonight," she answered. "They had no such assurance."

Samidar clenched her fists, no sympathy in her for people so cowed by fear. Stooping, she ripped the mask from one of the fallen. Only a man beneath, but a fine webwork tattooed his face from hairline to chin, from one ear to the other.

"The Blood Spiders?" she asked, receiving a nod for an answer. She looked down the road into the darkness. "Where would his accomplices go?"

"To their keep in the next valley," the old one said. "Back to their Faceless Mistress."

Rising, Samidar leaned toward the child and touched her tiny shoulder. A sweet, small face turned briefly her way; wide, frightened eyes, like cloudy emeralds, locked with her own. Another flash of memory came back to Samidar. "I had children once," she told the little girl. She struggled to hide the sadness of that memory. "You're going to be so pretty."

Her lips drew into a grim line as she turned from them and took to the road. The darkness offered no deterrent; she saw well enough. Well enough, indeed.

The Blood Spiders had destroyed the temple of her lord. Their arrow and their ropes were proof of that. And more, she despised them—murderers and thugs!—for the life they had needlessly taken, and for the smothering shroud of terror in which they seemed to rule.

She stood on the summit of a hill. Beyond, framed in starlight and against the moon that just peeked over the far horizon, rose a structure vast and black, a castle that radiated antiquity. Its towers lurched at precarious angles; a bulwark wall coiled about it like a serpent. It was architecture from another time; the concept and product, Samidar realized, of no human mind. Lamplight or torchlight shone through embrasures and mullioned windows that were grouped together strangely. They gleamed—leered!—like faceted eyes.

Still, she approached defiantly, shield on her arm, helmeted now. Men lined up on the wall, their numbers increasing as she drew nearer to the gate. The firelight from braziers sheened on their faces, on swords and arrow-points.

She felt the weight of Death's ring on her finger and recalled his promise: *All that you once had you shall have again!*

Extending her will, she gathered the night and called the wind. Clouds took shape; they drank away the starlight and the moon. It all came back to her, easier than she'd hoped or imagined. Power coursed through her; her body sang with it. She called, and thunder answered.

On the wall, the Blood Spiders reacted with terrified shouts. An arrow glanced off her shield. Then a cascade of arrows shot outward from panicked bows. She laughed. A wind swept the flimsy missiles from their flight. The sky split open with rain.

She had arrows of her own to hurl.

She stretched an arm to the churning heavens. A jagged bolt of lightning lashed downward, striking the gate. One of the two great doors splintered and twisted on its hinges. A second bolt followed the first. Wood, metal, and stone exploded. The parapet directly above the shattered gateway crumbled and crashed. Men screamed, and their cries were sweetest revenge for a murdered mother!

Samidar strode through the smoking destruction into a grand courtyard. A man rushed her, ax in hand, an expression of desperate fear on his face. Her own sword gleamed, its shining blade rippling with reflections of fire and fading lightning. Sidestepping his blow, she laid his red mask open with a slash and moved on.

Most of them ran from her. Some few cowered, whimpering wrecks of men, as she passed by. The foolish ones charged her. She dispatched them coldly with contempt.

Crouched by a well, sword hanging from a limp hand, a man hid his face and trembled as she neared. "It is Death Incarnate!" he muttered.

"Blasphemer!" she answered. But she did not kill him. Beyond the well, a motion caught her eye.

The great doors to the castle itself swung quietly open. Even the Blood Spiders took notice. A hush fell over the yard. The air tingled with expectation.

She turned her attention from the one-sided combat. Cautiously, she crossed the yard, coming to a flight of wide stone steps. She ascended them to the threshold, pausing only briefly at the top, then proceeded into darkness.

Dim light filled but a single corridor. Removing her helm, hanging it by its chin strap over her scabbard, she advanced toward that light. The hall smelled strange, of mold and dust, and of something more, something unidentifiable.

Another lamplit corridor offered itself, and the light behind her flickered out. Guidance, she realized. And sorcery not her own. No matter. With jaw set, she followed where the light led. At last, another pair of doors blocked her way. They, too, opened seemingly of their own accord. The light beyond those doors came from no lamp or candle.

The hall was vast, the ceiling reaching into soaring gloom. Above her head, an immense many-layered web, intricate in design, shimmered with a creamy radiance. Its geometries dazzled. Its scale amazed.

It was a thing of awe—and repulsion.

At the very center of the web, a gauzy, egg-shaped sac hung suspended. Through its veil-thin walls, a shape could be glimpsed. It stirred.

"Why do you attack my home and my servants?" The voice was feminine, polite, curious.

Samidar lowered her shield as she craned her neck upward. "You defiled my Lord's house," she answered sharply. "Death's temple. Though your men did the deed, you surely gave the order."

"You are mistaken," the Faceless Lady replied, for so Samidar deemed her to be.

"I found a red-marked arrow and your ropes," she answered. "Proof of your guilt."

The figure stirred again, and the web sac shivered with movement. "Proof of nothing," that soft voice said. "The hunting is good near the old ruins. That explains the arrow."

"Your men are brutes and bullies," Samidar said.

"Not hunters. I saw with my own eyes tonight how they attacked a house and killed a mother."

"Still they are men and must eat," came the lilting answer. "So must I."

Samidar thought. Hunting might explain the arrow, but what of the ropes, what of the destruction? She found it hard to think suddenly. The smell she had noticed earlier—she knew it now. It was the web itself. Its substance exuded a cloying perfume. "I do not trust your words," she said. "Why do they call you the Faceless Lady? Are you afraid to face me?"

A long rip appeared in the fabric of the sac. "The villagers call me that because I have not been seen outside these walls in seven hundred years."

"Seven hundred years?" Samidar said. She rubbed her nose, then pinched her nostrils shut. Still the odor assailed her.

A shadow moved in the sac's long rent, an unnatural shape that sent a shiver down Samidar's spine. A woman's face looked out, a young and pleasing face framed with silver hair. Then a torso. Her skin was pale, her breasts small and piquant. She had no arms.

What came next was nightmare. A bloated thorax with black and yellow markings, eight black articulating legs that grasped strands of webbing with graceful precision. Half-human, half-spider! Abomination!

Spinnerets wove and worked. The creature descended smoothly on a glistening line. "My name is Eetha," she said, dropping. "In another age, my father was one of the great artisan spiders in the northern forest called Etai Calan." When she reached the floor, she regarded Samidar unflinchingly, eye to eye. "Now put away your sword," she said. "Like my father, I cannot be harmed by the weapons of men, and my magic is as strong as yours."

Samidar doubted that.

"I did not destroy your temple," Eetha continued soothingly. "Nor did my men."

Samidar backed an involuntary step. Her senses reeled. "They attacked and killed that woman," she challenged. "Tried to take a little girl."

The soft weblight and Eetha's voice had a mesmeric quality. "Yes," Eetha whispered. "A sweet child. As I said, I must eat."

With a shock, Samidar snapped her head up. Eetha had worked her magic well. She found herself already ensnared by coils of fine webbing, lying nearly co-cooned, suspended high in the air in the great web itself.

Eetha straddled her on eight horrible legs, and she bent her face near to Samidar's. "The villagers are bound to me by spells and cannot flee. I know their flavor too well. You, an outsider, I shall savor."

Her sword lay far below on the floor. Samidar struggled against the webbing, striving to reach the dagger, Demonfang. Her fingers curled around its hilt, and she jerked it from its sheath.

A cacophonous wail of countless tormented voices filled the hall as the dagger's edge sliced easily through silken strands. Samidar freed herself and slashed viciously at Eetha's underbelly. Nimbly, Eetha sprang back as her captive plummeted to the floor. She followed on a fresh web.

Samidar fought to get up, the breath half-knocked from her. She spun about, grasping her dagger. The arcane blade trembled hungrily in her hand, its many voices demanding satiation.

Eetha's eyes burned with anger. "Your weapons cannot hurt me!" she shrieked. "Nor your magic prevail. In my castle, I rule, and your blood will feed me!"

Eetha attacked with startling speed. Knocking Samidar over, she straddled her once again, and spinnerets began to weave fresh bonds.

"No man, but Death himself, made this blade," Samidar said with bitter anger. "And the voices of Hell are calling you home!"

She plunged the dagger into Eetha's torso where she hoped the heart would be. The blade's unholy voices fell instantly silent. Eetha stumbled back; her eyes flashed wide with surprise, then with fear. Her lips parted to scream. Only it was the dagger's chorus of voices that issued from her mouth.

"Seven hundred years is long enough," Samidar murmured when Eetha lay still on the floor. She reclaimed the dagger and sheathed it. It purred against her hand, its hunger sated for the moment.

She fled the hall. Stumbling her way blindly through seemingly endless corridors, she reached a window and jumped. A few nerveless men still lingered in the courtyard, their tattooed faces turned to her in terror.

She gave them no more thought, but passed through the shattered gate and down the road. When she stood once more on the summit overlooking the valley, she called her storm again. Bolt after bolt of scarlet lightning stabbed at Eetha's castle, lanced it like a boil. At last, when no tower remained, when no stone lay unscorched, Samidar relented and turned away.

For three days, she labored in the ruined temple. Straining, she righted the altar stone. She pulled weeds that thrust through the cracks of the floor. With a bucket borrowed from the old woman, she filled the

Pool of Welcome Relief, and when she rested on its edge, the face of Death appeared to her.

"Are you prepared to name the enemy that destroyed my shrine?" he asked.

She extended a hand toward his image, longing to touch him, afraid to disturb the water. Did she dare to tell him how she ached for his caress, or how empty she felt on this side of life? She drew a breath and steeled herself against such sentiments. She would not, for her soul, have him think ill of her or think her weak.

"My Lord," she said. "I know the enemy now, and the destroyer of your temple. It was neither Eetha, nor her Blood Spiders."

Death nodded. "The name," he said.

"There were clues," Samidar said. "A girl child with my eyes and hair. An old woman with my face, but aged. Had I but looked closer at the state of this ruin . . ." She shrugged. Her Lord had tricked her, but she had the answer. Now she would take her time. It would keep him with her longer.

"The name," Death repeated. "Speak it."

Samidar smiled stubbornly. "Seven hundred years of solitude drove Eetha mad."

Death looked at her through the water, his eyes unfathomable to her. Yet sometimes she thought she saw something there, some spark, some hint of what he might feel for her had he a heart to feel with.

"You do know it," he said. "I have not tricked you, as you surely think. I have taught you, Samidar, a lesson that even Death must know. I am eternal. You might think it a great gift to live forever. But it is my prison and my unending nightmare."

"As it became for Eetha?" Samidar whispered. "As it will become for me?"

Death did not answer, but the water rippled for no good reason, and his image trembled.

She swallowed, wondering and fearing what lay before her. "The great and arrogant enemy," she said finally, using his own words, "is Time."

SACRIFICE
by Michelle West

Michelle West is the author of several novels, including *The Sacred Hunter* duology and *The Broken Crown,* both published by DAW Books. She reviews books for the on-line column *First Contacts,* and less frequently for *The Magazine of Fantasy & Science Fiction.* Other short fiction by her appears in *Black Cats and Broken Mirrors, Elf Magic, Olympus,* and *Alien Abductions.*

She reflects, in the darkness, the pain passing, that magic is something that cannot be caught or trapped. That a spell, some casting into the wild, is like fishing. Like fishing with a thin rope and no hook and a pole that is dry and brittle, when everything depends upon the catch.

It has been almost beyond her grasp for all of her life, and she reflects on that life in these shadows, wondering where the magic comes from, and why it is always so very expensive.

She is, of course, afraid.

She has always been afraid.

When she was a little girl, when she was young enough to be a miracle because she had survived the winter and the fevers that had come when the healers were so difficult to reach, she was fascinated by everything. And because the children had died across the length and breadth of the farmsteads that were only

72

barely enough of a community to be called a village, she was treasured, envied, cozened.

She was not beaten into submission; she got into everything, the way an unrestrained child will. The unknown made her squeal in a language that was no language, but understood by all. She remembers this.

The first time she saw magic was in the hands of an elderly man. He seemed the very casement through which she might look and see the knowledge of the world. She could not see how age bowed him; how his shoulders were not so straight or so strong as her father's, his steps not so quick, his eyes not so clear. She did not know that the snow-white streaks in his dark hair were signals of weakness and surrender to time. She thought they were like ice and snow, like the weather itself; she loved the lines in his face, the way his jaw had worked itself into a hard, brown shape over the years.

She knows that he came to her, his wind-creased hands open, his palms empty. And he asked her, wizened old man, for a hug. They laughed, the people in the crowded family room. She laughed. She could hug anyone without fear then. His breath did not smell of ale or wine; it was old.

"I'm going to show you some magic," he said, and the uncles laughed again, and they said things that she didn't understand, and she laughed because they were laughing, even though the words made no sense. Years later, she would remember the words, and they would destroy some part of what made the memory valuable. But comprehension could not destroy everything. "All magic has its price. All magic."

She could speak then, not in words that made sense to anyone but her Ma. But she did anyway, and he smiled.

"No," he said, "I want what *you* can give. Hug the old bear, and that will be payment enough; it's a small magic."

And she hugged him, not because she wanted to see the magic—she barely understood what he meant by the words—but because he liked her, and she knew it. She could ask him for anything and he would indulge her.

That was what she looked for in a grown-up.

She does not clearly remember when she discovered that there is no safety in indulgence.

"You are a good little girl," he said, when he was willing to let go. "And you've paid the price. Here. What would you most like to see?"

She shrugged a minute, and then said, "My Da."

"Look into my hands, look into my hands, weaver's daughter. Look hard, let the light fill the bottom of my palms. What do you see there? Do you see what you wished for?"

She nodded solemnly, and he smiled. "Sometimes," he said quietly, "what we wish for—no matter what it is—is danger enough. And sometimes, it is impossible, but it is worthy nonetheless."

She saw her father's face, hood fringed in snow; he was out in the woodshed. No storm tonight. In the cold, his forehead glistened; sweat, his skin too warm to let his body's moisture bead into ice. He'd lit a lamp, but it wouldn't last long. Oil was so expensive. He worked, to keep his family warm. He worked, and she was happy to watch him. It made her feel safe.

"I want to be safe forever," she said, in the broken syllables that meant nothing to anyone but her.

And the old man looked down at her from a height that must once have been impressive; he took her up in hands that had killed lesser men, and pressed her

a moment to a chest whose scars nubbled flesh she
couldn't see.

"No one is safe forever, little one. That's what
breaks us, over and over. No one is ever safe."

She didn't understand what that meant until she was
five years old and she found out that the old man who
had once led men into victory without flinching had
been waylaid by a band of drunk youths and beaten
to death.

She can see him now, in the darkness, his face an
old man's face. She wonders how he died; if he struggled; if he fought; if he curled up on the ground in an
attempt to shelter himself from the blows. He died far
from the village, and she was never shown his body,
although in the years to follow she would see many,
many deaths. War in the lands, much of it, and an
army to feed. No magic; no magic there. She wonders
what it was that he gave her that day, and if in using
it for the sake of amusing a small child, he sold his
life away.

And hates wondering. Hates it.

They have left her alone. The bleeding has stopped.
But they have not taken the child.

Her father was a miller. But her mother, during the
poor harvests, sold her skills in town as a weaver, and
although it made life hard for their family, it also
made it possible. As any other family did, they endured. Her father had help from his unmarried
brother, and help from his dutiful daughter; his wife
would leave and return, leave and return, like a season
of her own.

Mills were only good when there was something to

mill, and when the season was harsh, she wished for rain.

Rain was such a little thing to wish for. She understood its significance; it was, her father said, staring at the beautiful depths of perfectly clear sky, like the blood in a person's body; when it ceased to flow, the body was dead.

But it's clear, she had thought. Clear, and light; it gave life when it fell, rather than taking it away.

She walked the edges of her father's land, saw that the ground was hard. She'd have to go home soon; dinner wasn't far off, and she'd need to get started. Her father was in a foul enough mood as it was.

No, that wasn't fair. He was worried. The mill was all they had, and he could lose it if the year were as bad as it looked to be.

Think, her mother said, although her mother was in town, *of your father, your uncle. They don't know how to think for themselves; they've so much to do. Men don't notice the details, daughter. They never notice the details.*

"It's true," a voice said quietly, and she turned, and her jaw fell open the way that jaws do when you forget how to use them. "But you notice much, because you were taught to notice."

She nodded, she remembers nodding because she couldn't think of anything to say.

"Come with me," the woman said. "Come with me."

"Why?"

"Were you not thinking of magic?" Her smile was wonderful, was blessed.

Had she been? She couldn't recall it; she was in the presence of magic now; she felt it. This lady's hair was golden, as golden as the ring that her mother wore with such pride—her father's gift. *You see?* Her mother told her. *This band is unbroken, start to finish. It's about love, about your father's love for me.*

"The land," the lady said, "it's been dry this season. Very dry."

She nodded again, the feeling upon her. "And you've come to help us?"

"I've come to help you," the woman replied. But there was something in her voice that was as cold as ice in winter. "But you've had experience with magic before. Do you understand it any better than you did?"

She saw her father's face as it was, in the winter light, the wood splitting beneath the wedged head of an ax. "No," she said at last, because it did not occur to her to lie to the woman, even though she so very much wanted her approval.

"Well, it can't be helped. Is it rain you want? I can give you rain, child. I can drench the county."

"You can't give us too much rain," she said, eyes narrowing, cautious now in a way that she had not been cautious the last time.

"Not too much, no. You don't have to be careful with your desires." Her smile was full and red. "Not in that way. If you choose to offer what I request, you will have the power to do as you desire. It is not I who will use the magic."

"But you'll give it to me?"

The woman's smile was so beautiful it was hard to think.

"What do I have to do?" She knew, no child she, that the woman wanted more than a hug; more than delight, more than fingers across the underside of her delicate, perfect chin.

"Do?" She said. "Almost nothing. Promise only

that you will not interfere with anything you see this eve, and you will have rain in plenty on the morrow, and on the day after, and this season there will be no drought."

"And after this season?"

"There is always other magic," the woman said coolly, "and if you desire it, and you understand the price you've paid, you will be able to call the rain."

She wanted the rain. She thought of how proud her father would be if she summoned the rain; of how well they would do. She thought of her mother, of how her mother could tell the weaver that *this* season she needed do no extra work; her mother could come back from town and live with them. All would be well. All would be well.

"Yes."

"Yes?" the lady asked her quietly.

"Yes."

"I will accept that, although I know full well that you have no idea what you've promised to give up. That is what all of your life will be like. You'll have no idea of what you've given up until it's gone, and then, try as you might, you'll never get it back; something is always sacrificed for magic's sake."

That night, the woman went to the mill. Behind her, a young girl followed, possibly because she didn't want to let the magic out of sight for a moment; possibly because there was some promise, some desire the mysterious stranger invoked by presence alone that even a child could feel the edges of it. She saw the lady's back, and then the lady herself didn't matter anymore, for she saw her father look up, drop something heavy at his feet, and stare. She watched; it was almost as if she was incapable of looking away. Almost as if.

But when she started to turn away, something

caught at her throat, something pulled her around; she had to move in order to keep on breathing, the grip was so tight, the pull so merciless. She saw her father walk to the door and close it, and for just a second, in the narrowing gap between the door and the frame, their eyes met.

She did not understand, until that moment, what it was that the lady with hair the colour of her mother's wedding band had taken as her price; she understood it then, when her father's face reddened, when his eyes glanced off hers, when his expression shifted from a start of guilt to anger.

She knew what that anger meant.

But the guilt was worse.

She never called the rain again. But it was too late; the drought was absorbed, swallowed whole; it became a part of her. She is not certain why she has tears now, but they are falling. Perhaps that drought has ended.

The storm is worse.

In time, the weaver's daughter learned her mother's craft. No longer willing or able to sit like the good daughter by her father's side, she had begged her mother for permission to accompany her on her journeys to town, and when it was made clear to them all that she might indeed add to the family income, her mother relented.

In town, she discovered a life that was, in its way, magical—a thing of wonder. There were stores here, where the money that was hard won could be spent in the blink of an eye; where sweet food waited in small wooden bins and pantries; where bread, soft and white, was baked every day. Evidence of this came wafting up into the third-story room that she and her mother shared, its scent so much sweeter than cock's crow.

Dawn broke not on open field and the few animals they owned, but on streets wide across as several wagons, and packed flat by the weight of wheels and feet; it opened across the face of buildings, with windows the size of half walls in the large, grand buildings. Those buildings were not made of the wood slats or logs with which she was familiar; they didn't smell of the hewn tree. They came from the stone quarries to the far North of the town, and they were costly. And so, too, were the people who made them their home.

She met a boy.

She met a boy from a family in town, face fair, hair pale, eyes as dark as edge of night sky. She met him in the market, at her mother's watchful side.

He offered to carry their baskets, and her mother said, quietly and firmly, that no help was needed. She was glad of it, fiercely glad; she did not want that boy to know that they lived above the baker's in a single, spare room that held all of the summer's heat and none of its soft breezes.

But they met, and they met again, in the town's center, the market a map whose significant features she learned by heart because of those chance meetings. Sometimes he traveled in a fine carriage, and on those days her throat would close, and all air would momentarily refuse to make its way into her lungs. The horses were meant for show, and they were splendid; her own family could sell every animal they owned and not have enough money for a single such beast, and even if they somehow managed to own it, they could never afford to feed and keep it.

On days like that, a woman's harsh profile in the window at his side, she *knew* what was impossible.

* * *

She thought a lot about the nature of magic during those days. And during the nights, when she tossed sleeplessly beside her mother's still form, she thought more, and more deeply. She had not—would never—forget the look on her father's face when he had opened the door to the compelling, cold beauty of a stranger; she felt certain that she would never forgive it either, although she tried very hard not to think of the part she had played.

But she understood some of it then in uncomfortable, prickly ways, for when she saw the young man, everything else she had ever learned in her life—all manners, all behavior, all the warnings about the importance of propriety—left her; she could hear them as dim and meaningless echoes, although she *knew* that they had once been the center of her life.

She remembers, clearly, the first day he touched her hand. Remembers it in the darkness that is being relieved by the flicker of lights. The pain is almost gone, but some other nameless anxiety has taken its place.

She would rather have the pain; pain is, after all, certain.

They have not taken the child, but they have cleaned him and left him at her side, and he is beginning to open his eyes.

She wanted to believe in love.

She wanted to be smart.

In the end, she was neither; she walked the line between them both with the desperate obstinacy of a young woman who cannot accept that she cannot have what she wants, but who cannot force herself to believe wholeheartedly that she *can*. The first time he touched her hand in the market she pulled back as if burned, and then she regretted it, feeling like a stupid farm girl; her cheeks rose in blush, and she walked away quickly.

But the day after, she lingered, and he lingered, their silence an awkward, unspoken secret. They learned how to break it.

Her mother was furious.

His mother was never mentioned.

"Don't you wonder," he asked her one day, "what you're missing?"

They walked by the broad banks of the river around which the town had been built, casting long shadows in the dying light. "What I'm missing?" At his side, his eyes along the line of her jaw, the swell of her cheek, the contours of—yes—her lips, she felt as if nothing were missing.

"You can't read," he said. "You can't write."

She frowned, hating to hear any of the things that separated them spoken out loud.

"I'm not saying it to criticize you. I'm asking you: Don't you wonder what you miss?"

She rounded on him then, the blush brought by his attention replaced by some other color that looked, in the end, the same. "What point would there be," she said, her voice low. "You know that we could never afford anything *to* read." And she walked away from him, crossing the bridge, her anger and her hurt pride the shield behind which she hid.

But the next day . . .

The next day he brought her a book.

The baby mewls. She has never had a baby before, and no one is there to tell her what to do with the child, but she has had some warning and some advice, and she takes them both now, seeking to content the child. Dark here; too dark to read.

He loved her. Of that she was certain. Her mother's anger lessened; developing, over time, into pensive and terrible sadness.

He loves me, Mother, she would say, defiant.

And does it matter? Her mother would reply. *It's not you he'll marry.*

Would he have? Would he have married her had things gone differently? Bitter question. She asks it, when the seasons turn. Asks it, when her own situation seems too dark and she seeks solace in the thought of other paths her life might have taken.

She asks it now a moment, and then the baby, in the darkness, offers her solace of a different sort.

She had promised that she would never, never seek magic again. She had promised it because she was terrified that the most beautiful woman she had ever seen would come walking across the packed dirt of the open road, seeking to break the fragile belief in, and of, love. But something else came instead: a wagon, a frightened horse, a child under its feet. The horse veered; the wagon veered as well.

And the young man responded in a way that still made her proud: He saved the child.

He saved the child and then lay in the road, victim to the horse's hooves and the wagon's back wheel.

And at that moment, while voices were raised in screams—for doctors, for gods, for his parents—she stood feeling the chill take her. She knew death when she saw it; knew his.

It was another woman who came to her then, a

woman the age of her mother or perhaps older. No beauty she; but stern and wise, if heavy with years. Her eyes were clear gray, and her lips were turned down slightly in an expression that seemed to echo sorrow without being consumed by it.

"Well, daughter," she said quietly

"I'm not your daughter."

"No. I didn't say you were. But you are someone's daughter, and she will feel as I feel in time. In time you will be someone's mother, and perhaps, if you are very lucky, you will not feel what I feel."

"And that?"

"I am come to offer you what you carry within you."

"Magic," she said, watching blood pool.

"Yes."

She hadn't been afraid of death, although she saw it coming; she had been afraid of *this*.

"I would lie to you, daughter," the woman said. "Or perhaps tell you that you must give me something that you do not understand. But you are wiser than you were, and you have paid the earlier price.

"Let me tell you."

But the girl raised a hand, stemming the flow of words. Bitterly, because she could not speak any other way, she said, "Just answer this: Will he die if I don't use what you offer?"

"Yes."

"And if I do?"

"There are days," the older woman replied softly, "when you will wish he had."

"What do you mean?"

The old woman frowned. Started to speak, and then pursed her lips slightly. "Make your choice, and make it quickly; magic is a thing that will not touch the dead."

She knew, then, that she would save him. She ran from the older woman's side, and the older woman vanished like shadow in darkness; she knew it, although she spared no backward glance. She pushed the people aside; pushed them hard when they ignored her in a panic of their own.

She cried, *I can save him!*

But the words seemed to make no sense. There was no panic, no more panic, on her part; she had made her bargain; the spell had already begun, and as its completion all that was required of her was that she touch him.

And she did, as he lay insensible on the city street. She kissed his forehead, his cheeks, his street-bruised lips, weeping all the while.

When they came to take him away, they thought it was because she loved him and feared he was dead, and they were right and wrong: she loved him, and she knew that the price of saving his life was *his* love; he would leave her, in the end, for someone "suitable," just as her mother had always said.

He did. His love, which had been so perfect and so peaceful, which had isolated her from her environment and had offered her a world unlike the world her mother and father had been confined by, drifted in time, lessened by the absence of his convalescence.

When they met in the market weeks later they were once again separated by their station, and if he paused, if he stopped to stare a moment longer than necessary, it made no difference to the outcome. She wanted to speak with him. She wanted to beg and plead, to ask him what had changed in her that he no longer loved her, or no longer spoke to her of their future together.

But she already knew the answer, and she contented herself with that bitter knowledge, and a wealth of tears. Her mother was unexpectedly kind, although in part this was because she had not become so entangled that there was a question of children.

And perhaps because, although he did leave her, he did not leave her with nothing: she could read.

She doesn't remember the feeling behind the tears anymore; she remembers that she cried them. She remembers that she cried them into her mother's arms and shoulders, and that her mother's arms and shoulders—for just those awful moments—were as hard and as strong as they had been when she was a child.

They're gone now, of course.

In the year that the worst of the plague came to visit the village, she was still unmarried, and given her age likely to remain so. She was not, by this age, untraveled, for her ability to read made her useful in some situations, and she added a rudimentary grasp of numbers to her old lover's gift. The local merchants, especially those who dealt with the out-of-town buyers, came to her when they felt intimidated, and she agreed, for a small fee here and there, to aid them. Her father was failing, her mother healthy, when they found the first village to be struck by disease and narrowly avoiding dying in the panic.

But something died in her anyway; she could see, beneath the membrane of closed lids, the bodies that lay beneath the open sky, left there to rot in fear, or worse, left because no one remained who might offer decent burial. She had a terrible desire to pull a huge tarpaulin over the whole of the village—or of what she had seen of it; she was sick for days because the stench would not leave her nostrils.

Sick for days, waiting to see who would catch what the wind had carried.

Two of the guards caught the fevers that raged without cease; they turned red and then purple over the course of three nights, and on the fourth they were buried.

By the fifth day they were home. She left the caravan at the farmsteads on the towns outskirts, and found that her father had taken ill. Her mother was tired and gray, but her mother was strong; she knew that her mother would be fine. Her mother.

"What is it?" the older woman said, her voice sharp as she saw her daughter's momentary lack of breath. "Tell me."

"It's nothing."

It was the last time her mother struck her, but her small open palm left a mark in the silence that followed the sound of flesh striking flesh: symbol of weighty authority, and more. Implicit was accusation and command: You lied to me. *Don't* lie to me.

She told her mother about the plague. The disease and the deaths. The horror that she had seen. It came spilling out of her lips, words like bile, and her mother—her mother, like *a* mother—strong enough to stomach them.

Perhaps because she'd never had a husband, it didn't occur to her until later what it cost her mother to know that the man who lay abed was already dead.

That night, she went out to the covered porch, and in darkness, he came, and she said, "What do you want?"

And he said, "You already know me. Good."

She was not to be deterred. Time pressed on her; time and the deaths she had passed through. "What do you want?"

"I want what you can offer."

"And that?"

"After this passes, you will walk a little closer to death's dominion."

She was silent, contemplating the meaning of his words. Understanding them in a way she could not have had she been young. "Can I ask?"

"Ask who?"

"Her."

She thought he smiled; she thought, in the darkness, she detected the faintest glimmer of approval. "You are not the child you once were," he told her softly. "You may do or say whatever you like; the choice and the spell is yours. Cast it, or take the chance."

But she had seen what had happened. "How far?" she whispered, as she turned toward the house.

He did not pretend to misunderstand her. "Your heart and your home is here, in this town. You will save only the town. There will be some deaths, but they will be deaths, not carnage."

"And if I—"

"If you ruled? Yes, possibly. Possibly then you might save more. Nothing is guaranteed." His eyes were dark, like the whole of night. "And would you, little one?"

It had been many, many years since anyone had called her that. "Would I?"

"Would you pay the price necessary to save a kingdom?"

"You ask me for so *much*," she said, her voice low because she couldn't speak without a tremble, "I would have nothing to pay your price *with*."

"It is not my price," he said. "Never that. It is yours."

"And what would magic ask?" She said. And then she felt the night's chill pierce her cleanly like a blade. *There are some questions you must not ask.*

She walked into the house without looking back, and in her own way, she asked for her mother's blessing and said her good-byes. And then she went to town.

Five days later she heard word that her mother had passed away in her sleep. She wept, although she had expected it, and the loss of her first great love was nothing compared to the emptiness that she now felt at the loss of the only unconditional love.

But magic had not yet finished with her, although she swore—as she so often did when the pain was greatest—that she had finished with magic. It came to the attention of lords and ladies that the village had been spared the wrath of the gods; that the plague that destroyed whole villages had passed almost peacefully over this one.

The men came, in carriages that put the finery of the town to shame. And with the men came swords, and with the swords, fear. Hers. The town's.

The men were not careful and they were not kind, but they were held back by the presence of a man who—cold, cold eyes glancing over them all—called himself King. He was not satisfied with the answers the clerics of the town gave, and within a week, they were dead. He was not satisfied with the answer that the mayor gave, and he, too, joined the clerics.

She understood then that rulership and ownership are not so very different, although she thought she must have always understood it. Cold, this man.

It came to her that he was seeking something, and she understood it, although the understanding was bitter.

Magic.

She was surprised, given how very cold he was, that he had not the ability to summon magic of his own.

Ah, a voice said, and when she turned she saw no one at all, *but that is where you are foolish. How can he accept magic when he has nothing of value to sacrifice in its stead?*

But I, I have nothing of value to sacrifice in its stead.

Then people will die. His voice was as cold as the king's eyes.

She was silent; silence had become something that was valued for it attracted little attention. At last, she said, quietly, "What does he want?"

"What any man of power wants. Gold."

"Gold?"

"It will build his army."

She thought that she had seen her father, brought the rain, saved a single man's life; that she had held back the plague from the village. All of these, invisible, practical things. And she thought a moment of finding gold, of offering him gold, of anything that was as practical as these other things, but she knew that he wanted *magic.*

And what will it cost?

She thinks of the first man the King's men dragged away; older now, and worn by years, but still attempting to save a child. She thinks of the gift he gave her; a gift that she has returned to time and again, for escape, or wonder, or comfort. She finds the story, and she thinks and she thinks and she wonders what might satisfy a man of power.

In the dark, babe at her breast, her stomach turns; she struggles a moment to be free of burden, to *sit;* to clear the images that *will not leave.* For a moment— just a moment—the babe is no help. But she will live. She will live through this. Again:

The room is bare of ornament. She has been in it before.

There is a single window, high enough that birds might sit in the sill, and a single door; the door was fitted by a man who was good at his craft; it lets in the light only through bars. No faces come to break the light; no men to bear witness.

Across the floor, straws lie against the sanded wood. Poorly baled hay reaches up to the barred window, but some small mercy prevented the men who brought it in from actually barring moon's light; it reigns, here, the emblem of the night world. While the moon is in the sky, she is safe. While the moon is in the sky, the blood's flow is staunched; the straw, dry and capable of swallowing all moisture in its thirst, remains unsatisfied.

Tomorrow, the straw must be gold.

Tomorrow, the bales must become the stuff of which armies are made, and paid.

She promised them this: that she could weave such a magic. Her words, her words were a spell, her words were a softness that did not allow the greedy men listening to disbelieve her. And now, she sits, in a room that is little better than a dungeon, the smell of hay all around. A moment, she pauses; she brushes the grassbugs from her hair and her arms, although they return as if they were folds of silken shroud, as if they know the truth of her death before she does.

She has one night. One night, the weaver's daughter, in which to perform this promised act of magic. And she asked for this task; she made them believe that she could do it. Made them believe that with many more deaths in the Town itself, she would not have the anchor and the focus required.

He comes, then.

He opens the door, the big keys are in his large hands, his body covered by robe, his face shadowed by hood.

She rises at once; grass bugs go skittering into the shadows his sharp lamp casts.

Be careful, she thinks. *Be careful, you fool, where you set that lamp down; we'll burn in an instant if the straw catches fire.* But she says nothing.

He does not remove his hood. Instead, he lifts the lamp higher; the light brings out the golden color of the hay and shows that there is nothing to reflect.

"A question," she says at last. Softly.

"A question is always yours to ask."

"Why—why do you come?"

"Me?"

"All of you. Why do you come to *me?*"

His laughter is unpleasantly heated. He does not answer her with words, but after a moment, the laughter muffled by straw, he pulls the folds of his hood down. She does not like the look in his eyes; they leave her face briefly. "You've done little work, clever wordsmith. The straw is straw; the spindle is empty."

"It is not yet the appointed hour."

"No," he says softly. "It is not. The moon is full, but the hour does not yet mark the depth of night, when witches work." As if he knows that the fire will ignite them both and destroy all chance of magic, he approaches her, holding the lamp.

"Lie back," he tells her.

She frowns.

"Lie back, and it will be easy. Fight, and you will burn."

"I won't be the only one to burn," she says softly.

She lies back against the straw; he straddles her, forcing her skirts up. When they get caught on the rough boards, he strikes her; hard enough to bring blood to her face, but not hard enough that it breeches the skin; she is lovely, in the darkness. He holds the lamp; holds the lamp while he enters her, the hood a darkness across his face that cloaks all symptoms of desire or need or enjoyment or rage, things that speak of power.

But she closes her eyes anyway; grits her teeth; drives her nails into her palms. And so she misses the transformation, for when he is done with her, and the light of the lamp rises, it reflects the light in a cascade of sharp, painful brilliance. Her legs are dry, her skirts unwrinkled; there is straw on the sturdy linens, but there's straw on everything. The man with the hood is standing by the doorway. He bows.

"For everything, a price," he says quietly.

She feels too dirty to look at him.

Too dirty . . . and yet. Such congress, such a simple act, an exchange of flesh for gold . . . she is afraid that it is not enough.

No.

"Never ask," he said. "Never ask for power if you're not willing to pay the price. You won't like the result."

She spits. "I don't like the result now."

He laughs. He laughs loudly, and a little too long. "You will like it better in the morning. Sleep. You

have bought what you desired; your people are safe
by your actions."

"And me?"

He says, again, all trace of laughter gone, "There is
only one way to cast a spell, little weaver. And if you
are not the mistress of your magic, it does not mean
that magic does not flow in the veins. You paid a
price; that I chose it for you is of little consequence;
had I not chosen it, you would have perished, your
magic gone, your gift unused." He bowed.

She does her best not to throw up.

In the morning, they came.

She had not slept, and so, tired and frightened she
watched as their faces were transformed by the reflected sunlight. Gold; gold everywhere. She was surprised, for on the heels of the four men who had
come, no doubt, to drag her to the death that King
had promised her in such chilly, distant words, came
the King himself. As if he could not trust the men he
had brought with him to stay their hand from the treasure that was rightfully his.

She had thought she could not feel more degraded.
She was wrong. For he came to her as she stood in
the center of the room, stiff and gold as the gold that
he coveted, and he reached out and touched her chin,
pulling her face up to meet his eyes.

"You are," he said, "passably pretty. It is a pity
that you are so provincial. Come."

She knew that to speak the wrong words meant
death, but she spoke. "Where?"

"My dear," he said, "Did you think—if you survived the morning—that I would leave you in this sty?
No; you have proved yourself worthy of a far better

fate. It is a pity you are not a young woman, but if I judge correctly you are not too old."

To her great surprise, and her lasting terror, he married her. He had put aside two wives for their failure to produce an heir; the gold that she had produced pleased him well enough that he thought her worth the risk. For if she had magic, might she not give him the son he desired?

He was not gentle, but he was not cruel; he used her as he used all else that might gain him power; with care, but coldly.

To his great delight, she proved useful again: she became pregnant immediately; so quickly in fact that discreet inquiries were made about the possibility of sexual congress elsewhere before the wedding itself had been blessed.

No evidence was found.

For nine months she wandered like a caged bird. She was disdained by the nobility and feared by the commoners who formed the household staff; she was lonely, but she could bring herself to trust no one. This, she learned from her husband; there were daggers up every sleeve. Twice, during the nine months of her confinement, men had attempted to kill her, once by poison and once by the long winding fall of the stairs.

Even so—even so—she had pleaded poor health when her husband had attempted to keep her by his side for their executions; the deaths were long and horrible and she could hear them from half the palace away.

*   *   *

Yesterday, perhaps the day before, the pain started. The midwives came, and the physicians, and the King himself, and outside, from a distance that was never far enough away, she heard the rasp of metal against metal; drawn swords. He had posted guards at the door, and not a few of them.

She wanted privacy, but she realized that that was a vain hope; this child was the future of a kingdom, and its birth, live, must be witnessed. No opportunity must be left for substitution here, and no chance for last minute accident or assassination.

But she hated to show the pain to the watching world; she hated the gleam in the face of a husband that she would have been happy never to see again, his eyes the color of night, his expression just as hungry as it had been the morning that he had been robbed of her death by gold.

She did as he expected. She produced the child. Only then did he order them out.

She was afraid that he would take her son, for the child *was* a son.

She has been afraid of so many things, but this fear is a fear that speaks to gut and heart so loudly she can't think around it; her breath is short and her heart is loud and the long room's shadows contain all the nightmares that she has not beheld since she was a child herself.

She is thinking about the nature of magic; the baby has fallen asleep, his little mouth still attached to her breast. She is lying in the darkness when the door opens and the light in the distance falls against the gleam of readied swords.

But the swords are not in motion; they are at atten-

tion; they are decoration. And what swords could stop
this particular visitor from crossing the threshold?

And yet.

She thought to see a man; she does. An old man,
his face browned and weathered by sun and storm, his
forehead white only where scars have healed. If scars
ever heal completely. Behind him, a woman whose
beauty is so perfect, even now, babe in arms and ex-
hausted, she forgets how to breathe. And behind her,
an older woman, the matron. Behind her, a hooded
man, a man who might be death himself.

There are worse things than death.

They gather around her, expectant. She says, to the
old man, "But you died."

And he smiles. Nods. Yes.

The beautiful woman steps forward, the old woman
by her side; they look like sisters although one is so
plain she would hardly be noticed in a crowd. Then
they turn to the door again, and the man enters. She
thought she would be revolted by the sight of him,
should she ever see him again. But he is like a thun-
derstorm, like a blizzard, like a terrible accident; there
is nothing in him that is human. She has never seen
the same messenger twice, and she wonders, as her
arms tighten, why they have all returned now.

Because they have only ever returned when she's
about to face death or loss, and there is nothing in
the room but the child.

And the child cannot die. *Cannot* die.

But she has nothing left to offer them. Her life?
She would have given that up years ago, as a foolish
girl, as an older woman. It has never been her life
that they've been interested in.

"What do you want?" she asks them, holding the
child as carefully, as closely, as she can. The child's

breathing is quiet, but it is there: steady, as steady as her own. She wonders if her own breath ever smelled so sweet.

"Do you know what you hold?" The youngest of the men says intently.

She has so many answers, but they fight for her words and in the end, all she says is, "My son."

"Yes." The oldest woman answers. "Your son." She smiles softly. But not gently; never that. "And perhaps one day he will rule. Perhaps one day." She stared at him as if she could see beneath the surface of his wrinkled, wet skin. "Or perhaps one day he will be the means by which you might save a kingdom."

She holds him, arms frozen. "No."

They say nothing at all.

But their eyes are on her, in the darkness; on her and what she carries.

No.

The beautiful woman looks at her, eyes shining in the lamplight, with a light that lamps could never contain.

Not yet, she says.

SPELLSWORD
by Jane Lindskold

Jane Lindskold has frequently driven up to the Sandia Crest, where this story begins, but has yet to have anything unusual happen there. The author of over thirty short stories and several novels—including *Changer* and *Legends Walking*—she lives in Albuquerque, New Mexico with her husband, archaeologist Jim Moore. She is currently at work on another novel.

I hang in midair, breath tearing out of my lungs in great, shuddering gasps. My hands grip the hilt of a sword buried to the middle of its shimmering steel blade in the side of the sandstone cliff. Creatures that look like pterodactyls sweep just below me, snapping at my ankles. The light from a pair of glowering red suns makes their scaly hides seem pink, but I know that the flying monstrosities are actually a sickly corpse-white.

I want to scream, but I can't get enough air into my lungs, not if I want to keep hanging on. The worst thing is, I have no one but myself to blame for the position I'm in. And no one but myself to get me out.

Lucky Will, all on his own. William Zacharetti, Loner at Large. Hah!

Rocking back and forth like a gymnast about to try some fancy flip, I feel the sword blade grate against the sandstone, then a slight sag. Way below me, glimpsed intermittently between pterodactyls and what might be wisps of cloud, is something I'm pretty sure is a deep pool. I've based this brilliant deduction on its green color and the way light reflects off of the surface.

If I can loosen the sword, I'll start falling. Given the apparent height of this cliff, I should have some moments in free-fall. If I torque my body just right, I'll land in the water, rather than splatting on the rocks surrounding the pool. If I angle my body as I aim myself, I should cut through the pool's surface cleanly and not break my back doing the mother of all belly-flops. If I hold onto the sword, I should still have the strength to drag it—and me—to shore.

Lots of ifs, but what the pterodactyls have planned in their tiny little minds also involves my falling and with a lot less pleasant end-result for me.

Kick out the feet. Rock. Rock. Grating felt through the metal blade. Kick. Rock. Kick. Rocking faster now, almost a swing. Kick. Kick. Rock. Kick—hard!

With a tremendously shrill screech of tortured metal, the sword rips loose from the stone. My heart leaps just like it does when the roller coaster drops down the highest hill. Sure I'm prepared, but you're prepared for the roller coaster, aren't you? And most of us still scream.

I don't have the breath or energy to waste. Peering down past my feet, I try to aim for that pool. It sure as hell seems smaller now than when I was hanging over it, wondering if drowning was preferable to being a corn-dog on a stick for a bunch of flying reptiles.

The weight of the sword is drawing me off course; with tremendous effort I shift it parallel to my torso. That action pulls it below me. I'd envisioned entering the water feet first, but now I'm strung out behind the sword like a high-diver going into the plunge with his hands pointed out in front.

I check my descent again. Momentary relief. I'm going to hit the pool. Then a putrid stench envelopes me, clogging my nostrils like something tangible. Whatever fills that green oval down there isn't water. I manage to breathe a prayer that it's not acid. Then the sword blade, followed microseconds later by me, pierces the stuff.

Shit.

I'm not being profane—though I'm perfectly capable of that. I'm being descriptive. That's what the stuff is and I'd hate to meet the creature that shat the goo. The stuff reeks like human diarrhea mixed with ripe cow dung. The contribution my stomach adds after I've dragged myself to the bank doesn't help.

But I'm down off that cliff and I have the sword. I figure that—even in the condition I'm in—I'm ahead of the game.

I'm right—in a way.

Given how I stink, the pterodactyls give up the chase. That's almost a pity. With the sword, I could make them think better about nibbling on William Zacharetti, bearer of the Spellsword Arlen.

Hah.

Holding my prize tightly in one green-slimed hand, I stagger off around the base of the cliff, pushing my way through thorny shrubs and prickly bushes that remind me somewhat of the piñons and junipers back home in New Mexico. Underfoot, coarse sand grates against the soles of my hiking boots. Overhead, the glowering red suns show no sign of setting.

I locate something that might be a game trail and follow it, hoping that the predators that eat the critters that use the trail won't take a fancy to me. I suppose

I could just go cross country, but I need to feel like I'm heading somewhere rather than what I am—utterly and completely lost.

About the time I'm getting used to how I smell, the trail comes out into relatively open ground near a spring nestled into more sandstone. The rocks surrounding the water are polished into smooth, gentle shapes resembling clouds or pillows or billowing columns. I guess that sometime—maybe aeons ago—the water ran higher here.

I trudge over to the spring and discover, just before I'm about to plunge in, that it's steaming.

"Hot water!" I say aloud in delight. My voice echoes strangely off the rocks, coming back as a whisper: "Water . . . Water . . . Water . . ."

A test dip with my left hand—my right wouldn't have given a good reading; it's been a bit funny since I dunked that arm up to the elbow in the River Styx[1]—puts the water at about the same temperature as a hot bath. Not bothering to strip, I lower myself into the nearest pool. For a moment I feel like I'm cooking, then everything's perfect. As the sludge floats off me, I herd it down to a lower pool where it drifts away.

Carefully balancing the Spellsword on two nearby rocks, I dip my head under and give my hair a good scrub. Then I'm almost ready to continue on my quest.

First I need to clean Arlen, which I do with a rag torn from the tail of my flannel shirt. While I polish, I take a good look at my reflection in the blade. I guess I'm hoping that I'll see some big changes, but the guy I see is a bedraggled version of me: a young

[1] See "Hell's Mark" in *Wizard Fantastic*, edited by Martin H. Greenberg, DAW Books.

man of twenty, no hunk but at least less scrawny than I was six months ago. (Those trips to the weight room have helped). Fair hair of an undistinguished shade muddling between blond and brown. Gray eyes that hid behind spectacles until the surgery last month. Facial features that are just coming out from behind baby flesh I hadn't realized was there. I study them for a while, realizing that I'm being as vain as any girl—but then who is there to notice? I'm alone.

And by my own choice. I'd stayed in New Mexico over the Christmas holidays despite an offer from my father and stepmom to join them in the Bahamas— and an offer from my mom and her husband to join them on an Alaskan cruise. The offers were both sweet and sincere, but I'd stayed in Albuquerque, muttering excuses about needing to prepare for some heavy-duty courses for the spring term. The folks had been so pleased at my maturity that I'd felt like a real heel. Still, I couldn't tell them that I was really staying to take my wizardry ranking exam, could I?

And then I'd taken the test. The same test several of my closest friends had taken—and alone of all of us I'd failed. I'd known the results the minute I'd come out from under and seen the smirk of mock-condolence on Madame Alexandra's pinched features. She hasn't liked me since I refused to tell her stuff she wanted to know about how we got out of Hell that time. I knew any smile from her didn't mean anything good for me.

I'd left as soon as I could, hardly listening to anything either Madame A. or Lord Whatsis said to me. Lucia—who since she lives locally hadn't gone anywhere for the break—had been waiting for me. I'd brushed by her with a few grunted comments. She'd run after me, but I'd jumped into my old red Camaro and buzzed out of there.

Failure. Nothing. And deep inside I knew that the test hadn't told me anything I didn't know already. Lucia has powers that measure off the scale. Danny can heal with a touch and a song. Pedro can divine using rod or pendulum or even a few pebbles. Maddie talks to the animals—and they talk back. Me? All I can do is a bit of past-life regression work and I'd heard the muttering (not from my gang but from members of the High and Mighty) that what I do is nothing more than hypnotism.

Leaving the "shrine" where I'd taken my test, I'd sped up I-40 through Tijeras Canyon, then up the twisting climb to the crest of the Sandia Mountains— the big lump of granite and limestone dotted with valiant stands of trees that hulks at the edge of Albuquerque. Even in summer the trip to the crest is a bit like magic. At the bottom, the day can be warm enough that a T-shirt seems like too much clothing. Get to the top and you'll need a jacket. Amazing what a climb of several thousand feet can do.

On that day—today, I guess—it was late December. Even the city below still had a dusting of snow lurking in shadowed corners. The road up to the crest was slick with damp and patches of ice. I drove like a madman, spinning around curves and pushing the Camaro to ever greater speeds. The blacktop snaked through evergreens that stood with their lower trunks buried in snow, their needles white with hoarfrost. Deciduous trees traced black lacework against the fading blue of the sky. It might have been a lovely sight. I was in no mood to consider.

Failure.

Reaching the crest, I slid the Camaro into a parking

space. Not many other cars were here. Folks had better things to do a few days after Christmas than go up a mountain for a look down, and I was already higher than the ski area. I trudged up the slick ice-and-snow-covered path to one of the places where you can view the city, but today Albuquerque had vanished beneath white clouds. I could hardly see fifty feet down the slope. Standing there in the quiet and the cold my anger began to fade, replaced by a sorrow as biting as the icy wind.

I'd failed. I couldn't believe it. I'd been to Hell and back. I'd fought Hell's renewed force when it came after us in revenge.[2] How could I be no sort of wizard at all?

Because the others carried you, I seemed to hear Madame A. saying in her mincing tones. *You didn't contribute even the slightest spell—just a strong body and something of a steadying influence. There's not a trace of magic in you.*

"I don't believe it!" I yelled into the mist.

And the mist said back, "So, are you willing to prove differently?"

I glanced around, but I was alone on my icy perch. Everyone else must have taken refuge in the gift shop. Still, I looked carefully. Like I said, Lucia has power to spare. She could have tried something, gotten Pedro to track me. Then I remembered that Pedro wasn't around, had gone to visit relatives in Española for the holidays. And anyhow, the mist was still talking to me.

"Are you willing to prove differently, William Zacharetti?"

---

[2] See "Hell's Bane" in *Battle Magic*, edited by Martin H. Greenberg and Larry Segriff, DAW Books.

"Will," I muttered, not knowing what else to say.

"An auspicious name," the mist said approvingly. "Will—the force of intellect and personal resolve. Are you going to give up, then, Will?"

"No!" I said, more forcefully than I'd intended.

I'd kept studying the mist while we talked. I was pretty sure now that I could discern features in there done in white on white. Masculine with a sweeping beard and long eyebrows: Jehovah on a benevolent day or maybe Merlin. My heart leaped with hope.

"Are you saying that I've still got a chance?" I added.

"You say you don't believe the results of the test."

"I don't."

"Then you have a chance."

"What must I do?"

"Take a leap of faith. Seek the Spellsword Arlen where it is bound. Free it. Bring it home. None will doubt you then."

I never even asked if I could have help. Idiot me. Even Lucia—rated with the power of six Chinese wizards and possessed of more than that besides—was allowed help on her quests, but I was too messed up, too angry. I wanted to prove myself. Alone.

Dickhead.

So all I said was: "And how do I take this leap of faith?"

"Step onto the wall before you and jump," spake the mist.

And, ass that I am, I did.

I finish polishing the Spellsword Arlen, admiring it quite a bit as I do so. It's about the size and weight of a saber: that is a real sword, not one of those effete long-piece-of-wire-with-a-hilt fencing foils, but not one of those incredible how-the-hell-did-anyone-ever-use-one-of-these? metal monstrosities either.

The dragon-shaped hilt is shaped to protect the user's hand, but practicality doesn't mean that it isn't beautiful. The long-necked dragon glowers up the blade, its backswept wings making something like a basket hilt. Each individual scale on the dragon's bronzed hide is detailed and the beast's eyes are tiny but perfectly faceted rubies.

When I rub the now gleaming blade with my rag, tiny sparks trail after, silver and gold mostly, with a trace of moonlight blue. The sword feels alive, and so I guess that's why I say: "I wonder how you ended up embedded in that cliff face?"

A voice, androgynous, but with the ringing undertones of metal upon metal replies: "I was placed there by gods who feared my power and sought to keep me from a wielder's hand."

I've read enough fantasy novels that I don't yelp and drop the sword, but I must admit that this *is* my first impulse. I manage not to say, "You talk!" either, but it takes a real effort. No matter how much you've read, when the real thing happens to you, it's a shock.

"Arlen, what is your power?"

The metal-on-metal voice replies serenely, "I am a Spellsword, one of nine crafted when the sun was but one and still burned bright and gold against a sky of cerulean blue."

A rational corner of my mind wonders if a solar system could survive if its sun was split in two, but I push that aside. Clearly different rules are in effect in this place.

"Arlen, my name is William Zacharetti. I freed you from where you were wedged in the sandstone."

My voice is steady, and I'm pretty pleased. Given

how my heart still gives an involuntary leap when I remember plummeting through the clouds, seeing the sword stuck there, grabbing it and hanging on despite aching shoulders and pterodactyls, I hadn't been sure I could mention the events with any composure.

"I know you, Freedom Bringer," Arlen says with a trace of some emotion I can't place. "You I shall serve."

I feel really good about this. *Just you wait until I get back, Madame A.! Then we'll see who you're smirking at!*

"Tell me, oh Spellsword Arlen," I continue, "just what *is* a Spellsword?"

"A Spellsword makes the will of the bearer manifest."

"Go on."

"Usually, William Zacharetti . . ."

"Will."

"Usually, Will, in order for the Talented to shape their power into the forms of their desire they must employ some ritual."

"Or spell," I say, thinking of all the spells I'd watched Vanessa and Cindy laboriously committing to memory.

When I'd tried spellcasting a couple of years ago it had seemed tedious and at times downright silly. Even Vanessa—who's a smart lady in her first year of graduate school these days—admits that she doesn't know the necessary parts from the unnecessary. All she knows is that spells work for her and her coven. They never did for me.

"A spell, that's right," Arlen says. "My role is to take desire and, within the limits of my power, provide the shape within which it can work."

My majors are math and economics. I've worked a

lot with software for generating statistics or random numbers or whatever. The similarity is obvious: the Spellsword Arlen is a spell-generating program!

I express the thought, and the sword seems confused.

"I know nothing of computers, Freedom Bringer, but as you explain it, yes, this could be the case. However, I simply provide the means to make your will manifest. You must supply desire and power."

That last makes me think—especially with recent failures fresh in mind. Do I have power? I ask the sword.

"Oh, yes!" This time I'm certain I hear metallic laughter. "You have power. We are using it at this moment to converse. Since I rest in your hand and you are focusing on me, the amount of power I need draw from you is the least grain of sand from a vast beach."

"Does everyone have power?" I ask, suddenly jealous of the answer.

"No," Arlen assures me. "Not one among a thousand but perhaps more than one among two thousand. Powers are finicky things as well and respond only to the correct forms."

This fits in with what I've already been taught. The reason that there are so many magical systems worldwide isn't just a reflection of various cultural backgrounds. They're different tools for different jobs: sometimes better or worse, sometimes just different.

"Right!" I say, pleased. "And you can provide the form for my power."

"That is so."

I recall what the mist on the mountain had said to me. Finding Arlen had only been the first part of my quest. The second had been to free it. The third was to bring it home. I've completed two-thirds, then. On to the last!

"Arlen, can you make a spell that will take us home?"

"Yes, Will, but before you command me so, let me tell you that the powering of it would kill you."

"Oh."

Arlen adds kindly, "It would kill a god."

I feel a bit better. "But it is possible for me to get home?"

"Yes."

"Can you tell me how?"

"I am just a Spellsword. I make the will of my wielder manifest. I have some sense of the limits imposed by power. That is all."

"Right." I gnaw a knuckle for a moment, setting up this challenge like it's an elaborate mathematical formula.

"As I see it," I say to Arlen after a time, "if you had the power, you could get us back to where I was. Can you use power other than my personal power?"

"Yes. First I would use your power to create a conduit between myself and the power source. Then I would tap the power and create the spell."

"And we're home?"

"Yes."

"Do you happen to know how much power you would need?"

I get the feeling that the sword is embarrassed, but it replies nonetheless. "Do you see how the suns hang fat and red and cold in the sky?"

"Yes."

"Once they were one sun: young and bright and hot. In powering a spell such as you desire, the sun was split in two and lost much heat."

"Wow!"

"Nor were there always pools of sludge where there should be fresh water. Nor did monsters flap their leathery wings where proud eagles once flew."

I laugh unsteadily. I'm beginning to understand why the gods embedded Arlen in a cliff.

"Time to think of another option."

"I would prefer so."

After more knuckle chewing I say, "Arlen, we've been talking about your taking me home in basically one jump, right?"

"Yes."

"What about doing the trip in stages or by means of some transportation device?"

Sparks fly along the blade as Arlen analyzes my request. Fascinated, I watch the dancing silver and gold; the force of Arlen's working tingles along my nerves like the rough tongue of a cat.

"The latter option," Arlen says, "would be preferable. Then the power inherent in the means of transportation itself would be at our employ."

"So you don't mean to create this transportation device?"

"Summoning would serve as well and add the summoned creature's resources to your own."

"I don't want some vicious slave," I hasten to put in, thinking of trapped genies or summoned demons.

Arlen vibrates with what I hope is laughter. "Very well. That rules out the options that first comes to mind, but there remain the Flame Steeds of the Void. I can ensorcel one to your service, but you must address it with great courtesy or the binding will break."

"I promise."

"The Flame Steeds set great store in ritual," Arlen says with a trace of delicacy—like when someone's about to tell you your fly is unzipped and doesn't want to embarrass you. "Might I take the liberty of completing your grooming? The power used would be a minimal investment toward what you hope to gain."

Thinking of myself clad as I am in the stained, steamed, and crumpled jeans, shirt, and jacket in which I'd fled up to Sandia Crest, I grin at the image I must be presenting.

"Make it so," I say grandly and Arlen does.

There's a rush of that cat's tongue feeling. Sparks of silver, gold, and pale blue dance over me. The one place they don't touch, I notice, is the lower portion of my right arm—the section I dunked in the River Styx last spring. This is only of passing interest, I'm too busy gawking at the figure in the mirror that Arlen thoughtfully supplies.

I'm dressed like a character right off the cover of a fantasy novel: close cut trousers in matte black leather, an off-white shirt that manages to show off my shoulders without making the rest of me look chunky, a vest of some brocade fabric in shades of forest green, a wide belt from which depends (I mean, that's the only word for it) a sheath for Arlen, and riding boots polished to a high gloss.

My hair is a bit longer, just brushing my shoulders and I have a short, neat, but full beard—something I've wanted for years but have never been able to manage. My hair color's the same, but now the blond seems to highlight the brown rather than mixing in and making it all look wishy-washy. I guess the best thing about what Arlen's done is that all of it's still me—just me like I've never managed to look, no matter how hard I try.

"Wow!" I say.

"You are pleased?" Arlen asks anxiously.

"I'm blown away," I assure the sword. "Ready to summon the Flame Steed? And can you create a ritual to make certain the right etiquette comes to mind when I speak to it?"

"I am ready and, yes, I can A wise choice, that last. Flame Steeds can be difficult."

"So you said."

Again the sparks flow, and this time exhaustion wells into me. I struggle to keep my balance. It wouldn't do to fall on my butt just when the Steed—whatever it is—appears.

"Easy, Arlen," I mutter.

"Yes, Freedom Bringer. With your permission, I will tap a bit of power from this hot spring."

"Any long-term damage?"

"Just a slight lowering of the temperature."

"Do it."

I feel better instantly. Squaring my shoulders, I follow an impulse and raise Arlen above my head in both hands. Lightning crackles around us. The mirror shatters, but not before I see myself haloed in sparks and lightning (all but my right arm, of course). God! I didn't know I could look so dramatic.

From the dark heart of a thunderhead high above comes an orange-red light like a tongue of candlelight. As I lower my arms and hold Arlen point down in front of me, the candlelight becomes a bonfire, becomes a firestorm, becomes the most magnificent horse of which you could ever dream: a pinto stallion colored in pale orange and eye-searing red.

The Flame Steed is the size of the Percherons I've seen at the State Fair—that is, its rear end is nearly as tall as my head. Its eyes are fire opals, its mane and tail molten gold. Heat washes over me, but something Arlen's done keeps it to a manageable level. That only seems sensible. It would hardly do to dress me up all fancy and have me melt into a grubby sweat moments later.

Remembering courtesy, I address the Steed:

"Greetings, noble Void Voyager."

"And to thee, Wizard," comes the Steed's reply. Its voice blends muted brass trumpets with the crackle of burning juniper.

"I have a challenge for thee," I say. "Bear me across black velvet reaches where the stars are but cold diamonds, bear me back to the place from whence I came."

"And how will you honor me if I do this service?" asks the Steed with a toss of its mane and a stamp of one hind hoof.

"In song, in poetry, in tale," I say, glad that Arlen's spell provides the right price. "A world that knows not your glory will dream of you for aeons to come. Children will weep that they cannot know you, laugh with joy that you exist."

"This delights me," the Steed admits. "Show me whither we go, and I shall bear you there."

I wave Arlen through a single elegant arc and images trail behind the blade's passing. I feel a whisper of weariness and know that seemingly effortless conjuration is taking its toll.

"That far?" is all the Void Steed says. "Leap astride, Wizard, and begin your singing. I would have its heat to warm me against the chill."

My singing voice is what folks call a pleasant, light baritone. Nothing to write home about, but nothing to cause the shudders either. For a moment I toy with the idea of asking Arlen to enhance it, but that last shudder of weariness had been a warning. Trusting the etiquette spell to continue supplying the proper

turns of phrase, I sheathe Arlen, grasp the golden
mane in my right hand, and mount the Flame Steed.

It's easier than it should be—even though I'm a
pretty good rider—so I figure that Arlen's concern for
my dignity is still in full effect. Once I am astride, the
Flame Steed gallops on the wind into the vale between
the stars where its own heat warms me as my song
warms it.

As we gallop from bright point to dark to bright
once more, I alternate singing with chanting poetic
praises to the Steed. Mostly it's rhymed couplets and
mostly pretty bad, but as long as the praise is fulsome
the Void Traveler doesn't seem to mind at all.

My heart is full of my success and fuller with imag-
inings of what I'll say to Madame A. and Lord
Whatsis, so the journey—one of those eternally time-
less things—seems to take no time at all. Some time
must have passed, though, because when the Flame
Steed deposits me and Arlen on Sandia Crest, I glance
down at my car and notice that several inches of snow
have accumulated on it.

"Sing of me," the Flame Steed says as I dismount,
more a reminder than a request.

"My heart will recall your beauty, even in my
dreams," I reply. "Farewell! Fare-ever!"

"The same to you, Wizard," the Steed replies, leaping into the clouds, "and look out behind you!"

I do. From within the swirling white clouds en-
shrouding the mountaintop emerges the man whose
face I had only glimpsed before. This time he doesn't
look so wise or so kind, though he is robed in purest
white. He bears in one hand a sword I recognize as
kin to Arlen, but this blade is shattered along one
edge and no sparks dance along the battered remnant.

The dragon on this sword's hilt is white with glittering blue topaz eyes.

Back-peddling a few steps, I realize that I might just have been had. Battling the sinking sensation in my chest, I grasp Arlen's hilt—hard.

The man strides toward me, long hair and beard tousled by a rising icy wind. As he closes, a mist rises and thickens, cloaking us in shades of pearl and frosted breath. I know immediately that if I yelled for help no one would hear me—not even the people fifty feet away in the gift shop.

"Give me the Spellsword Arlen," the man commands, avarice in his glittering gaze, "and your quest will be complete. The approval you desire will be yours—as will be a wizard's ranking quite satisfactorily high."

"Giving you the sword," I protest, sliding my new boots back a few steps on the slick stone of the walkway, "was never something I agreed to do."

"Nevertheless," the man demands, "I will have Arlen *now!*"

The last word is half-shouted, half-sung, dropping on a falling note to a near bestial growl. The power in it nearly stuns me. If I hadn't let myself be the test subject for several spells Cindy has been designing, I think it *would* have flattened me.

The man from the mist is striding toward me, walking as if the snow and ice underfoot bother him not at all. Now that he is closer I realize that his white robes glimmer with silver, gold, and just a touch of palest blue—the same colors as the sparks that run up and down Arlen's blade.

"Who are you?" I demand.

"What right have you to ask?"

"I jumped off a mountain at your suggestion. I think it gives me some rights."

The man chuckles. "You may call me Trandolin God-Trembler. It is not a name to conjure with, but I have answered to it. I am the wizard who forged the Spellswords. At first, the gods were amused by my crafting. I caused them to fear. In their fear, they destroyed or imprisoned many of the swords. I myself was captured, bound, and cast out into the Void. Even then the gods feared me, so that they left me only the broken end of my favored sword."

"Really?" I manage, figuring that if Trandolin's talking about himself—a thing he seems quite happy to do now that I've got him started—he's not focusing on me and Arlen.

"Why would I lie?" Trandolin replies tartly. "As I swam within the Void I was summoned by a wizard of this world. I slew him for his temerity and only too late found myself trapped here."

"Tough breaks," I say—trying to put a sympathetic note into my voice—a hard thing since I'm scared out of my mind.

"For centuries I have sought to make my way back to those I left behind," Trandolin continues and something in the nasty tone in which he says it makes me think he isn't planning on a quiet homecoming. "Each time I have failed, for the craven gods have blocked all the gates and roads against my return. In the course of my magical workings I came into contact with the organization you refer to as the High and Mighty. Through them, I learned of a human possessed of power such as I needed."

Me? I think with wondering hope. Then I understand. He means Lucia. Even with the December wind whipping me I feel a flush of heat at the thought of her in this maniac's hands.

"Too late," Trandolin continues, edging toward me as if he thought I'd be so caught up in his tale that I wouldn't notice, "did I learn that her power was of a kind even she could not use freely. By then I had laid the groundwork for my return. Lest that be wasted, I must use another to walk those roads."

Or jump off that mountain, if we're being strictly accurate, I think. Whatever else he is, Trandolin strikes me as a raving lunatic.

"Me," I say, knowing that this time I'm right. "Why me? I'm no powerhouse."

"No, you are not," he says, dashing my last dream that I might be otherwise. "But you have courage, William Zacharetti. Twice you have gone against forces far more powerful than you are and prospered. You have defied the wishes of those such as Madame Alexandra who have the power to do you harm."

"What," I ask, knowing that I'm right, "did you bribe her with to tell me I'd failed my test?"

"A trinket she desired," Trandolin answers lightly. "I needed you susceptible to manipulation: angered, in pain, yet unwilling to turn to your friends for comfort."

And I wouldn't put it past you to arrange a little push, just to make certain.

I'm getting increasingly angry—a stupid reaction I should have learned by now that anger doesn't do me much good. Trandolin extends his hand.

"Give me the Spellsword Arlen."

"No."

"It is my property."

"Possession is nine-tenths of the law," I retort, wondering in the back of my mind if that's really true.

"Give it," Trandolin says, "or I will take it."

"I bet," I reply, "that you *can't* take it. I don't imagine you'd waste your time chatting with me if you could."

A cruel expression spreads across the wizard's features. He says very, very softly:

"I can make you wish to give it to me."

"Try!" I say, drawing the sword. "Arlen, do you want to go back to him?"

"Not particularly," the sword hums dryly.

"Then," I command, "defend me!"

I thought that was pretty clever of me, given that outside of a couple of fencing lessons I hardly knew which end of a sword was which. Arlen, however, had shown a considerable amount of smarts—and a lot more initiative than it'd admit to.

"By any means?" asks the sword.

Awkwardly raising the blade to block an ice-spear that Trandolin hurls at me, I grunt at the shock, then reply, "Within reason. No stripping the sun of its power or anything like that."

"There are other powers I can tap," the sword says with infuriating calm, "if I have your permission. Powers that are not of this world or even of this universe."

Ignoring us, laughing mirthlessly to himself, Trandolin is sculpting raw power into what even I can tell is a major working. The monstrosity taking form under his hands could be a Rottweiler but it's twice as large, has armor plates, long teeth, twisting horns, and loads of bad attitude.

"Do whatever it is you have in mind!" I shout. "I need help fast—or he's going to get you from me."

The ground shakes. Warmth blossoms from the sword in my hand and fans out to surround me, a blast of heat so intense that the snow and ice I've been standing on instantaneously transpires into steam.

"Not," comes a rumbling voice both familiar and not, "if I get him first."

It's Arlen's voice, but deeper and more majestic. It's a good thing that I had given the order for Arlen to defend me, otherwise that moment when I heard the Spellsword's voice change probably would have been my last. But Arlen plays fair, even when it stops being a sword and becomes—you've guessed it—a dragon.

Dragon Arlen towers over me, its arching neck cresting at something like thirty feet. The bronze scales are living now, glowing with that silky gloss you see on snakes. The eyes are ruby-red and burn. The feet between which I stand have long, curving claws that score deep gouges into the stone.

What happens next is really ugly.

Arlen flaps huge bat-style wings a couple of times, angles his long neck and breathes fire the color of molten bronze over the wizard. The first time the dragon exhales, Trandolin encapsulates himself in a bubble. The flames shunt off down the sides, melting what snow remains. The creation Trandolin had been working on pops out of existence.

The second time Arlen breathes, naked terror sears Trandolin's face, for the sphere in which he has taken shelter bends like a soap bubble right before it pops. Scrabbling frantically, Trandolin pulls the broken sword from its sheath.

Raising it in shaking hands, he cries out in a voice no longer majestic but thin and shrill with terror:

"Breathe once more, Arlen, and my power will be broken, but know that I will take this with me. You, not I, will bring your hatchmate to the final death."

"She still lives?"

I hear the disbelief in the dragon's bellow.

"Damaged, yes, but capable of being healed by those with enough power," the wizard shrieks. "In my hands, as a Spellsword, you will give me that power. Come to me. I will heal her and together we will return and take vengeance on those who have done me harm."

Remembering split suns and pools of sludge, thinking how I'd feel if someone told me that my sister would live or die on my action, I dart out from the shelter of the dragon's forelegs. Dashing forward, I thrust my right arm through Trandolin's protective bubble. If I'm wrong, I figure I won't have much time to regret it.

But just as Arlen's spellcrafting couldn't touch whatever the waters of the Styx had done to my arm, so it proves immune to Trandolin's magic. I reach through and wrench the broken sword from the wizard's hand. Despite my arm's immunity, I'm blasted by the backlash. I go flying through the air, stopping only when I crash into the stone wall bordering the path.

Lying there with my head ringing, I see what happens when Arlen breathes a third time. Trandolin's bubble bursts and well, what's left there on the snow isn't pure and gleaming any longer. The only white on the wizard's corpse is where bone peeks through blackened flesh.

Rolling over, I dry retch, but there isn't enough left in my abused system for me to vomit. When I lift my head, I find myself facing the dragon Arlen. He flicks out his tongue and takes the battered white dragon sword from my hand.

"Well, Freedom Bringer," Arlen says in tones

mocking and ironic. "I have taught you something of the price of power. Trandolin thought he was above paying those prices, that he could bind others to pay them for him."

"You," I say, "and others."

"Dragons are highly magical, highly intelligent, and very clever," Arlen agrees. "We made the perfect bound sentience to guide the Spellswords. Other creatures who were less versatile were simply drained and transformed—destroyed."

"Do I still command you?" I ask.

"Perhaps," the dragon says, bronze flame flickering within his nostrils.

"Then could you please do something about my head? I've the grandmother of all headaches."

"You should," the dragon chides, "be more careful how you phrase such requests. I could solve your problem by killing you."

"True," I say, "but I'd rather trust you."

"Dangerous."

"Dealing with dragons is," I grin. "At least that's what I've always heard."

"Flatterer," Arlen grumbles, but my headache vanishes, as does the incipient sensation of nausea, and all the aches from crashing into the wall.

I get to my feet. "Do you think you can do anything for her?" I ask, gesturing toward the white dragon sword.

"Yes, if I take her to the realms of dragon magic," Arlen replies. "We were drawn from there to serve Trandolin and are even more powerful in our own land."

"Good. Now, you admit that I can still command you."

"Perhaps."

"Oh, you've admitted as much. Very well. I command you to seek healing for your sister, then to find and rescue the remaining dragons bound into Spellswords. That should not only make you happy, it should make the gods of Trandolin's world happy."

"True," Arlen rumbles. "And what about you?"

"If you promise not to harm me or mine—and to clean up this mess—I'll be glad to release you from whatever still binds you to me."

Arlen laughs, a really amazing sound. "And so bind me further—dragons have a strong sense of indebtedness. That is one means by which Trandolin first captured us."

I shrug. "If so, at least it will be by your own choice."

"I accept your terms," Arlen says, "but what about you?"

"Me?" I grin. "I think I'll go see Madame A. about a retest. I may not be much of a wizard, but Trandolin said that I have some power. After I learn what, I'll see what I can do about building it. As you said, you've taught me quite a bit about the uses and costs of power."

The dragon flaps his wings preparatory to taking off.

"Do you regret the loss of the Spellsword?"

I nod. "It would have made me amazingly powerful—I'd be a liar if I didn't admit I would have enjoyed that, but in the end lots of raw power hurt Trandolin more than it helped him."

"Wisdom in that little head."

"Like Trandolin said," I shrug, "I've been through a bit."

"And will be through more," Arlen predicts. "The Flame Steeds will dance your world's ether, for their vanity flourishes with praise. Come visit sometime."

I hold out a hand and Arlen offers me the tip of his tail.

"Deal."

And we shake on it. Two beats of his wings launch Arlen into the sky, a third removes the evidence of our battle with Trandolin, a fourth sweeps away the mist. Then I'm standing alone on a path bordering one of the scenic overlooks on Sandia Crest. Snow is falling. In it, I see the promise of white dragons.

CURSE OF THE DELLINGRS
by Mickey Zucker Reichert

Mickey Zucker Reichert is a pediatrician whose science fiction and fantasy novels include *The Legend of Nightfall, The Unknown Soldier,* and several books and trilogies about the Renshai. Her most recent release from DAW Books is *Spirit Fox,* with Jennifer Wingert. Her short fiction has appeared in numerous anthologies, including *Battle Magic, Zodiac Fantastic,* and *Wizard Fantastic.* Her claims to fame: she *has* performed brain surgery, and her parents *really are* rocket scientists.

The ceiling fan whirred and clicked rhythmical circles, stirring cool air through Michael Coglin's room. The newborn snuggled in his father's arms while his mother, Jillian, slept in the bedroom across the hall. Fading sunlight spilled over the Sesame Street trim on the walls and the black-and-white mobile disks dangling over the crib. Dan Coglin stirred a finger through the infant's fine brown hair, slightly lighter than his own curly mop, and marveled at the pouty pink lips, pudgy cheeks, and baby-irregular breaths of his new son. Love seemed tangible, riding with the breeze the fan sucked through the screen, sending curtains festooned with Elmo, Zoe, and Big Bird fluttering. He wanted to sing the praises of the tiny life in his hands, a miracle that only days before was just a kicking bulge that stretched his wife's pants.

The doorbell chimed. Afraid a repeat might awaken

Jillian from her well-deserved rest, Dan reluctantly pulled his gaze from his infant. He rose, careful not to jostle Michael as he shifted his grip. Still clutching the baby, he eased down the stairs to the door at the bottom. He opened it.

Dan's father, Aaron Coglin, stood on the concrete stoop. The setting sun sparked red highlights in his coal-black hair, and blue eyes glimmered in his large-boned face. He held his lips in the tight purse Dan recognized from childhood as a prelude to something serious. A Florida T-shirt stretched across broad shoulders that Dan had never shared, and he wore his favorite soft gray shorts, white gym socks, and stained suede sneakers. He carried a leatherette portfolio tucked beneath his left arm.

"Dad." Dan stepped aside, smiling. "Couldn't stay away from your grandson?"

The corners of Aaron's mouth barely twitched upward as he stepped into the hallway. "We need to talk."

The somber tone of the father's bass voice sent a shiver through Dan. Possibilities flew through his mind, and he could not help voicing the most worrisome. "Is Mom all right?"

"She's fine," Aaron tossed over his shoulder as he wiped his feet on the mat and trod two steps across the black-speckled dark jade carpeting, then turned right into the living room. Dan trailed him. The blue-striped couch stood against one wall, opposite a combination entertainment center and knickknack shelf. Two solid blue chairs graced each corner, on either side of the speakers; and a coffee table strewn with magazines sat in the middle of the room. Aaron sat stiffly on the couch, looking more uncomfortable than Dan ever remembered.

Dan sat beside his father, his heart pounding. He cradled the baby. "What's wrong, Dad? You can tell me."

Aaron did not look at his son. He set the portfolio on his lap. "Where's Jillian?"

"She's sleeping." Dan leaned forward. "Come on, Dad. What's wrong?"

Aaron sighed, closed his eyes. "I wanted to tell you this when you were little, but I promised Pete on his deathbed. He was so insistent, and I—"

Dan did not understand. "Pete?"

Aaron opened his pale eyes and looked at his son. "Your birth father."

The unfamiliar word refused to register. Dan stared through hazel eyes that perfectly matched his mother's. "My what?"

Now, Aaron continued to study his son. "Peter Leverton. Your birth father."

"You're not my real father?" The words shocked from Dan, unconsidered.

Aaron's expression turned dark, almost angry. "Oh, I *am* your *real* father. I adopted you when you were only a year old, six months after Pete's death. I shared your every triumph, your every illness, your every failure. In every way but genetics, I *am* your father."

Dan looked at his newborn son, his blood heating. His cheeks felt suddenly on fire. Betrayed and fuming, he blurted words he never bothered to consider. "Genetics matter." He thought of the tangible aura of love that seemed to ooze from him whenever he even thought of his son, the pride of accomplishment at having created Michael, the realization that, with Jillian, he had made a tiny version of himself. "How could you possibly love me as much as I love Michael?"

Aaron Coglin reared back as if slapped. He glanced at the ceiling, clearly considering the words and his reply. Finally, he placed an arm around Dan. "So, you're saying that you could never love Jillian as much as your Aunt Patricia."

"What?" Dan did not see the connection. He ran a hand over Michael's slumbering head, reveling in the warmth of the contact even as his thoughts tumbled crazily. He wanted to scream, to pace, but he would not awaken his son. His mother's sister, Patricia, was a skinny, pinch-faced woman whom he had hated visiting as a child. She kept plastic slip covers on her furniture, dolls on every shelf, and huge jars of marbles she would not allow him to touch.

Aaron explained. "Your Aunt Patricia shares your genetics. Your wife doesn't." He forced a strained smile more like a rictus. "If genetics determined love, we'd all be inbred morons."

Dan shook his head, too foggy with shock to fully appreciate the point. "So Mom is . . ." he trailed off, allowing Aaron to finish.

". . . your mother and your birth mother," Aaron explained. He shifted toward Dan, training the full vigor of his sapphire stare on his son. "Look, I admit there's nothing magic about a legal contract declaring you my forever son that creates love." He continued to stare. "But I think, if you look back on your life, you'll realize I loved you as much as any father could. And that there's nothing magical about DNA either."

Dan sat woodenly, uncertain what to think, to feel. "Tell me about my . . . birth father."

Aaron's demeanor softened, even as Dan's did not. He finally smiled. "Peter and I were friends from grade school. Great guy, but ungodly serious for a kid.

He shared your interest in art, but the intensity of his drawings tended to freak out his mother and teachers. He was tall, but you've outgrown him, too. He had hair just a bit darker than yours and green eyes." Aaron dropped the portfolio on top of the magazines. His picture's in here. Along with the papers he asked me to give you within a week of the birth of your son."

Confusion wormed through the blank of Dan's emotion. "He asked you to tell me after I had a son?"

"Yes."

Dan blinked. "What if I never married? What if Mikey had been a girl?"

"I asked the same things." Aaron grinned slightly at the similarities between himself and the son with whom he shared no genes but twenty-two years of joy, trials, and love. "He said it was impossible. He knew you'd have a child and that it would be a son. Just like he knew he would. And that he would die exactly six months later under suspicious circumstances."

Dan forced himself to process this new discovery, still reeling from the previous several. "Suspicious? How?"

Aaron cleared his throat. "Dan, your birth father was murdered."

"Murdered," Dan repeated vacantly.

"In junior high, he told me in confidence he would be killed exactly six months after the birth of his first child, a son." Aaron lowered his hands to the portfolio. "We were on a backyard campout. Telling ghost stories. I thought he was just trying to scare me. But, just before your birth, he brought it up again. I tried to talk him out of what seemed like a delusion, but he became desperately insistent. Said he'd get murdered and there was no way to prevent it. Said he had nothing against his murderer, that the guy wouldn't be able to help it. If the police thought it was suicide or an accident, I wasn't to try to dissuade them. Made me promise to look after you and your mother. I didn't expect to fall in love with her. It just happened while we mourned Peter together."

A hideous thought filled Dan's mind, and he could not banish it. He asked directly. "Did you murder my . . ." He couldn't say the word. "Peter?"

"Me?" Aaron laughed. "You know me. When your mom asks me to kill a spider, I secretly let it go out the window. When Pete died, I was at the theater watching *Star Wars.* It had just come out. I had sixty-some witnesses who heard me loudly remarking to my date: 'This'll go nowhere. It's just a B-Western with ray guns.' I still haven't lived that down."

Dan could not help smiling. A group of his coworkers had taken a week off to stand in line for tickets to the *The Phantom Menace.* Then, he recalled the purpose of their conversation, and his grin disappeared. "So how did he die?"

"Somehow, your mom's curling iron wound up in the bathtub with him." Aaron shook his head at the memory. "Didn't make much sense. Pete talked Mom into visiting Grandma and Grandpa that evening, and I can't imagine him curling his hair. And he always took showers." Aaron shrugged. "But there wasn't any sign of forced entry. No resistance. It was ruled an accident." Aaron rubbed a hand across the leatherette covering. "Your answer's in here, I believe." He rose. "I think I've given you more than enough to think about. I love you, Dan." He gave his son a hug turned awkward by the differences in their positions and the baby, then showed himself out.

Dan sat in silent emptiness for a long time. The sunlight faded, disappeared, and the dusk-to-dawn lamp shone like a beacon through the living-room window. Michael continued to slumber, chest rising and falling in arrhythmic but reassuring constancy. Dan carried the baby upstairs, slid him into his crib, and turned off the rattling ceiling fan. Slowly, he glided down the staircase, wishing he could feel something, anything. Anger continued to gnaw at him, wholly undirected. Aaron had been, still was, a great father. At times, especially when a parent had made him angry, Dan had wondered about the possibility of adoption. *All children feel that way. Don't they?* Armed with new information, he had to wonder if he had known all along. Then, the realization that he had as often questioned his biological ties to his mother proved the perfect answer. His doubts had been normal, universal, his father more than capable.

Dan Coglin returned to the living-room couch, flicking the light switch on as he entered. The two pole lamps flared to life, revealing the portfolio like a black splotch against the table, amidst scattered copies of gardening, news, and parenting magazines. With one arm, Dan swept most of the magazines to the floor, hauled the portfolio directly in front of him on the coffee table, and unzipped it.

A puff of stale air wafted to his nose, and he gained a new respect for his father. Aaron Coglin had not only obeyed his best friend's last wishes, he had resisted what had to have been urgent curiosity to read the contents. Dan received a message loud and clear. This information belonged to him and him alone. Just as Aaron would not have entered the teen-aged Dan's room without a knock and permission, he would not violate the privacy of his biological past.

Dan reached inside the portfolio and drew out three sealed manila envelopes, each with a number from one to three. He picked up the first and reached to open it. His fingers froze mid-movement, as if beyond his control. Once he broke that seal, his entire life changed, for better or worse. He considered letting secrets remain secrets, to find a stronger time to unleash a past that he never knew haunted him. *My father . . .* He corrected the thought, for Aaron, . . . *my* birth *father believed this the best time for me to know this. He didn't desert me; he died. If my father trusted him, I can, too.* Hands trembling, Dan broke the seal and removed a stack of perfectly preserved papers.

The one on the top sported lines with unfamiliar handwriting and had a picture paperclipped to it. Dan recognized his mother in the picture at once, hair feathering from her young face, her eyes aglow. A small baby stared from her arms, looking dazed and uncertain. The male stranger at her side kept one arm looped across her shoulders. Longish hair curled around his ears. Aside from a tall and lanky frame, he little resembled either of the Coglin men, though Dan thought he distinguished similarities between his birthfather's cheeks and smile and his own. He pulled off the picture and turned it over to read: "Pete and Samantha Leverton with baby Daniel Dwayne" in his mother's loopy scrawl. Dan pushed it aside to read the letter:

Dear Danny,
You don't know me, but I was your father. Please understand that I loved you dearly, and I would not have left you if I could have helped it. But when you turn exactly six months old, I will be murdered by a

man whose actions are as inevitable as my death. Trust Aaron. He's been a loyal friend for more years than I can count. And I hope you grow up with a father. I never did, and I always regretted it. You see, Danny, my father died when I turned six months old, as his did before him, and his before him. My story will sound crazy. It did to me, too. But the information I've sent should convince you. I'm sorry, my sweet perfect little baby. The curse of the Dellingrs lives on.

The letter continued, but Dan lowered it, needing to catch breaths that had turned to wild panting. He knew where this had to go, with warnings about his own death on Michael's half-year birthday. He tried to soothe himself with the knowledge that such a thing was ludicrous, that his birth father must have convinced himself of a nonexistent curse, then committed suicide. Like a placebo, his belief in a certain course of action had forced him to carry it out. Yet Dan could not help huddling into himself, assailed by the tense shocks of terror that filled his chest in the dark of night when a horror movie still lay fresh on his consciousness. He forced himself to continue reading:

My father left me information about the curse that I read as a young child. It colored my entire childhood. I carried a sense of future doom through everything I did. I did not want that for you. Although you will die young, I wanted you to enjoy your life without that threat hanging over your every moment. Through the centuries, our ancestors have chosen to tell their sons early, late, or never. They have attempted to avoid pro- creation through intended abstinence and every form of birth control, even vasectomy and castration. They

*have chosen "barren" women. On the fated day, they
have surrounded themselves with family, sought law-
men, locked themselves in "safe" places, to no avail.
Your great grandfather hanged himself before he im-
pregnated a wife or girlfriend. It left him vegetative but
alive. Your bereaved great-grandmother, ignorant of
the curse, had herself inseminated with his sperm. He
died when my father turned six months old, suffocated
in his sleep.*

*Always, a son is born. And always, the father dies
when the child turns six months old, killed by a descendant of Lonn Cearnach. And always before the age of
twenty-six.*

*Danny, it's up to you, now, to end the curse. I have
come to the terrible conclusion that there is only one
way. Like my father, I was too weak to carry it through.
Perhaps you will have the strength, or your son. After
an, albeit brief, lifetime of study, I have brought all the
information together. The curse strikes the child the day
his father dies. You are already damned, but those after
you might be spared. I believe that to break the curse
you must kill your son before he reaches six months
old. If you wish to continue the bloodline of Olief Dellingr, you may then use your remaining half year of
life to father another child. Or, you might find it best
to let our cursed bloodline die.*

Peter Leverton, 1977

Heart slamming in his chest, Dan Coglin dropped
the letter. It fluttered to the floor, ghostly pale against
the dark blue carpeting. Driven to movement, he rose
and paced with the wild desperation of a newly caged
animal. *Kill my son.* The thought was berserk, dirty.
He wanted to wash it from his mind. Though he had
done nothing worse than read the words, he felt driven

to bathe just for allowing the idea to enter his head. *I won't kill Michael. I couldn't harm a hair on his tiny, perfect, little head. Better a short life than none at all.*

A cry froze Dan in his tracks. From upstairs, Michael let out a series of hungry wails. For an instant, Dan's blood felt as if it had turned to ice in his veins, as if the baby had read his biological grandfather's murderous thoughts. He let Jillian handle the baby, glad she had managed four hours of sleep. Only she could breastfeed him. He looked at the two unopened envelopes, terrified they might convince him to do the unthinkable. He would never open them, would read nothing further. *Kill Michael.* Tears filled Dan's eyes at the bare thought, anger mixed with fierce anguish. Too many would suffer. Not only his innocent baby but Jillian, his parents, himself. He looked at the papers and envelopes, despising them and everything they represented. *Is it too late to pretend this night never happened?* He shoved everything back into the portfolio, not caring that a copy of *Parent's Digest* got shoved inside with the rest.

Giving the zipper a ferocious tug closed, Dan hid the portfolio beneath a decorative compartment in the coffee table. Forcing his mind back to an unfeeling blank, he headed upstairs to assist his wife.

A month passed before Dan Coglin succumbed to the allure of his history again. On a rainy Saturday, Jillian had gone to visit her parents for the weekend. She planned to spend most of her time catching up with a clique of girlfriends, showing off Michael, and exchanging stories about husbands, boyfriends, and children. Though Dan felt certain no words could ever cause him to harm his son, it reassured him to have his baby a three-hundred-fifty-mile drive away.

Though it seemed foolishly superstitious, he could not shake the fear that the paper itself might hold some ability to hypnotize him, some deep magic that might force his hand in a way common sense could not overcome.

A lemonade in hand, his feet crossed on the coffee table, Dan sat back with the sheaf of papers his birth father had packed away some twenty-two years ago. It began with the story of a young man named Olief Dellingr, clearly written by a competent storyteller. It drew Dan in like the best fiction he could remember. As he read, he became the eighteen-year-old of tall Viking stock whose family had settled in Celtic lands long before his birth. He could feel his father's broadsword, a bit too big, slapping against his knee as he walked. The description of the ancient tunic, breeks, and cape became vivid enough to feel as well as see. Filled with ancient hatred sparked fresh by the recent death of his father, Olief called to his father's killer on a grassy knoll dotted with sheep.

Lonn Cearnach answered the challenge, charging from his family's cottage with a drawn sword and a bull bellow of fury. Dellingr had never fought a real battle before that moment. Its looming actuality filled him with unexpected terror. The killer rush of his opponent dispelled the triumphant silver interplay of weaponry in his mind. Suddenly, the image of his newborn son flashed in front of his eyes. He should not have started this; he could not afford to die.

Only a few years older, Cearnach reached Dellingr in a twinkle, but an instant later than the sword rasped from its sheath. Dellingr ducked a bold strike for his head. He countered with a sweep that slammed its target. The blade slowed to a crawl as it sliced tendon, organ, and jarred against bone. Blood splashed his face, warm and salty. Cearnach collapsed with a screech, and a farther scream echoed the sound. Dellingr looked up to see a young woman clutching a baby several months older than his own, surely Cearnach's wife and son. A wizened old crone stood beside them, as grim and still as a statue.

Cearnach shrieked again, thrashing in mindless agony. Dellingr found himself frozen in place. His stomach lurched. His hands seemed to thrum with the impact. The odors of blood and bowel soured the air. The battle had ended much too soon. He had not managed any of the pretty, heroic swordplay he had imagined would overcome this enemy. Weak to the point of vomiting, he back-stepped and suddenly found the elder beside him.

"A pox on you!" the woman nattered, spitting. "Faeries curse your black heart for stealing a father from the six-month-old son who needed him. Your son will suffer the same, and that babe . . ." She spat again, gesturing a withered arm toward Cearnach's wife, lying in the grass, rending her clothing beside her wailing infant. ". . . Will slaughter your son like you did his father, leaving your grandson fatherless, too. His death, and that of every Dellingr father, will damn you for eternity."

The rest of the first packet, and the second, proved drier: Peter Leverton's lifework to chronicle every descendant of Olief Dellingr, made easier by the fact that each and every one created one and only one offspring. Their reactions to the curse, however, spanned the spectrum: confusion or denial, active attempts to thwart it, even a trial or two of happy acceptance. Where available, Dan's birth father supplied the rationale, or his interpretation of it, for how and when every father informed his son about the curse. In some cases, they fully hid the knowledge, but it always reemerged. Every father died exactly six months from the day of his first-born's birth, before the age of twenty-six. And that first-born was invariably male.

An interesting pattern emerged. Though several exceptions existed, most of the sons informed their own offspring in a far different way than their fathers had. Traumatized by the news no matter its delivery, each apparently tried to spare his son the same horrible method. The paradigm held true to this day. The father who had dedicated his life since late childhood to intimately researching and chronicling the devastating nightmare that haunted his bloodline had withheld the information from his own son until the last six months of his life.

The realization stopped Dan Coglin cold. He dropped the sheaf of papers in his hand, staring at the assortment of bric-a-brac on the entertainment center shelves. A jointed wooden monkey hung from a shapeless ceramic sculpture, wedding gifts from relatives and therefore undiscardable. A picture in a simple frame perched in front, Jillian looking ragged and tired but happy, baby Michael lost in the hospital blanket. *I have six months to live.* All the terror that had failed to come before erupted now. Dan's thoughts scattered like sea birds charged by a toddler. Shaking started in his toes and quickly seized his entire body. He sat in wild, uncontrollable panic, unable to move, think, act.

Dan did not know how long he sat, his mind and body frenzied but inactive. He no longer doubted the curse. To deny its reality seemed folly of the worst kind, the kind that would condemn not only himself, but his descendants, through eternity. He imagined this was what it felt like to enter a doctor's office with an unexplained lump and leave with the certain diagnosis of an aggressive, untreatable, genetically determined cancer. *Six months.* He knew science dictated that he go through stages now, and he tried to recall them all. Denial, he remembered. Anger, bargaining. And, finally, acceptance. *I don't have time for all that.* Dan fished for determination through terror. He looked at the picture again, Jillian's tired ecstasy, innocent Michael with his whole short life ahead of him. *The curse has to end with me.* But it would not end with him killing his baby. *There has to be another way.*

Dan forced aside thoughts of parks, Little League games, plays, and concerts. Fate had already decreed he would miss all of those. He would have time enough to mourn them in the wee hours of the morning when sleep fully eluded him. Denial, anger, bargaining, even acceptance. He could face those stages when they crept up on him while he attempted to work, in quiet moments when he tried to enjoy the short time he had with his son. Convinced by his reading that the curse truly struck from the moment the father died, Dan knew he could not save himself. Another realization abruptly slammed him, with express train speed. *And if I'm already slated to die, maybe I can't save my son, either. Only my grandson. And every future Coglin . . . ,* he corrected . . . *Leverton . . .* It still did not fit. Because of the early deaths of the fathers with frequent remarriages of the mothers, and because of distant attempts to "hide the child from the curse" in other families, the last name of Olief

Dellingr's descendants had changed a myriad times over the centuries. *Dellingr offspring.*

If an answer existed, it lay in the missive of Peter Leverton. Gathering his courage, and the fallen papers, Dan returned to his reading. The remaining chronicles of his most distant male relatives added little, except that they more openly discussed the curse. Over time, it had become a family secret, then a divulgence not even always passed from father to son.

Still without an answer, Dan sighed and reached for the third packet. Dinnertime had come and gone, yet he knew no hunger. Obsessed with finding an answer, he broke the seal, wondering what this last, thick sheaf could possibly contain after the first two had detailed the lives and deaths of every Dellingr offspring. The first thing that tumbled from the envelope was a high-density 5.25-inch floppy disk labeled "Family Research, disk copy" that surely contained all the information Dan was reading now. A quick scan of the papers revealed two remaining topics: attempts by Dellingr progeny to have the curse removed and the history of the Cearnach descendants.

The first pile interested Dan more, so he dived into it like a starving man at a feast. His predecessors had, apparently, put at least as much work into escaping the curse as he planned to do himself. Some, like his birth father, had dedicated their lives to the effort. Women a decade barren miraculously conceived. Birth control, cajoling, hiding, and suicide failed. Rigid vows of abstinence became meaningless. One Dellingr descendant had even endured castration, only to discover his wife pregnant days later. Though none had succeeded in foiling the curse, several had penned down their attempts for future generations. Pete had carefully compiled their findings, translating many of the dissertations from ancient Norse, Celtic, and Old English. Even the Dellingr ancestor who brought the family to America had done so in a vain attempt to escape the curse of the Dellingrs rather than for any opportunity or freedom. A soothsayer had told him that the curse would stay with the Faeries who honored it. The soothsayer, it seemed, was dead wrong.

Potions and poisons had likewise failed, along with carried, printed, and spoken charms. Exorcism had accomplished nothing. Witches and warlocks of diverse nationalities, cabals, sects, and covens invariably proved weaker than the Cearnach's curse. Visionaries who named themselves fortunetellers, prophets, oracles, and seers gave mysterious advice that seemed without merit. Nevertheless, Dan focused his attention here. It made sense to him that, having brought the curse upon themselves, it would take one of the Dellingr clan to remove it. The counselors of the psychic stripe at least gave cryptic recommendations for the Dellingr men to act on rather than claiming their personal powers or brews would remove what the family's own sin had invoked.

Worried for the terror that would ruin his sleep if he turned his attention from this obsession, Dan continued to read and consider through the night. Dawn light snaked rainbow patterns across the living room wall when he finally discovered a clear and consistent understanding. Not every soothsayer had claimed the same thing; but, when their advice came together, one thing seemed decisive. Removing the curse would require a deliberate joining of the feuding families into one. Coming to that place had required Dan to discard some of the seers' advice, however. By comparing the circumstances and the words, he felt he had eliminated the quacks rather than just the ones that did not support his theory.

Dan yawned and stretched, muscles cramped from too long in one position. Oddly, he did not feel tired, his mind surprisingly precise for one who had missed meals and a full night of sleep. He knew adrenaline drove him and that, once depleted, he would regret his decision not to sleep. Yet, he also knew that he would have worried himself awake all night anyway. Total, inescapable exhaustion might well prove his only chance for rest.

Food was a whole other matter. Hating even the moments it took him to walk to the kitchen, pour a mixing bowl full of Cheerios, and add milk and two spoonfuls of sugar, Dan hurried back to his birth father's lifework as he ate.

To Dan's surprise, the Cearnach's history proved as heartrending as the Dellingr's own. Dulled by time and distance, the original cause of the curse had become lost. Most were young, moral men, some already fathers themselves, damned to murder innocent strangers. Like the Dellingrs, the Cearnach descendants had often changed names, locations, and families of rearing in an effort to escape a curse initially cast in their behalf. Their information proved more sketchy than the Dellingr ancestors. Far more often, the Cearnachs were kept in ignorance. Many had served jail time; some had even succumbed to the death penalty. But they never died before creating first-born male offspring and sometimes other children as well.

Dan sat back. Tears stung his eyes, and he marveled at the realization that he could feel sympathy for the man destined to slaughter him. *This is insane. This can't be real.* For a long moment, he dismissed the whole as an elaborate prank. Peter Leverton, if that was his real name, probably languished in a mental institution somewhere, laughing at the son he had scammed or, perhaps, believing every word of the schizophrenic world he had concocted. *I can't believe I was so taken in by this. Curses, warlocks, soothsayers.* Another thought followed, as if placed there by a stranger. *Congratulations, Daniel Dwayne Coglin. You've reached denial.*

With a shiver, Dan continued reading. The next page of the missive dismissed the happy idea that had allowed him to attribute a day and night of savage discovery to madness. Copied directly from an Internet genealogy site, it traced the Leverton ancestry directly back to Olief Dellingr and further confirmed the strange single male child lineage, the multiple adoptions, the early deaths. If Peter Leverton was insane, so then was ancestortrace.com.

Perhaps it is all an elaborate scam, Dan told himself. *But it doesn't hurt to prepare for the worst.* The Cearnach history revealed that he had not reached the "combining of the feuding families theory" first. Those who had elicited oracular advice had followed it to their own interpretations. Some had befriended their future murderers, which only made the deaths more tragic and painful for the Cearnach clan. A short police confession penciled by one Cecil Orball (Cearnach) described a desperate and unwinnable battle against sudden, unexpected obsession that forced him to drown his best friend, leaving the man's six-month-old son without a father. Twice, Cearnach daughters had married Dellingr sons, loveless marriages that both ended tragically and barren. In an attempt more desperate than logical, a heterosexual Dellingr had forced a gay relationship with his killer.

Left without an answer, Dan replaced the papers in

their envelopes. Rising, he walked to the kitchen, put his empty cereal bowl and spoon in the sink, and headed out the back door. A brisk walk took him around the entire neighborhood, thoughts swirling. Caught in a dizzying limbo between panic and pluck, he arrived back home hours later without any memory of where he had gone or whom he had passed. Fatigue finally caught him, however. He crawled into bed. The legacy of Olief Dellingr and Lonn Cearnach, forever bonded together, followed him into his dreams. He slept through the rest of Sunday.

Weeks dragged into months. Dan Coglin took a leave of absence from his job under the auspices of spending more time with his newborn son. He did that, trying to cram a lifetime of experience into his remaining months. Yet, in the background, his mind wrestled continuously with the curse. Ironically, the more he tried to live every moment, the more they seemed to blend together, to race too fast, to blur into one mind-numbing effort to understand, to have it all, to break a centuries-old curse that seemed too far beyond the efforts of a single man doomed to a grave rushing ever more swiftly toward him.

One evening, four months after the fateful news that had changed Dan Coglin's life, he sat in his usual place on the living room couch, scanning his birth father's writings for some detail he might have missed. Having placed the baby in bed, Jillian perched on the cushion to her husband's left and laid her head on his arm. Her physical closeness reminded him of the intensity of his love for her. He placed his arm around her, drawing her close. Her long blonde hair tickled his cheek, and her shoulders felt dainty and helpless in his grip. His father's words, which had faded into the desperate boil of need, returned to him now: *So, you're saying that you could never love Jillian as much as your Aunt Patricia.* Dan smiled at the thought. No one in the world, blood-related or not, had ever moved him as deeply as his wife. "I love you," he said.

Dan expected Jillian to echo him, her standard response. She surprised him. "Then why won't you let me in?"

Startled to full attention, Dan gazed into her blue eyes and oval face, the cheekbones low and prominent, her nose small and freckled. She looked tired but beautiful. "What do you mean?"

Jillian shifted in his grip. "I mean, I know your father laid a big shock on you. I've let you handle it alone, respected your privacy. You're moping around like a zombie. Don't you think you'd feel better if you had someone to share that burden with?"

Share the knowledge that I'm going to die in just a few months? That our beloved son will, too? That our grandsons through eternity are doomed? Dan pulled Jillian closer. "I'm sorry. I'll be more attentive. I promise."

Jillian managed a wiggly smile. "If you got any more attentive to Mikey, I'd have to have him grafted to your chest. Attentive isn't the problem." She buried her face in his chest. "This is the 'worse' part of 'better or.' I promised to stick with you. I will. I can imagine what you're going through, but I'm probably wrong. I can't help you if you don't share your feelings."

Dan's heart felt like squeezed lead. Pain snaked down his left arm. *Am I having a heart attack?* The irony almost forced a strangled laugh. *Impossible. I can't die for another two months and six days.* "All right, Jillian. I'll tell you. But you'll probably wish you didn't know."

Dan's shirt muffled his wife's reply. "I can handle anything but ignorance."

The first words came hard. Then, suddenly, the story practically poured out of Dan, the simple act of sharing bringing a cold wash of relief he could never have anticipated. Jillian listened raptly, never interrupting, seeming to accept a curse that sounded more like madness than the logical interpretation of a rational man. Dan reached for the envelopes, sharing the papers that had to convince her, though she had revealed no evidence of her doubts. The copy of *Parent's Digest* fell to the coffee table.

"What's this?" Jillian Coglin spoke her first words since the story began, examining the magazine.

Dan pushed her hand toward the table. "That's nothing. Just got caught up with the papers."

Jillian continued to examine it. "Look at this. There's an article on adoption myths." She looked up. "Seems appropriate."

Thoughts of his adoption had banished themselves to the deeper reaches of Dan's mind as the more pressing problem of his imminent murder replaced them. Now, he realized, he still suffered a trickle of anger, betrayal. The very same curse that had stolen his birth father from him had damned him to the fate of his bloodline. Intuitively, he knew that if genetics played the massive role most people assigned it, then parenting became meaningless. All children might as well grow up in nameless institutions.

Jillian scanned the article. "Says here adoptive parents like people to realize that adoption is just another way to build a family. That it's not second best. That the terms 'real parent' and 'natural parent' should not be applied to birth parents because it makes the adoptive parents sound 'unreal' and 'unnatural.' "

Second best. Dan's mind stuck on the phrase because it seemed not to apply to his case at all. Aaron Coglin had not adopted him because of infertility but because of love and as a favor to a friend. Yet Dan realized how often situations that had initially disappointed him, second best, often proved far better than if he had actually gotten what he thought he had wanted. If he had won the lead in the senior play, he would have missed the comic relief role that granted him a permanent sense of humor which, until recently, had brought him through the worst times of his life. If Crystal Johanson had accepted his proposal, he would now have Ricky Meros' fat shrew of a wife—no Jillian, no Michael. Long ago, Aaron Coglin had told Dan that he loved him more than any other boy in the universe, that he would continue to do so forever. Dan had believed it then, and he believed it now.

Oblivious, Jillian continued. "The magazine surveyed three hundred biological mothers raising their biological children. It asked them to directly consider their actual sons and/or daughters. If they found out today that those children had been switched at birth, would they trade them. You know how many answered 'yes?' "

Dan shook his head.

"Zero." Jillian replied. "Most said they'd like to meet their biological children, but not one would trade. They also said it wouldn't change anything about the way they felt about their current children."

Jillian's words sparked the idea that had, thus far, eluded Dan. "That's it!"

Startled, Jillian sat bolt upright. "What's it?"

Dan laughed, suddenly freed from the grim obsession of the last four months. "Here's what I think we have to do. . . ."

*   *   *

Six months to the day after Michael's birth, Dan
Coglin had all his affairs in order. He sat alone on a
stool in the garage, plastic sheeting spread neatly beneath it and a gun he had personally purchased sitting,
loaded, on the work bench. He stared through one of
the gritty windows at the note he had taped to it, a
ruled page affixed with a single piece of tape. It faced
outward, but he knew it read: "Descendant of Lonn
Cearnach—Knock and I'll admit you. Please, can we
talk first? Sincerely, Descendant of Olief Dellingr
(Dan Coglin)." Dan did not know the name or appearance of the man he would confront. His father's
and grandfather's deaths were ruled accidental. No
one had seen, or named, their murderers.

As the morning stretched to afternoon, then evening, Dan breathed a sigh of relief. Though Jillian
had reluctantly agreed to his plan and supported him
through his dark moments, she could not wholly hide
her skepticism. She apparently believed that nothing
worse than Dan's own imagination threatened his life.
Like him, she did not believe in the supernatural and
barely indulged his Sunday night television guilty pleasure: *The X-Files*.

Then, just as gray twilight fuzzed Dan's vision and
he turned on the workbench light, a knock sounded
through the garage's confines. Startled, he leaped from
his chair, heart pounding. He barely stifled a scream.
Only then, he realized that, deep-down, he had always
truly doubted. Although he had accepted his inevitable death, he had never wholly released denial.
Bravely, he thumbed the garage door opener and
watched the door ratchet upward. Dressed in a
sweatshirt, jeans, and a denim jacket, a neatly slender

stranger stood in the opening. He wore gloves on his hands. "Daniel Dwayne Coglin?"

"Come in," Dan said, his voice tremulous despite long-gathered courage.

The man obliged, and Dan pressed the opener again. The door glided shut behind him. The stranger waited until it fully closed before speaking. "My name is Gene Reed. I have to kill you." He spoke unself-consciously, without fear of hidden witnesses, videos, or tape recorders. Dan got the idea he wanted to be caught, though he would not be. Dan's plan depended on it.

"I know." Dan hid his fear behind a bland mask. He held up the pistol by its barrel. I've put my finger-prints all over it for you. It'll look like suicide. No reason to ruin both of our lives for a curse neither of us can control."

Reed blinked, shifting nervously. "I'm sorry. I really am." His face screwed up, but he still approached. "There's no need to protect me. I can't live with this. I'd rather be caught and punished."

"No." Dan lowered the gun to the work bench. "You have to go on. For the good of our progeny."

"I have no progeny," Reed said. "Yet." They both knew he would father a son, at least.

Thank God. Dan's plan had hinged on that contin-gency, although, if Reed had already sired a child, Dan could still have presented his idea. Their sons could have arranged the situation so Michael's child was born at least six months before Reed's grandson. "I would ask only two things of you."

Reed nodded his willingness to listen.

"Please make this quick and painless."

Reed's nod became more vigorous. "I'll do every-thing I can to assure that."

"And after I'm . . ." Dan swallowed. ". . . gone, I want you to . . . adopt my son."

Reed stood, clearly shocked. "Your wife—"

"She knows. And she agreed. For the good of our children's children . . ."

"Our children's children," Reed echoed.

Dan placed the gun barrel against his temple, hand shaking so hard it took all his strength just to hold it in place. "Go ahead. Pull the trigger."

No matter how much Reed wished otherwise, there was no way he could resist.

In a spacious courtroom overlooking the Mississippi River, Judge Heatherman gestured for the justice of the peace to proceed. Gene Reed smiled, his arm around Jillian Coglin, his other clutching squirmy, fourteen-month-old Michael. In metal folding chairs, Aaron and Samantha Coglin sat quietly, watching.

The justice of the peace intoned, "And now, with the power invested in me by the state of Iowa, I now pronounce you husband and wife."

Placing Michael on the floor, Reed wrapped both arms around Jillian and kissed her. At that moment, he realized his love for her made every previous relationship seem like silly infatuation. He marveled at how such a thing could happen. It had seemed like awkward convenience at first, visiting Coglin's son to make the boy legally his own, presumably never to see him again. Reed could not have anticipated the way things had blossomed and changed; now, he celebrated the moment he had opened his heart to the boy, his grandparents, and his mother. He could still scarcely believe they had forgiven his heinous, albeit uncontrollable, crime against the younger Coglin. Grateful, he envied their heroism and silently vowed to cherish Jillian and to keep the Coglin elders a full and daily part of Michael's life.

Judge Heatherman cleared his throat.

Reed broke the kiss, cheeks turning scarlet. "Sorry to waste your time, Your Honor." Aaron chased after the toddler, scooping him up in his arms. He dumped Michael into Reed's waiting arms.

"Thank you," Reed told Aaron warmly, simple words that meant so much more.

Judge Heatherman grinned as he took over the proceedings again. "No hurry. This is the only thing a judge gets to do where all parties leave the court smiling." He continued on a more serious note, "You understand that by adopting this boy, your relationship becomes that of father and son forever, with all the responsibilities inherent in a blood relationship?"

"Yes, Your Honor."

"You understand that, upon your death, your son will inherit as per every federal and state law applicable to natural fathers and sons."

"Biological," Jillian corrected under her breath.

"Yes, Your Honor," Reed said, meaning it.

"And if your marriage ever failed, whoever did not gain physical custody of Michael Harris *Reed* would have to pay child support as per state law."

Reed hugged the boy, grin unstoppable. "Yes, Your Honor."

Judge Heatherman nodded. "The adoption petition is granted."

Michael struggled in Reed's grip. "Dada," he said on cue.

A massive burden seemed to fall from Gene Reed as Michael legally became the first-born of both the Dellingr and Cearnach lines. No massive fanfare accompanied the change. No ancient witch cackled over the destruction of her curse. Yet Reed knew that, thanks to a father's sacrifice, the curse of the feuding families had ended. "Dada, indeed," Reed repeated. "Forever and ever and ever."

FOR THE LIFE OF SHEILA MORGAN
by Dennis L. McKiernan

There ain't no such thing as a free lunch . . .
nor a free *spell* for that matter

Dennis McKiernan is the best-selling fantasy author of *The Voyage of the Fox Rider, Eye of the Hunter*, and *Caverns of Socrates*. His latest novel, the second in the *Hel's Crucible* duology, is entitled *Into the Fire*. His short fantasy fiction has been collected in *Tales of Mithgar*, with other fiction of his appearing in such anthologies as *Weird Tales from Shakespeare* and *Dragon Fantastic*.

"**D**jinn 2000? Never heard of it. Who makes it? IBM, Compaq, Dell, Gateway: who?"

The grubby night clerk at Harry's All Night Used Computers and Pawn Shop stuck an index finger into the pages of his *Hustler* to mark his place and leaned back in his chair and scratched that part of his beer gut which blobbed out over his belt buckle from under the edge of a dank T-shirt stained with swipes of french-fry grease and copious oozings of sweat; he wrapped his words around an extinguished, wet stub of a cigar. "I dunno, lady. All I know is that when I came in, it was sittin' back there. It ain't got no ticket, so Arlene must've bought it outright or took it in on a trade."

"Arlene, eh? Not Harry?"

"There ain't no Harry, lady. Just Arlene, and

she's—" He snorted a laugh, nearly losing his cigar.
"Hey, that's funny: Harry lady; hairy lady. Get it?"

Well, duh!

He flicked his moist eyes at the *Hustler* and mumbled, "Hairy lady," then looked back at Sheila, a leer
on his face.

Eww!

Repelled, Sheila turned away. She wouldn't even
have been here in this fly-by-night hole-in-the-wall if
her bloody laptop hadn't crapped out, and she on a
deadline at that—due at eight in the morning. Sheila
glanced at her watch: three AM. *Procrastinators R Us:
that's what it ought to say on my web page, rather than
Freelancer Extraordinaire. Now here I am at the only
place in town that has computers and is open at this
time of night—probably to fence stolen 'puters and
other such. —I wonder if I should make an effort to
work in the daytime rather than . . . ? Naah!*

"Look, is it okay if I try it out?"

"Do whatcha want, lady," said the clerk, turning his
attention again to the magazine.

Sheila walked back to the bench where the Djinn
2000 sat. *The only blooming machine in the place that
doesn't look to be beat all to hellandgone. I wonder if
it even* has *a word processor. And what kind of*—Sheila
hit the master switch on the power director—*Whoa!*
The screen instantly came to life, a toolbar displayed
at the top.

Hmmm . . . This looks to be—she clicked on the *W*
icon, and a menu came up: Word99, WordExcellent,
WordMagic, WordPower . . .

Ah, it does have a "werp," several in fact. Sheila
clicked on *Word99*, and the familiar toolbar—*Crikey,
but this is fast*—instantly came on. A few more quick
checks of W99 and she was satisfied.

Then she keyed in another command: *Good! It's got plenty of RAM and hard drive. Ah, a modem and a Netscan browser; I can get up on the Internet and transmit the file to Joe. No speakers, though. No soundcard.*

Sheila continued her survey. Finally she yelled back to the clerk, "How much do you want for this thing?"

Grunting in exasperation at being disturbed in his libidinous fantasies—"Lady, there ain't nothin' in this store higher than three hundred bucks." He swiveled about. "Of course, if you don't have that kind of money, we might arrange a little, um, *business* on the side, if you get my drift."

Ugh!

Sheila fished $264 out from her fanny pack—*Every last penny I've got*—and stepped to the counter and dropped it on the glass. "This'll have to do."

The clerk stood. "Well, then, there's always the alternative, lady."

"No way. It's this or zip."

Disappointment flickered across the clerk's face as with sweaty palms he counted the bills: crumpled tens and twenties for the most part.

Moments later, the Djinn 2000 was loaded in the Honda's trunk, and Sheila was outta there.

At 6:57 A.M., the magazine article was finished. *Ha! An hour and three minutes to spare. Now to spellcheck this sucker.* Sheila looked at the toolbar. *Hmm . . . Where in the—? There was no spellchecking icon. She searched all the drop-down menus. Still no bloody—* Growling, Sheila clicked *Help* and keyboarded *Spell*.

The CD-ROM drive began to spin up.

What th—?

Frowning, she punched the eject button. The tray

slid open, revealing a CD. Picking it up, Sheila read the handwritten label: *Spell*.

What's this? Some kinda bootleg program? Oh, well.

Returning the CD and punching the drawer closed, Sheila triggered the drive. Again it spun up, and within moments the screen read *Spell*.

Hmm. Same handwriting.

Sheila clicked on the word.

What spell? popped up.

It wants to know what to spell? Okay. Sheila typed in the name of her file: Titantic.doc.

Instantly the screen read: *That is not a spell. What spell?*

If I knew how to spell, idiot, I wouldn't need you! Again Sheila keyboarded in Titanic.doc.

That is not a spell. What spell?

Arrgh! What's going on here? Sheila glanced at her watch. *Six fifty-nine. Plenty of time.*

Frowning, she sighed and keyed in *Help?*

What kind of spell? Love, fame, wealth, death, power, resurrection, war, health for another: these are among your choices.

Rats! Not a spellcheck, but a game. Again she glanced at her watch. *Seven oh one. Still plenty of time.* She looked at the screen speculatively. *Let's give it a go.*

Sheila smiled wickedly and clicked on *Death!*

Who?

Who? Hmm . . . How about that lech of a clerk at Harry's? Clickety-click went the keys as her fingers flew.

How? Accident, murder, suicide, sudden illness, lingering illness, the death of a thousand cuts—

Still grinning, Sheila clicked on *death of a thousand cuts*.

Six months for that particular unnoteworthy person: Accept? Reject?

Sheila again glanced at her watch. *Seven oh five. Enough of this. I gotta get Titanic spellchecked.* She started to reach for the CD-ROM eject button, but upon impulse she clicked on *Accept.*

The nausea overwhelmed her.

When she came to, she was slumped down in her computer chair. Late afternoon sunlight shone through the west-facing apartment window. And the phone was ringing. As she groaned and stiffly reached for the handset, she glanced at her computer screen.

Done! Would you like another? Yes; no.

Lifting the phone to her ear—"Hello."

Moments later she slammed the phone down. Angry tears sprang to her eyes. *Sorry, doll—that scumbucket called me doll—but this was on spec and you missed the deadline. Worm! No kill fee. Clementine made her deadline, and we're going with her article. Well, screw Clementine! Screw Joe, too, the no-kill-fee, on-spec bastard! And the car payment is overdue and the rent, and I've no food and I'm maxed out on my credit cards. . . .*

Raging, she stood, a wave of dizziness washing over her. *I've caught a bug of some kind. Just what I needed, right?* Despairing, using the walls for support, Sheila tottered out of the computer room and down the hall and into the apartment kitchen and to the fridge. Sucking down a glass of V-8, she flopped onto the living-room couch. Drained by fatigue, she clicked on the TV: *The universal soporific.* Moments later she was sound asleep.

". . . Tucson, Arizona, police are still searching for clues as to the horrific, early-morning . . ."

Grunting, Sheila sat up; she seemed to be over whatever bug she had caught. *How long have I been—? * Starlight shone through the window, adding faint luminance to the glow of the TV. On the screen a CNN Headline News reporter stood in daylight somewhere—*Must be on tape*—talking to some woman at a small, run-down strip mall—*That looks like—* Sheila slapped on her eyeglasses and focused on the—*Hey! It* is *Harry's All Night—*

". . . is how I would describe it. Just gruesome. Blood everywhere. It looks like some pervert took, like, some kinda whirling blade—like, say, a blender blade—to him. What kinda sicko would—"

Holy crap!

"—do that to Karl?"

"Was anything taken?"

"No. I mean, like, there was two hundred or so dollars in Karl's wallet. And the store money, like, well it was untouched; in fact there was fifty bucks in addition."

That sleazeball pocketed all but fifty of my money.

"Oh, and, like, one of the computers was gone, so Karl must have sold it. It was an off-brand of some sort—"

In that moment a police officer stepped into the picture and held out a hand to block the camera as he said, "Sorry, but the details of this case are confidential—"

Sheila didn't hear what else he had to say, for she was up and stumbling toward her computer room.

The screen still read: *Done. Would you like another? Yes; no.*

"You lousy, murdering piece of junk!" shrieked Sheila. "You killed that—"

Done. Would you like another? Yes; no.

Wait a minute. What the hell am I thinking? How could a computer game—?

Done. Would you like another? Yes; no.

But what if it isn't a computer game? —Ah, come on, Sheila. How could it be anything but? . . . Even so, what if it isn't just a computer game?

Gingerly, she sat down at the keyboard. Taking a deep breath, she gripped the mouse and guided the pointer to Yes and clicked on it.

What spell?

Sheila keyed in *Help?*

What kind of spell? Love, fame, wealth, death, power, resurrection, war, health for another: these are among your choices.

This is ridiculous. A bloody computer game can't cast spells, grant wishes . . . not in the real world, it can't. It's got to be coincidence, right? And yet . . .

Her mind shied away from the clerk and the death of a thousand cuts.

What kind of spell? Love, fame, wealth, death, power, resurrection, war, health for another: these are among your choices.

But if it could . . . Jesus. Just what is it I want? A Pulitzer! That's what. —But what I need at the moment is money. Yes. Money.

Sheila clicked *Wealth*.

How much? And for whom?

For me, you fucking idiot. A million bucks. Sheila keyed in the amount and her own name.

Five years for that particular amount. Accept? Reject?

Again Sheila keyed in *Help?*

It will cost you five years of the remainder of your life for that particular amount: Accept? Reject?

"Five years!" shouted Sheila. "As Demi Moore

said, 'Suck my—!' " *Whoa! Wait a minute. No wonder I passed out. This pile of silicon sucked away six months of my life just to kill that poor—*

Angrily, Sheila snapped off the power, but the screen was a long time fading.

Five years for that particular amount: Accept? Reject?

Five years for   Accept? Reject?

Fiv   rs   Acc t? Rej ?

Fi   AC   Re ?

A   R ?

?

The phone awakened her.

"Hello. . . ."

"What? . . ."

"Go to bloody hell!"

Slamming down the phone—*Damn all collection agencies!*—Sheila groaned out of bed and made her way to the refrigerator. *Nothing but stupid V-8.*

At the computer she brought up Netscan and the modem and keyed in the phone number and her ID and password for her Internet service provider.

What th—?

Access denied. Account canceled.

Canceled? But I'm only three months— Greedy bastards!

Fuming, she swallowed the last of the V-8, then looked with distaste at the pulpy red streaks oozing down the inside of the glass.

Sheila closed her eyes and leaned back. Through the open window she heard the muffled whine of hydraulics echoing in the complex. After a moment it stopped. Then a diesel engine revved. *Sounds like a— Oh, my!* Leaping up, she ran to the sliding door and out onto her apartment balcony . . . to see the wrecker hauling her Honda around the corner and away. "Hey, wai—!" But then it was gone.

Brushing tears of despair from her eyes, Sheila plodded back to the computer and slumped into her chair.

She sat long moments staring at the glowing monitor.

Access denied. Account canceled.

At last she stirred. *What the bloody hell, it's the same as $200,000 a year.* Still she hesitated—

Five years! That's—what?—ten, five, twenty, eighty, or who knows what percent of what's left of my life?

—but finally triggered the CD/ROM drive and keyed in *Spell.*

What spell?

Sheila sat back and looked a long time at the words on the monitor. . . .

. . . Her stomach growled. . . .

. . . She could hear someone coming up the steps to her apartment. . . .

. . . *What spell?* demanded the screen.

THE SAGEBRUSH *BRUJO* MEETS THE LAST OF THE PLATTERS
OR
WHY DO WE LIVE IN LA?
by John DeChancie

John DeChancie has written more than twenty books in
the science fiction, fantasy, and horror fields, including the
acclaimed *Castle* series. He has also written dozens of
short stories and nonfiction articles, appearing in such magazines as *The Magazine of Fantasy and Science Fiction*
and *Cult Movies* and many anthologies, including *First Contact* and *Wizard Fantastic*. In addition to his writing, John
enjoys traveling and composing and playing classical music.
His most recent book is *Other States of Being*, a collection
of short stories.

This is the city: Los Angeles, California.
Remember how *Dragnet* opened? Jack Webb as
an anal-retentive cop with a flat affect. Did you know
that "Just the facts, ma'am" deadpuss shtick of his
went back to radio? In stark contrast, do you remember him playing a beatnik writer in *Sunset Boulevard*?
Great movie. Great story. No, that's not the story I'm
about to tell you. But it will be an story about LA.
It was Friday night. It was cold in Los Angeles.
Never mind.
It was Friday night and I'm working on a screenplay
for a direct-to-cable, do not pass Go, do-not-buy-that-

Porche-yet movie. Budget? It is to laugh. I won't tell
you the title, but it's now playing on HBO 2 and you
won't see it before midnight, if you get my drift.
Though it's a T & A potboiler, I'm wasting my time
giving it a plot and even a bit of characterization, but
maybe you won't be able to recognize them, awash as
they are in a sea of rippling saline implants. You've
seen my byline on a raft of late-night cable movies,
but it probably didn't register, popping on and off the
screen in less time than it takes to crunch a nacho
chip. I've written scripts for about two dozen flicks,
have a hand in about an even dozen more, with two
credits in arbitration with the Writers Guild. Credits
mean very little, really. In the movies in which I get
sole screenplay byline, upwards of fifty percent of the
dialogue comprises words I never wrote. Who wrote
them? The director, the producer, the actors, the leading man's personal trainer (that brings to mind something that happened the other day; I was at a cell
phone store in Beverly Hills paying my bill, standing
in line, and I had just quaffed a double mocha latte
and was feeling kind of bloated and I was standing
there in line with my stomach kind of hanging out and
this thin young man in front of me turns around and
says right up front, no preamble, no overture, no conversation striker-upper, no prelims at all, man, he ups
and says to me, "Do you need a personal trainer?"
and I say something like "Duhhhh . . . wha?" and he
repeats it and I can't believe this guy and I think he's
maybe coming on to me, but then I think again, because he is indeed eyeing my middle-age beer belly in
a clinically nonsexual way, and I admit to having one,
a small paunch, a nicely rounded hillock of belly-flesh
that has no function on earth but to push out the
nether regions of my shirt just the slightest bit, just

the slightest eensy bit, mind you. Do I need a personal trainer. This guy is just oozing solicitude for my holistic wellbeing, and I want to cut this short, I want to get shed of this Rodeo Drive dweebmeister right quick, and I say forthrightly, taking great care not sound the least bit hostile or defensive or put off, no negative vibes, sweetheart, and I say, "I really don't go in for that sort of thing," thinking this is safe, this is cool, this is the Chardonnay-and-cheese-fundraiser, limos-double-parked-up-and-down-Wilshire-Boulevard way of saying, "Mind your own fucking business, mate," but this guy gets over on me by quipping—get this specimen of West LA wit—he wisecracks, "Well, *that's* obvious," and I want to take a Qualcomm phone and shove it so far up his butt he'll be tasting lithium ions at the back of his throat, but that might be interpreted as overreacting, and I'm not at all violent; I just hate gratuitous rudeness, so I play it even cooler; however, I'm digressing all over the freaking place), the leading lady's agent, whoever, you've heard this all before anyway, like the one about the actress who was so dumb that she slept with the writer; doubtless this is yesterday's *USA Today* to you, and anyway this Hollywood stuff is not what this story is about. It is about Hollywood in a way, though, and I'll get to that in a minute, but I want to establish myself first and set the scene. We need an establishing shot.

Interior, my apartment, night, and all that. No, let's not do it in script format. I'm taking a break and writing a short story here. I'm finishing up the *nth* rewrite of this potboiler script, this so-called "erotic thriller" which shall be titleless but which we will refer to as *The Last Ripoff of Basic Instinct*, complete with obligatory lesbian scene, knifing the lover at orgasm

scene, and police interrogation/seduction scene—anyway, let's get on with this—and my aforementioned
cell phone tinkles, and I answer, and it's my girlfriend,
who is mightily pissed off.

"Where the hell are you?"

A picosecond's interlude of anomie. Again, it's
duh . . . wha? time and suddenly it hits me and my
right palm slaps against my forehead with a meaty
thwack.

"I was supposed to meet you after you got off work!
Jeez, I'm sorry. I got to working, and I just . . . jeez,
I'm sorry, sweetie."

"It's okay."

She's great, really. She indulges me all to hell and
back. She's more battle-hardened than Audie Murphy.
My ex-wife would have gone into a two-week snit. My
ex^2 (two wives back) would have essayed to give me
a vasectomy with a machete (she was a Philippina—
and I've always wondered, does that make the guys
Philippenises?—never mind), but Jennifer, unlike the
psycho bitches in the scripts I write, is sanguine.
She's cool.

I say, "Are you sure you're not mad? You are,
aren't you?"

"Nah. But I'm getting kind of worried."

"Why? What's going on? Where are you?"

"I'm at that Denny's in Burbank that you said to
meet at. I've been sitting here for an hour."

"Oh, Jesus."

"And there're some creepazoid types lurking
around and I'm feeling just the slightest bit creeped
out. I want to get out of here."

"Meet me at Mel's Drive-In."

"Which one?"

"The one on Ventura in Sherman Oaks, so you

don't have to leave the Valley. The one on Sunset is more Hollywood, but you don't want more Hollywood if you're creeped out. And it's just up the freeway from me."

"Okay."

"When?"

"I have to stop at a Ralph's and pick up some orange juice. I'm out of orange juice, so I'll be there in, like, half an hour."

"Plenty of time," I say.

But I know it depends on traffic on the freeway. Sure, it's late, but it's Friday night, and despite reports to the contrary, LA has night life. The freeways are thick with traffic on weekend nights. A real snarl is rare this late, but all it takes is one accident, and traffic clots up for miles.

But if that happens, there's always the "surface streets," as they're called. Translation: any thoroughfare that's not a freeway, and the reason they're called surface streets is because most of the freeways run atop colonnades of concrete pylons, raised above the rest of the sprawl. These pylons have been known to crack and crumble during earthquakes, and every once in a while, when I'm shooting through an underpass, I think about that. Think about tons and tons of concrete dropping on me. It's happened to people. You don't think about it much. Earthquakes are one of the givens in this region of the country. You expect them, you even plan for them. You live with them. And chances are you won't die from them. More of a chance of getting killed in a pileup than of being crushed by a thousand tons of ferroconcrete. There is more than one way of ending up looking like a Budweiser can run over by a semi. I worry about pileups. You can be the best defensive driver in the world, but if a car six or eight carlengths down the road spins out, hits the median, and careens out to the middle of the road in front of you, you are going to hit that sucker at fifty mph even if you stand on the brake. No avoiding it. And then brace yourself, because two hundred cars behind you are going to smack into your rear end.

But again I digress. Actually, not so much, because all of the above relates to the issue at hand, which Jennifer is about to state in its most succinct formulation. She'll do that shortly, so hang on.

I grab my jacket and slam out of my second-floor two-bedroom, and head down the stairs. Out in the courtyard, I walk past the swimming pool, still full in the middle of winter—oh, did I mention it was what passes for winter in LA?—yes, I did say it was cold. But LA cold is not what you guys back East think of as cold. I'm talking fifty Fahrenheit, maybe a degree less. Bracing, but no more than light jacket weather.

As soon as I get outside, it hits me. What's the first thing you think you'd smell as you step out into a Los Angeles night?

Exhaust fumes.

Gasoline.

Burning automobiles.

Cordite. C-4 high explosive?

No, no. What I smell is . . . well, you might not believe it.

Vegetation.

Sure. Green things. Trees, flowers, bushes. Eucalyptus, live oak, bottle brush trees, palms, hibiscus, jacaranda, mimosa, bird of paradise, piñon, mesquite, chaparral, prickly-pear cactus.

But mostly what I smell is sagebrush. I don't know why, because I don't see it much down in the city.

Sage has a unique smell to me, and I seem to be able to pick it out on the breath of the breeze blowing down from the Santa Monica mountains. Sagebrush. This is the West, and there's sagebrush out here.

I fire up my Saab and back out of my parking slot in the garage, head toward the electric gate. I stab the electronic key, which is clipped to the passenger sun visor, and the gate creaks open. You have to have off-street parking in LA, and it helps if it's gated.

I roll westward and get on the 405 Freeway, the San Diego, heading north. I get to the top of the ramp and find to my satisfaction that traffic is relatively light, moving steadily at an average of about fifty-five. Not bad at all. I'll make the Valley in fifteen minutes, get off on Ventura Boulevard, and I'm there.

My Sprint PCS phone rings. It's Jennifer.

"I'm going to be a little late," she says. "The supermarket lot was filled with cop cars. Looked like a robbery. So I got on the 101 and hit a jam."

"Christ. How's it look?"

"The radio says there's a big wreck out at Topanga Canyon and it's backed up all the way to here."

"You have to get off onto Ventura Boulevard," I tell her.

"I know. But the next exit is a mile away. I should have taken the Laurel Canyon exit but who thinks of a tie-up this late at night?"

"No hurry," I assure her. "Take your time, get there in one piece. Get off anywhere you can."

And that's when she says it.

"Jesus, why do we live in this town?"

"You love it. You wouldn't live anywhere else."

"Try me," she says. "I've been wanting to move to Oregon. Eugene, Oregon."

"Nice college town," I say. "It's beautiful up there. Even more beautiful in the Cascades or on the coast."

"You better believe it. You can be sure there're no tie-ups at eleven o'clock on a Friday night."

"Not unless out-of-work loggers are blocking the highway in a protest. But tell me, what's there to do in Eugene, Oregon on a Friday night?"

"What are we doing? We're going to a diner. There aren't any diners in Eugene, Oregon?"

"Truck stops," I say. "Ground mystery meat patty smothered in gravy with the viscosity of STP Oil Treatment. Country-fried cholesterol."

"Don't be silly. There are plenty of nice, late-night places. Microbreweries. Salmon burgers with avocado and alfalfa sprouts. Stuff like that."

"All right, it's a nice town. You win. We have no reason to live in LA."

"You do. You write."

"Yeah. But that's not the reason, really, I live in LA. I'd live here anyway. Remember, I moved here years before I got work in movies."

"You did. Why did you?"

"The question all my friends asked. 'Why the hell do you want to live there? Isn't it all concrete and asphalt? The smog, the crime. Yadda yadda.' "

"Yadda yadda. The endless strip malls."

"The endless strip malls. A Starbucks on every corner."

"Didn't Starbucks start in Oregon?"

I say, "I think so. No, it was in Seattle."

"Same part of the country. Anyway, you haven't told me why we live in LA."

"It's the magic," I say.

"The what?"

"The magic. Spells cast everywhere you turn."

"Have you ever considered taking St. John's wort?"

"That's for depression," I tell her. "I'm not depressed. I'm crazy."

"You sure are. Magic, my fanny. Don't tell me you're talking about Hollywood."

"No, about the whole town, even the environs. It's a special magic. Kind of cheap and tawdry, but magic all the same. And your fanny is what I especially like about you."

"Get serious," she says.

"I'm serious. See you at the restaurant," I say.

The exit to Mullholland Drive is coming up, and I weave over to the right-hand lane. It's a clear night, and I have some time to kill. She'll be stuck on that freeway for the next half-hour unless she can find an exit, and I know pretty much exactly where she is, and she's right, there isn't another exit for about a mile.

I'm almost at the summit of the Sepulveda Pass on the 405, called thus because Sepulveda Boulevard parallels the freeway and tunnels through the summit not far ahead; in fact, Sepulveda was there long before the freeway. I pull onto the ramp and make a right onto Mulholland Drive, a two-lane country road that winds along the crest of the Santa Monica Range. You'd think you were out in the middle of nowhere instead of smack inside one of the biggest cities in the world. It's a clear night, and I want to look out. Great scenic vistas up here, especially at night.

Something off to the side of the road, barely visible in the headlights. Crosses, flowers, a makeshift plaque. This is the spot where young Ennis Cosby, Bill Cosby's son, was killed by a lone gunman, for no earthly reason that anyone can guess. The kind of totally senseless killing for which LA is notorious. The incident happened several years ago, and people are still marking the spot with garlands, spontaneously, no organized effort. Just people wanting to remember the young victim.

Another reason not to live in this town. Some people cite less serious reservations. No seasons, they complain. But they're wrong. We have four seasons just like anywhere else: earthquake, fire, mudslide, and high-speed chase.

Trundling along Mulholland, going east, sneaking brief glances at the panoramic scene to my left, the San Fernando Valley at night, laid out like a luminous net. It sprawls for miles, a grid of light and shadow bounded by mountains in the distance, all under a purple-red sky. I've seen it before, many times, but it's no less spectacular. At one point along the road it's possible to see both sides of the range, the Valley side and the LA side. The LA grid at night is even more extensive, but farther away. The drop on the Valley side is more abrupt. I tool along, making sure not to gawk so I don't run into a slow-moving car or run down a late-night jogger. Or a coyote loping across the road. Or a roadrunner. As I said, this is The West.

There's some shoulder up ahead and I pull off and shut down the motor.

It's quiet. Unbelievably quiet. There are homes along the road, big, expensive homes, most of them. These are the upper regions of Bel Air, I think. Or Brentwood. Someplace ritzy like that. Huge houses with conspiratorially glowing windows, behind which who knows what perversions are going on. The obscenely rich live by their own rules.

But I'm not thinking about them. I get out of the car and cross the road. I stand on a dusty shoulder and look out into the Valley night. The smell of sage is strong. I look around. I carry a little penlight, and I fish it out, sweep the beam at the brush growing along the side of the hill. I see a bush and stoop over it. It's sage, all right. I reach down and snap off a twig, examine it in the penlight. Sagebrush has long needles like pine. It might be a pine, for all I know. I tear off a few needles and crush them, rubbing them between my fingertips, which I then bring to my nostrils.

Nothing like the smell of fresh sage. Nothing says The West to me like that smell.

Maybe you think Arizona or New Mexico is The West. Or Utah. No, because as I look way out there into a valley of shadows I can see the backdrop of every Western movie ever made. I see the rocky buttes of Chatsworth, home to every movie ranch that ever served as a set for six-gun shootouts and cattle round-ups. To my right are Studio City, Universal City, and Burbank with their backlot Western streets of fading false fronts.

So it's quite literally The West, the West of legend, not reality. You think you're in the West but it's beyond the West, all the way to Munchkinland.

Okay, enough, back in the car.

Let's not let this devolve into a travelogue. You don't want to move to LA; you might not want even to visit. So I'll stop trying to persuade you that you should pack the family into the truck and migrate like some Okie. I'm just warming up to telling you why I live here. I'm getting there, really. The route is as twisty as one of these canyon roads, but we'll get there, we'll get there.

But maybe I'm not convinced myself. That guy in the cell phone office is still pissing me off, weeks later. I should have at least told him off. Only in LA would someone make a crack like that.

But aren't we big enough to take some gratuitous sniping at our body image? Or have we really succumbed to the Zeitgeist out here and think that the worst thing people can say about us is that we're pudgy and undesirable? That we are, shall we say, unprepossessing? Which is to say not photogenic. Out here, looks are everything.

The traffic, the riots, the crime. The pollution.

The perpetual sunshine. The mild climate. The magic.

Hey, it all balances out. Wait a minute. What magic? What kind of hocus-pocus am I talking about? All that movie stuff? Forget that fluff. That's old, *old*.

Oh, maybe it's old. Maybe it's cheap and tawdry.

Hold on. Hold on a bit longer.

I roll down the other side of the mountain, following Beverly Glen Canyon Road. I'm far from the freeway, and the road twists and gyrates, following a canyon cut over centuries by runoff rainwater. Down it winds, and I coast in second gear.

At the bottom, Ventura Boulevard. I turn left and head west. Toward Ventura, in fact, which is way the hell out there on the coast in another county. But I'm only going up the street.

Mel's Drive-In. Or . . . actually it's officially *Mels*, no apostrophe. The disappearance of the apostrophe in our language is a little-noted fact. But it is as endangered as any snail darter.

It's a chain, and it must have been engendered by the merchandising that grew out of the success of the film *American Graffiti*. Stills from the film cover the walls. The place looks like a typical drive-in burger palace of the nineteen-fifties—stainless steel, glass block, jukeboxes, red leatherette stools, and all. There are lots of modern chains capitalizing on the revival of the Eisenhower years. This is one of the best, and the name does indeed go back a few decades, but all of it smacks of a replica, a bit of merchandising, a copy of a copy, a movie adjunct. False, ersatz, fake, phony.

What do I give a crap. I like it, and the burgers are big and juicy. The place is better than your average McChainburger any day.

In the lot I see Jennifer's car, a navy blue Saturn. She struggles to make the payments, alternating between office temping and extra work in TV and movies. Those are the weekday gigs. Weekends, she makes good money as a cocktail waitress at a hotel near the Burbank airport. Tonight she's worked noon to nine. Most of the time she works six to two in the morning.

"You made it before me after all," I say as I slide into the booth. She's looking especially pretty tonight. There are highlights in her dark hair. Her face is bright and her luminous eyes, those almond eyes so artfully, so Orientally folded, no mistaking her heritage, are especially lovely.

"It started to move just after I hung up. What took you so long?"

"I was in search of magic," I said in my best imitation of Leonard Nimoy. "I was picking flowers up on Mulholland."

She glances at her watch. "At midnight? Looking for St. John's wort, no doubt."

"St. John had piles, not worts."

She forced a smile, literally, using two index fingers to push her cheeks up. "Amelican humor velly funny," she said.

"Laugh at this, Dragon Lady," I say, throwing down the sprig of sagebrush.

"What's this?"

"How long have you lived in this area?"

"Born and raised in Glendale. It's a bush. So what?"

"It's sagebrush."

"That's sagebrush?"

"Born and raised, and you don't know what sagebrush looks like?"

"What do I look like, Roy Rogers?"

"You don't even look like Dale Evans. This is sagebrush. Native Americans set great store by the stuff. Their shamans . . . the magician . . . the *brujo*, as he was called . . ."

"Carlos Castenada."

"Huh?"

"Don Juan, the magician, in those books. He was a *brujo*."

"Exactamiendo."

"That's not a Spanish word."

"I know. Pay attention. They used this stuff in magic spell casting."

"Really."

"Really. Here, smell it."

I did the crushing and rubbing thing, and she sniffed my fingertips.

"Ooo, I like that. Nice. Smells like sage."

"I wonder why?"

"So what's the smell got to do with anything?"

"Not a lot. But I bet the Indians liked it, too."

"Native Americans," she insists.

"What does that make us?"

"Huh?"

"If Indians are Native Americans, what are we, we who were born in this country?"

"Resident aliens."

"Right," I say. "Let's not go there. Back to the sagebrush."

But we can't get back to the sagebrush just now, because the waitress is there to ask for our orders.

We order while the jukebox blares and a bunch of people two booths away laugh and scream. It's an odd group. A bunch of Latino-looking kids, teens, maybe a little older, and one black guy who looks neither old nor young. But he has the air of a relic. His hair has been colored and straightened and he has it slicked over a bald pate. Unless the practice has enjoyed a recent comeback (and for all I know it might have), it's a rare black man who straightens his hair these days. Back in the fifties, black singers used to as a matter of course. In every publicity photo of a black R & B group you saw huge piled pompadours and duck's-asses worthy of Elvis. Not one kink in a mile of hair follicles.

This guy barely has a follicle left, but what he has he defiantly zaps with miracle hair-straightening Congolene (do they still make that stuff or has some new, gentler product come along?) and plasters it over the parched desert of his scalp. It's admirable, in a way, this nose-thumbing at political correctness.

But I'm not admiring him so much now, because he and the kids are making noise. The laughs from the girls are shrieks and out of the boys it sounds like dogs baying at the moon. Or maybe I'm just irritable tonight. Anyway, they are making a hell of a racket, so much so that conversation at our table is a little inhibited. I put the sage aside and the subject shifts to something else, mutual friends and their problems, until the food comes.

The jukebox, loaded with selections from the period under consideration, ceases to blare as I eat, and I hear a familiar tune. "The One and Only You," sung by the Platters.

Mellow harmonies, sweet, sentimental lyrics. The essence of the nineteen-fifties. Love, heterosexual love only, please, was the proper subject, almost the only subject, of a popular song; not like today, when a tune can be about killing cops or the desirability of suicide. I'd like to run the lyrics by you here, but I'm not about to go out-of-pocket for the rights. You remember the tune. Play it in your head. It's nice.

And I notice that the elderly black guy . . . okay, he's pushing sixty at least. His face is still young, though. Not young. There's a kind of perennial look to him. He's been around, but he still likes to think of himself as in Late Youth. Anyway, he's singing along, and he's doing it pretty good. In fact, pretty darn good. And he's singing harmony.

I watch, I listen, I eat.

"So what about sage and Native American magic? By the way, is sagebrush the same as the sage that's an herb? You know, that you cook with?"

"Eh?"

"If you're cooking out on the desert and you need some sage, like for a stew or something, can you go out and tear off some sagebrush and use it?"

"Hmm? Uh, I dunno. I don't think so. They're related, but probably different species."

"Oh, so this is poisonous?"

"I didn't say that."

"Okay, but what about the magic?"

"Oh, they burned it. Like this."

I've finished my burger, so I take out a butane lighter. I smoke a pipe when I write sometimes. I take the branch and I flick the lighter and apply the flame to one end of the sprig. The stuff isn't dry, but it flames up right quick. It's mainly hydrocarbon, I'm guessing.

"Hey, we're going to get into trouble."

You can't smoke in restaurants in California. State law. You can't even smoke sage, I'll bet.

Actually, nobody notices. The little sprig just lies in my dish and smolders. It goes out a few times, and I have to relight it, but mostly it all gets burnt. The smoke is fragrant. I'm enjoying it.

"That's it?" Jenn asks.

"That's what?"

"That's the magic?"

"Oh. Yeah, sort of. You burn it and say magic words."

"What magic words?"

"You know what the Indian name for the San Fernando Valley was?"

"Oh, I used to. Fire Valley?"

"The Valley of Smokes. There was smog in ancient times, it seems. Dust and camp fires, I guess."

"That's interesting, but what about the magic part?"

"Hey, look at that."

The black guy has gotten up to let someone out of the booth, and on the back of his white satin jacket there is lettering. It's strange. It says *THE PLATERS*.

The Platers? Not the Platters. The Platers.

Wait a minute. Could that be the correct spelling? All these years I'm thinking . . . I check the jukebox. Nah. It's "The Platters," all right. But maybe the jukebox is wrong.

I watch him laugh and talk some more. He's the right age. Actually not much older than me. I'm older than I look. (Again with the looks.)

Eventually he gets up and walks the teens to the

door, says good-bye, then heads back to his booth. As he passes I say, "Hey, dude."

He turns and smiles. It's a natural smile but very show biz.

"Excuse me, but the name of the group on your back . . . did you belong?"

"I'm the last one," he says. "They're all gone. I did all the arrangements and sang backup. They're all gone now, man. All dead. I'm the last man."

I'm amazed. Jesus, here's a guy whose voice has echoed in my head for . . . forget the time element . . . something something years. And he's standing in front of me.

I get up and stick out my hand. "I'm pleased to meet you." I'm so nonplussed I don't even ask his name. And I never found out either.

"I did a lot of studio work back then. I was a side-man on piano. I played keyboard on 'Chances Are.' You remember that one?"

"The Johnny Mathis tune? Do I remember? Sure I do."

"I played piano on that. I quit music to play base-ball. And you know who made that possible?"

"No."

He points to more lettering on the jacket. This is an interesting garment. Red embroidered lettering on the right lapel reads JESUS.

"Oh," I say. "Yeah."

"That's who made it possible. You can do anything if you want it bad enough. Anything."

"Well, you sure did a lot," I say. "I really enjoyed your music."

"Stick around, and I'll sing it again."

"Really. Let me put in the quarter. Will you sing 'The Great Pretender,' too?"

"I wasn't the lead singer. He's dead. But I'll sing it for you."

And he did, belting it right out. He did a beautiful job.

And when he was done, the restaurant exploded in applause.

"What did I tell you?" I said to Jenn. "This is a genuine LA moment. A magic occurrence."

She didn't take much convincing. "And at first you wanted to go over and ream them out for making noise."

"That was before I burned the sage. This kind of thing happens all the time in this town. Little spells, gratuitous bursts of magic that come out of the woodwork and weave a spell. A cheap thrill, granted. But a spell nonetheless."

Jenn laughs, but that's what living here means. Moments of unexpected low-level magic. Little memorable moments, snippets of cut-rate epiphany. I've been inside the studios in this town. I've seen the old scene docks, what's left of the back lots, the warehouses full of old costumes from many a production. It's my life. My interior life, my imaginative life. Out in the high desert, at Vasquez Rocks, I've stood where the Lone Ranger's horse rears up in the opening sequence of that show. I knocked on The Beaver's front door. I dipped a toe in Gilligan's lagoon.

Like it or not, I have a head full of cultural trivia, and most of it originated here. And a hell of a lot of it is *still* here.

And this guy's part of my life, too. The music part. LA's a movie and TV town, but it's also a music industry town. That plinky-plink piano in "Chances Are." Jeez, how many times have I heard it? It's stamped into the pulp of my brain.

"It's been a real thrill," I say to the guy. The nameless guy. Maybe he said his name, but I didn't get it.

"Thanks." He shakes my hand warmly.

"What about the spelling, though? On your back?"

He laughs. "Oh, that was my girlfriend did that. She can't spell too good." He grins sheepishly.

An LA moment. Oh, sure, something like this could happen in, say, New York, or New Orleans, or Chicago, or Detroit, or Nashville. They're all music towns, too. But this sort of thing seems to happen on a regular basis in the Big Orange.

We walk out. It was funny, and sad, and touching, and great. This town with all these little people with one claim to fame, nursing it through the years. One claim, one little role to play in our lives, and almost nobody knows who they are. They spend their lives in total anonymity, for all that they'd be instantly recognized if the memory gets jogged a little—and sometimes it just gets to be too much for them and they have to go to a diner, throw a quarter into a jukebox, and proclaim their identity.

It could be a music thing, it could be something else. "Hey, do you know who I am? I'm the guy that played whatshisface on that TV sitcom that you watched for umpty-ten years. Yeah, that one. On CBS. Back in the fifties, the sixties, the seventies. Remember me? Of course you do. I'm him! And this is her. And that's me, here, in this picture. See? See?"

Funny, sad, touching, heartening, happy-making, and magical.

But more. To live in this town is, in a real sense, to live in the interior of one's own psyche. The place resonates with Jungian significance. Not just your psyche, but just about everyone's. It's a town of collective memory.

And the sage did it. I believe that. The magic goes back, far back. Who knows what form it took in antiquity. It didn't conjure pop culture figures out of your psyche. Or, hey, maybe it did. Maybe it always conjured ghosts of some sort.

We drive our cars back up Beverly Glen, turn on Mulholland and go to the lookout. You're not supposed to park here after dark, but the road is deserted, the stars are bright, and the lights of the Valley flare with an almost eschatological glow.

Jenn gets out of her car and into mine. We kiss for about five minutes.

"How did you know about all that stuff?" she asks in time. "About the sage and all?"

"I made it up."

Her easterly eyes are wide. "You . . . ?"

"But they must have done something with sage," I say.

"You total phony baloney!"

"Show biz is my life."

"What if that guy was lying? What if he wasn't one of the original Platters?"

"Phenomenologically, it was still a magic LA moment."

"Fa-whatically?"

"Appearances are everything. Let's watch the movie."

She sat back and looked out the windshield, puzzled. "What movie?"

I pointed to the lights of the spell-enthralled city. "That one."

TO CATCH A THIEF
by Lisanne Norman

Born in Glasgow, Scotland, Lisanne Norman began writing
when she was eight years old because "I couldn't find
enough of the books I liked to read." She studied jewelry
design at the Glasgow School of Art before becoming a
teacher. A move to Norfolk, England, prompted her involve-
ment with the Vikings, a historical reenactment group,
where she ran her own specialist archery display team. Her
writing takes center stage now, with her creation of the Sholan Alliance, a world where magic, warriors, and science all
coexist. Her latest novel from DAW is the next in the *Sholan
Alliance* series, *Stronghold Rising*.

The small demon hunkered down on its haunches,
peering through the chinks in the flat wooden
roof. Strips of light from the room below bathed his
wrinkled brown face, highlighting the two tiny horns
that poked through his thick curly hair. From her van-
tage point, Mouse could clearly see the white underside of his nub of a tail as it began to stir. He leaned
closer, hands resting on the unstable surface as he
listened intently, his pointed ears twitching to catch
every word.

Mouse waited patiently. She had to be sure Kadron
actually had Cullen, and that he was still alive.

Deep within her mind, something alien stirred. *This
is foolhardy,* came the silken thought from the jewel
that lived within her. *The boy is nothing to you—a*

beggar, a cripple, what use is he? Why risk your life for him? Leave him to this Kadron.

Anger surged through her. "Leave me alone!" she hissed. "Get out of my head! I don't want you inside me!" How could she have been so stupid as to break her own rules and accept a contract from a Mage? Served her right for cheating on Kadron and taking on a private job in the first place. She focused her attention on Zaylar, using her anger to force the jewel's alien presence back down into her subconscious.

Zaylar glanced uncertainly in her direction. Of late, he'd developed a knack of knowing when the jewel was speaking to her. He stood up, and as surefooted as any mountain creature, trotted back across to her, his tiny hooves barely making a sound on the rickety wooden surface.

"Boy there," he confirmed quietly. "On floor, in ropes."

"Is he alive?"

Zaylar nodded vigorously as he crouched down beside her. "Must be. Squirms lots."

"How many men?"

"Four. One fat man with loud clothes, and another, stand over boy. Two more hide behind cases opposite door. Is a trap for sure." He peered at her, his ancient seamed face wrinkling in concern. "Why go save boy? Leave him. Then you no need to sign Kadron's papers, lose Kolin's house, everything, maybe even life."

Even the demon agrees with me, whispered the jewel, taking advantage of her distraction.

"Shut up!" she muttered, scrubbing the palm of her right hand against her pants leg as if by doing so, she could remove the jewel itself. If only she hadn't picked the damned thing up, or worn gloves, then it couldn't have seared its way into her flesh and become part of her. How was she supposed to know it was alive?

Zaylar pulled back and began to chitter in distress until Mouse put a hand on his shoulder. The heat from his bare flesh warmed her. "Not you, imp. The jewel," she said, shivering. But the coldness she felt had nothing to do with the chill night air.

Zaylar touched her knee with his small, clawed fingers. "You all right, Lady? Must fight jewel, not let it control you!" His panic was palpable in every line of his body.

"You do this every time I go out on a job!" she muttered, brow furrowing with the effort of fighting the jewel's increased efforts to dominate her mind. Her head had begun to ache and she felt light-headed and nauseous.

You are wealthy, there is no need to steal. All Kolin owned is now legally yours, even the magistrate confirmed this. Let Kadron kill the boy. Why risk your life to save his? Think of all I cold teach you about magic. You could become the greatest Mage on Jalna, the only female in nine hundred years to achieve this.

"He's my friend! It's my fault Kadron kidnapped him. I owe him!" she said, putting her hands up to massage her aching temples.

"Must not listen to jewel, Lady," said Zaylar urgently, his hand tightening on her knee till his claws pricked her flesh. "We save Cullen, then find book. I teach you demon magics, then jewel no threat to you."

With the demon still touching her, she could feel his fears as if they were her own. He was afraid that if the jewel dominated her, he'd have no chance of gaining back the magic his King had stripped from him before casting him out of the Demon Realms and into the world of Jalna and its battling Mages. Nor would he be able to get her to make him the talisman that would prevent him ever being bound by another—demon or Mage—again. He'd have to continue his life of servitude to her, then the next four wizards after her. Between him and the jewel, she was being torn in opposite directions in a battle for her very soul.

Impatiently, she pushed his hand away and stood up, her anger finally providing enough force to drive the jewel's presence back.

"Let's get moving," she snapped, her hands automatically checking the sword that hung over her left hip. "We got Cullen to rescue."

The day had gone badly from the start. A high-pitched chittering, interspersed with the sounds of objects hitting a wall, had brought Mouse to wakefulness. She groaned. What the hell was Zaylar up to now? The demon had been a pain in the butt from the night she'd inherited him.

Throwing back the covers, she sat up and swung her legs out of the bed. As her toes hit the richly carpeted floor, she curled them in pleasure. Not for her the bare floorboards of her old digs above the tap room of the Packrats' Inn, nor the noise of the rowdy drunks celebrating below. That had all changed the night she'd killed Wizard Kolin and she'd inherited this house—and his small demon.

A loud crash preceded a shriek of rage, bringing her back to reality. Sighing, she reached for her pants and tunic, hauling them on before bending to scrabble on the floor just under the bed for her socks and boots. This needed her personal attention. She couldn't leave it to Cullen. One foot done, she hopped toward the door while trying to do the other. The Gods knew what Zaylar was up to now, but it didn't sound good. On a sudden impulse, she stopped, returning to pick up the slim volume from her night table.

As she flung open the door to the late Mage's study, the sight that greeted her was one of total chaos. Books, obviously flung in temper, littered the floor, lying in every state of disarray, some with their spines broken and the pages floating loose.

"Zaylar!" she yelled, looking around the room for him. "What the hell are you doing?"

He emerged from behind Kolin's desk. "I look for book," he said scowling.

Mouse surveyed the mess. "That's an understatement!"

"Must find. You need."

She looked back at him, eyes narrowing. "I need, or you? You're supposed to be helping me learn magic, not wrecking my house!"

The demon's brow furrowed beneath the mass of dark curls. "Need Kolin's diary," he insisted. "Magics in there help us. I need them to teach you. Tidy later."

"You damned well better! What's it look like? Maybe I've seen it," she said, picking her way through the piles of books till she was standing over him.

Zaylar made a rude noise.

"What do you mean by that?" she demanded, aware of his contempt for her.

"I read, you can't," he snorted, his brown face becoming even more wrinkled as he frowned. "Jalnians don't teach females to read, everyone knows that!"

Her hand darted out to catch him by one of his pointed ears, as with the other, she pulled the slim book from her pocket, holding it high above him. "Is this the book you want?"

"Yes!" he shrieked, clawing at her hand as he peered up at it. "Let go! You hurting Zaylar!"

"You didn't tell me the truth about yourself, did you? That you were bound, not just to Kolin, but to the next five Mages after him. That he only allowed you small magic spells because he considered you untrustworthy."

"He lied! Am trustworthy! Kolin hated Zaylar even though Zaylar did everything he asked!" He stopped, his small body becoming suddenly stiff and rigid. "How you know what Kolin thought?"

"I never told you about my mother, did I?" she said conversationally. "She was from a wealthy family till she got me, then they threw her out." She pinched his ear hard, making him shriek even louder than before.

He danced from hoof to hoof in pain, hands once more scrabbling at her in an effort to free himself.

"Mother taught me to read." She let him go and returned the book to her pocket.

Zaylar scowled up at her, rubbing his ear vigorously. "No need to hurt Zaylar. I trying to help you. Promised, I did. You make me amulet, I teach you magic, stop jewel from taking you over."

"The jewel's not bothered me in a while," she lied. "And just how are you going to teach me magic when you barely know any yourself?" She raised a questioning eyebrow at him.

He looked at the ground, shifting from hoof to hoof. "Used to know lots of magic, but King took it away when he banished me here," he mumbled. "Know how to get it back. When I get it, same time I teach you."

"A failed rebel, some useful demon you are," she snorted. "You can start earning your keep by tidying up the mess you made. You know enough magic to do that, don't you?" she asked sarcastically as she turned to make her way back to the door. "I'm going to the kitchen to get some food. Join me there when you're finished."

He muttered something unintelligible.

Mouse stopped dead and rounded on him. "I didn't hear that."

"Yes, Mistress," he said, baring his needle-sharp teeth at her in a parody of a smile.

She grunted. "Hurry up. You got a bargain to seal with me when you're done."

After having read the contract aloud to Zaylar, Mouse put it down and signed it, then pushed it over to him.

"Your turn," she said. Beneath the table, she slowly slipped her boot knife out of its scabbard and laid it flat against her thigh, ready for the final part of their deal. She'd read Kolin's diary carefully and knew exactly what was needed to bind Zaylar to this agreement. The fact he was bound to her by the terms of the Demon King's punishment wasn't enough: she wanted her own, personal insurance, just as Kolin had done. Except her contract was more comprehensive.

Muttering beneath his breath, the imp glared at her, his eyes taking on a reddish glow as he snatched the quill from her and scrawled his name on the bottom of the page. He tossed it down on the table when he was done. "You not trust Zaylar," he said. "Offended, I am."

Mouse brought her hand up onto the table, knife tucked against her palm, ready to use. "Damned right I don't. Pass it back to me," she said, watching his every movement. Timing was vital in this.

As Zaylar slid it across the table toward her, she

pounced on his hand, nicking it with her knife so it bled onto the contract, right over their signatures.

He squealed like a stuck pig, grasping his hand to his chest as his eyes glowed red as coals in a fire. "You cheat me!" he howled. "Insult my honor! I promise you, I sign your precious paper, then you stick knife in me!"

Mouse snatched up the contract and sat back in her chair, regarding him with a faint smile. "Now it's sealed with blood, Zaylar. Yours. There's no way you can break this contract, or betray me, even when our deal is over, because I'll still have power over you." Very carefully, she began to fold it before putting it away in a leather wallet and placing it inside her tunic. Later, she'd find a safer place for it.

"It'll heal in a few minutes," she said, unconcerned. "You know that. It isn't as if I did it after you'd bled on the contract. Then you'd have been in trouble."

His hiss of anger was low, like a kettle beginning to boil. She could feel his resentment. It disturbed her and she looked away, knowing that the sensation would cease when she did.

"So, what do we do first?" she asked, returning the knife to her boot.

"Could help Mistress more if I had more magics," he said sullenly, still nursing his hand. "Kolin only allowed me small ones that enhance his."

"You'll get more magics the more you help me," she said, pushing a plate of sliced meat toward him. "Here, have some food. You must be as hungry as I was."

As he took the plate, she saw the cut on his hand had already vanished. She'd learned a lot about the demon from Kolin's diary, including his ability to heal rapidly.

His mood had changed already, and as he stuffed the meat into his mouth and gulped down the weak ale she poured for him, once more she was reminded how childlike he was.

Deep within her mind, the jewel stirred. *Don't be misled by appearances,* it whispered. *He's older than you can imagine, and with age comes deviousness.*

She ignored it, pushing the presence down till she could feel it no more.

"We need book," said Zaylar, his voice muffled by the food. "Tells where other demons are. Those trapped here on Jalna by Mages like Kolin."

"There're others? Your King must be very unpopular."

Zaylar shook his head. "No. They were called from our world and trapped here by Jalnian Mages."

"Trapped? How?" This was news to her. There had been nothing about this in Kolin's notes. She leaned forward to hear him better.

"Mages make amulets to trap us in. Keep amulet near them always, then there to use when needed. Demons can never leave here while Mage holds amulet."

"The book gives their location?"

He nodded vigorously, picking up his tankard and taking a large swig from it. Putting it down, he wiped the back of his hand across his mouth. "Says which Mage has which demon. Kolin wanted this book, was planning to get you to steal it after he got Living Jewel from you. He control jewel, make him powerful enough to steal amulets."

"He needed the jewel to control the demons."

Again Zaylar nodded. "Told you. Only Mage-born can carry jewel. It enhances their magics, makes stronger. One demon safe for Kolin, but more is dangerous. He wanted many."

"Any idea where the book is?"

"No," he said regretfully. "Was hoping in book you have."

"There was nothing about it in there," said Mouse thoughtfully. If she were Kolin, where would she put this information, if not in a diary? "How recent was this plan?"

Zaylar shrugged his naked shoulders. "A day, maybe two, before he ask you to steal jewel for him."

"Must be somewhere in his study. There were still plenty of blank pages in his diary so he can't have started a new one."

"I looked. Found nothing."

"You cleared the books away?" she asked.

"Mistress told me to do it. I did," he said, his tone faintly reproving.

"Stop with the Mistress bit," she said, irritated by his use of the word. "I don't like it. I'm a thief, not a Mistress."

"Yes, Lady," he said. "Zaylar not call you Mistress again."

She grunted. Lady was only marginally better. Letting him call her something respectful meant he didn't forget who was in charge.

She got up from the table. "Let's go look properly this time. If it's not among the books, perhaps it's in his desk."

Zaylar looked up at her sharply. "Never thought of desk," he admitted. "Kolin always writing there. Maybe there."

It was. She'd even looked at it the night before when she'd taken a sheet of the expensive reed paper from the desk to draft out her contract with Zaylar.

Resting her arms on the desk, she examined it carefully. *"Demonic Amulets,"* she said. "That must be its name. Written by someone called Belamor."

"Mage up in mountain town," supplied Zaylar. "Kolin say book copied and sold to those with amulets. Some Mages cooperate, not all fight duels."

"That's comforting. Can't read the next bit," she said, squinting at the spidery writing. "He scribbled it down in a hurry from the looks of it."

"Let me see," said Zaylar, leaning on her thighs and squirming his head and upper body between her arms till he could see over the top of the desk.

Amused, she looked down at him. She could feel his body heat through the fabric of her pants. Though his brown-skinned chest was naked, his lower limbs, resembling those of a mountain sheep or goat, were covered with dense fur as dark and curly as that on his head.

"In house of Human Kris Russell, it says."

"A Human has it?" That surprised her. Cullen had spoken about him only the night before.

Until two years ago, the spaceport that adjoined Balrayn had been held by Lord Bradogan. His brutal reign had forced several of the local Lords to lead an uprising against him. Somehow, the Humans and another species of aliens, not unlike the felinoid U'Churians who helped police the Port, had gotten involved. With their aid, Bradogan was overthrown and Lord Tarolyn had replaced him. He'd immediately relaxed the rules governing the flow of off-world goods, and under his more benign rule, the shanty town where she lived had mushroomed in size, becoming a bustling, thriving community. Both species were to be seen more frequently now in the Port and around the safer street and inns of Balrayn.

"Not know. Want me to find out?" Zaylar asked hopefully, squirming away from her again.

"No. You're just a little too noticeable," she said, putting the paper down. "I'll get Cullen to see what he can discover." She stopped, realizing she hadn't seen him yet. "Where's Cullen?"

Zaylar shrugged. "Not Zaylar's job to know that."

That's when her nightmare had begun.

Cullen lay trussed up on the dirty warehouse floor, Kadron and his main henchman Raithil, standing over him.

"She won't fall for your trick," he said, trying to put more bravado into his voice than either he felt, or his twelve years of age warranted. "I mean nothin' to her. She'll never come."

Kadron nudged him in the ribs with the toe of his boot. "Oh, she'll come," he said. "You been living up at that wizard's house with her this past week or more. Think I don't know about that, Cullen? You might have been out on the street begging for me like my other brats, but you ain't been sleeping at your usual doss-house."

"What's it to you?" asked Cullen, straining at the ropes that held his wrists firmly behind him. "You get your money every day. What you leave me ain't enough to live on, you knows that. What if I do stay up at her place? Least I can afford to eat now."

The boot kicked him harder this time. "I don't pay you to eat, I pay you to beg and snout for me!"

Cullen tried to muffle his cry of agony. Already bruised and cut by the beating Kadron's men had given him earlier, he felt the rib give under the blow.

Kadron turned away from him to Raithil. "Go see if there's any sign of her yet," he ordered.

"You want me to look out the door?" Raithil asked. "She'll see me."

"So what? She won't expect me to be alone."

"You told her to . . ."

"I know what I told her! Just go and look," snapped Kadron, exasperated.

Cullen heard Raithil's metal-studded boots heading away from him, then the sound of the door opening a fraction.

"She's coming," he confirmed.

"She alone?" demanded Kadron.

"Yeah, no one with her."

"Then get back here and watch the boy for me," he said, moving toward the case he intended to use as a desk. "I don't want anything going wrong. And keep him quiet!"

Stifling his groans, Cullen twisted his head around till he could see the door. Somehow, he had to warn Mouse! As Raithil stepped past him, he saw the door begin to open.

A slight figure, barely five feet tall, stood framed in the doorway. Dressed in faded dark pants and tunic, with her cloak hanging back from her shoulders, she blended into the darkness of the night behind her. Mid-brown hair framing an oval face fell to her shoulders, and from beneath the ragged fringe, her dark eyes cautiously surveyed the room.

Ignoring Kadron, she looked past Raithil, locking eyes with him. " 'Lo, Cullen." Her voice was low, almost cultured by comparison to Kadron's and his men.

"It's a trap!" he yelled, struggling furiously against the ropes. "Get outta here, Mouse!"

Kadron spun around and kicked him again, this time

aiming for his crippled foot. Cullen screamed, his body convulsing in agony.

"I told you to keep that gutter brat quiet!" he snarled at Raithil.

Instinctively, Mouse started forward, then stooped, knowing it was exactly what Kadron had intended. She would have to play it cool now, ignore anything he did to Cullen to get her riled up.

She watched impassively as Raithil stopped to grasp the whimpering boy by the front of his tattered clothing and haul him upright.

Cullen staggered, crying out again as he was forced to put his weight on his damaged foot.

Raithil shook him viciously. "Shut up! One more word from you and I'll finish you right now!"

Cullen choked back his cries as Raithil spun him around, grasping hold of him more firmly.

"I see my prodigal Mouse has returned," said Kadron, returning his attention to her. "Come in, my dear. We're all friends here." His voice was oily, patronizing.

"You're no friend of mine, Kadron," she said, taking half a dozen careful paces into the warehouse. Beneath her feet, she heard the floorboards creak softly.

His flaccid gray face assumed a look of regret. "I'm sorry to hear you say that, child, after all the work I've put your way."

"I've come for Cullen. You've no right holding him like this."

"He'll be released as soon as you and I reach an agreement on the property of the late Wizard Kolin."

"Why should I give you what's legally mine?"

"You'll give me it if you want your little friend to survive, that's why," he snapped. "You're mine, Mouse.

When that shiftless mother of yours died, I took you in out of the goodness of my heart, trained you up, and found you work so you didn't end up in the brothels like other girls your age! Treated you like you was one of my own, I did. No sleeping at the doss-house for you, you had a room at the inn! And how do you thank me? By taking independent contracts you had no business to take! You. Owe. Me." His voice was cold now, the last words spat out like individual stones from the narilla fruits he loved eating. "And I aim to collect right now."

"I owe you nothing. The Mage sent for me himself. What was I to do? Refuse him?" She took several more steps, this time toward the high stack of crates on her left. She knew it was a trap, knew exactly what was in his mind just by looking at him. Kadron intended to get her to sign the paper, then he'd kill them both to avoid later complications. Her hand clenched over the pommel of her sword, taking comfort from the feel of cold steel.

"You work for me, Mouse, you don't go thieving on your own. You steal from whom I say, no one else! Someone asks you to do a job, you come to me about it! You're going to sign Kolin's property over to me," he snarled, pointing to the chest where paper, pen and ink lay. "It's mine by rights, and you know it."

"Don't do it, Mouse!" Cullen tried to yell as he twisted in Raithil's grasp. "Leave now while you can!"

She heard the sound of a blow and a yelp of pain from Cullen. Inwardly, she cursed him. Why couldn't he shut up and leave this to her? He was only making matters worse for himself.

"What do I get to keep?" she asked, taking three more steps. She could sense the other two men now, both of them hiding behind the tall stacks of crates that lined the warehouse. One was waiting in the shadows beyond the crate Kadron was indicating, the other was moving slowly around to the door to cut off her escape.

Kadron began to laugh, a deep braying sound of almost genuine amusement. "Your lives, Mouse! Your lives!"

From the corner of her eye, she saw a flicker of movement, heard the creaking of floorboards, then the door as it was closed. She risked a glance over her shoulder, but he'd already vanished behind the crates again.

As she slowly moved further into the warehouse, Mouse's fingers were checking the quill pen concealed up her sleeve, praying that the color in it matched Kadron's ink.

"You'll let us go if I sign it? We'll be free of you?" She was level with Cullen and Raithil now. He had the boy in front of him, holding him firmly by the back of the neck and one arm.

Kadron continued chuckling. "You'll be free of me, all right. You think I want to keep a dishonest thief and a useless beggar?"

"He's lying!" shrieked Cullen. "Don't do it, Mouse. I'm not worth . . ." Abruptly, his voice was cut off as Raithil began to throttle him.

"Harm him and the deal's off, Kadron!"

Kadron gestured to Raithil. "I said shut him up, not choke him."

Raithil removed his hands from the boy's neck, placing his forearm across Cullen's throat instead.

Heart pounding, she covered the remaining distance between her and Balrayn's leading criminal. Her fears chased one another around inside her head. Would his men jump her now, before she signed the document? No, if they did that, Kadron couldn't be sure she'd sign it properly, and her signature was registered at the courthouse as the legal owner of Kolin's estate. The magistrate would check it for sure when he saw she was giving everything away to Kadron.

"Clever of you to pretend you killed Kolin in a duel. They couldn't get you for murder that way. How'd you do it anyhow?" demanded Kadron. "You got about as much magic in you as one of those wild tarnachs they use to guard the spaceport! You probably walked in and found him lying dead at the foot of the stairs!"

Mouse stopped a few feet away from him. "He got angry and came at me, then he tripped like you said. He vanished a few minutes later."

"Vanished?"

She shrugged, feigning indifference. "Vanished. In a puff of smoke."

Kadron looked appraisingly at her. "Right. What you do to get him angry? Dupe him like you did me? And what happened to that jewel he sent you for?"

Startled, Mouse looked up at him. How'd he known about the jewel?

Eyes narrowing, Kadron reached out and grasped hold of her arm, pulling her close. "Where's the jewel?" His fetid breath was hot on her cheek.

"What jewel?" she asked, forcing herself to remain still.

"The one you stole from Haram the merchant, that's what jewel!"

"Never asked me to steal a jewel. He wanted me to get him something from the temple at Galrayn. I refused."

"You're lying," he snarled, raising his other hand to hit her. As she flinched, he remembered why she was there and lowered it. "Haram came to me squealing like a stuck pig about being robbed. I got him that Living Jewel in the first place, Mouse. You had no business to go thieving it from him. I said I'd get it back. So where is it?"

Mouse thought furiously as within her mind, the jewel began to stir again. She couldn't return it, that was why she'd had to kill Kolin. The jewel was part of her now, only her death would release her from their symbiosis.

"I took it," she admitted sullenly. "Gave it to Kolin. That's what killed him."

"How? How could a jewel kill him?" demanded Kadron. "It didn't do anything to Haram or any of the others that handled it."

"How should I know? I gave it to him, he lit up like a torch and vanished, that's all I know," she said, trying to pull free. "Damned thing was magic."

For the space of several heartbeats, Kadron held onto her, then he pushed her toward the wooden crate where the paper and ink lay.

"Maybe you're lying, maybe not, but you got nowhere to sell the jewel except through me. Now sign the papers and let's be done with this!" he ordered.

She picked up the document, trying not to let Kadron see how badly her hand was shaking. This was not going the way she'd planned. Haram hadn't reported the theft of the Living Jewel to the port authorities, and Cullen had heard nothing about it on the streets, so she'd assumed the merchant had kept quiet out of embarrassment. That he'd gone straight to Kadron had never occurred to her. How many more would come after her just for the jewel?

"What the hell d'you think you're doing?" demanded Kadron. "I said sign the damned thing!"

"I need to read it first."

He grinned. "Read it? You don't need to *read* it, girl, even if you could! Doesn't matter what it *says*, you got no option but to sign it!"

"I want to know what I'm signing," she said, looking over the top of the page at him. "I'm not having you claim later that I signed a contract saying I'd work for you for nothing for the next ten years."

"Hear that, Raithil? Mouse reckons she can read!" But his grin was fading and he snatched the document from her, slapping it back on the crate. Picking up the quill pen, he thrust it at her. "Sign it now, or I'll let Raithil play with your little friend again."

As Cullen let out another moan of pain, Mouse felt the blood drain from her face. It was no subterfuge when she dropped the quill. Bending down, she let her cloak fall forward, concealing her movements just enough so she could switch Zadron's quill for the one Tallan had prepared for her.

"Cut Cullen loose first, then I'll sign," she said, straightening up.

Kadron gestured to Raithil. "Do it. He's not going anywhere with that lame foot of his."

Raithil removed his arm from across Cullen's throat and, holding him upright by one arm, pulled his knife and slit the rope round the boy's wrists.

Freed, Cullen staggered, clutching his captor for balance. Raithil grasped him firmly by the shoulder, holding his knife under the boy's ear. "You keep still," he snarled. "And keep that damned mouth of yours shut!"

"No more delays," ordered Kadron. "Sign it now."

Mouse stepped closer to the crate and bending over the document, pretended to dip her quill in the pot of ink. Surreptitiously, she pressed the hollow spine, releasing the special ink just as Tallan had shown her. As she wrote her name at the bottom of the page, she prayed his magic would work.

As soon as she lifted the pen, Kadron grabbed the document and examined her signature. Folding it carefully, he placed it in his belt pouch.

Mouse could only stand and stare at him in horror. His pouch? He was putting it in his pouch? She'd assumed he'd leave it on the crate. How could the magic work shut up in there? As she took a step backward, his hand snaked out and closed over her sword arm.

"Oh, no, you don't," he said. "I've not finished with you yet."

She felt herself jerked forward till she was pressed against Kadron's greasy robes. This close, the aroma of stale sweat and beer was overwhelming.

"Think I'll keep you around for a while yet, girl," he said, grasping her chin in one fat hand and forcing her to look up at him. He leered down at her, revealing his broken and stained teeth: his rank breath made her gag. "I was going to kill you and the cripple, but I hadn't realized till now that you'd finished growing up. Raithil, take her weapons."

Shock paralyzed her; she offered no resistance as Raithil, still holding onto Cullen, grasped her sword and pulled it from her scabbard. Then Kadron ran his free hand over her body, looking for knives. Suddenly Mouse could sense his naked lust flowing over her as if it was a living thing. She felt unclean, dirty, as Kadron's hand lingered over her slight breasts before moving lower till he found her belt knife.

"You're a bit skinny yet, but I can live with that."

Fighting down the panic that surged through her, she felt the jewel waken fully.

Give me control, it sent. *I can kill this one, and the others, with a thought!*

She gritted her teeth, muttering "No!" under her breath as Kadron pulled her knife from its sheath and tossed it onto the crate beside him.

You want this one to rape you? It won't matter to him that you're not a woman yet. Will you let him kill this boy you value so highly? There is no way out unless you give control of your mind to me.

"No," she repeated, turning her face aside. "If you don't let us go, Kadron, you'll never find the best pieces from Kolin's house. I hid 'em in case you pulled a stunt like this on me." That Kadron would see her as a woman had never occurred to her.

"You double-dealing little . . ."

"Let us go, Kadron," she said, her voice shaking slightly. "You gave your word that if I signed your paper you'd let Cullen go and leave us alone."

"So I lied! Kill the brat, Raithil! I'm keeping the girl for now," he laughed, running his hand across her cheek before grasping hold of her other arm. "You'll tell me what I want to know, Mouse, never doubt that!"

"Kill him and I'll never show you," she said, trying to pull away from him while desperately trying to think up more excuses for Cullen to be kept alive. "Stuff's protected. Magically. Needs Cullen and me both to release the spell."

Kadron's fingers bit deep into the flesh of her arms as he shook her violently. "Wait, Raithil. Spells? What spells?"

A faint smell of burning leather teased Mouse's nostrils. The Gods bless Tallan, his ink spell was working! She risked a glance down at Kadron's belt and saw a faint thread of smoke escaping from his pouch. "Kill

Cullen and you'll never get it." She had to keep him talking long enough for the pouch to catch fire.

"Where is it?" he demanded. "Where d'you hide the stuff?"

"My room, at the inn," she said.

"You're lying again! Your room's been let. Nothing but garbage was found in it!"

"I had a hiding place." The coil of white smoke was thicker now. Someone would notice it if she didn't distract them. She struggled, kicking at Kadron's legs.

Kadron gave a snarl of rage, releasing her arms to grab her by the throat. "You're lying! Where would you get a spell like that from?" He began to shake her like a rag doll.

Hands clawing at his in a desperate effort to prise his fingers apart, Mouse choked out an answer. "Money. Bought it." As the blood pounded in her ears and her vision started to fade, she heard the jewel again.

You'd die rather than submit to me? Foolish child! Give me the power to . . .

The roaring in her ears grew louder, drowning the jewel's voice. She felt a surge of power, heard a commotion—swearing and shouting—then suddenly, a weight slammed against her shoulder, knocking her to the floor. She lay there, sucking in deep breaths of air to relieve her heaving lungs, aware of a dark, four-legged shape just beyond her turning and launching itself on Kadron. A tarnach? How in all the demons of Jalna had a wild tarnach gotten in?

Kadron's high-pitched scream of terror filled the warehouse. She couldn't stay on the floor. Raithil still had Cullen, and the tarnach would go for anything that moved. Coughing and gasping, she pushed herself to her feet, reaching for the knife that hung down the back of her neck as she turned to face Raithil.

He'd dropped Cullen and her sword and was backing away from her, a look of frozen terror on his face.

From behind the crates, two men dashed out, swords drawn, but they ignored her and rushed to Kadron's aid.

Mouse dived for Cullen, grabbing her sword up from the ground as she hauled the boy to his feet.

You're not free yet. What of the tarnach? Let me use you to destroy them all, whispered the jewel.

"Come on," she hissed to Cullen, ignoring the jewel. "We got to get out of here!" The smell of burning leather was stronger now.

"My crutch," he moaned, clinging to her as he looked wildly around the room. "I can't walk without it!"

"You'll have to!" she said, looping his arm across her shoulders as she began to drag him toward the door. "Kadron's pouch is about to burst into flames and that'll send the tarnach over our way!"

The tarnach, then. Let me destroy the tarnach. The tone was sharper now, demanding.

Cullen tried to hop, clutching his side and whimpering in pain as he jarred his broken rib with every step.

Why was the jewel so set on destroying the tarnach? Mouse risked a glance over her shoulder at Kadron and his thugs. The wolflike beast was straddling Kadron's chest, holding the other three men at bay. Around its neck, the long spines stood out like a collar of deadly spikes: its jaws were wide and slavering as it snarled and howled its anger at them. Then she saw its glowing red eyes, and realized how small it was.

Let me kill the tarnach!

Again, she felt the surge of power, but this time she was ready for it.

"Damn you! Leave it alone!" she hissed, concentrating on increasing her pace till she was almost bodily dragging the injured boy. "Stop trying to control me! I want nothing from you!"

Abruptly, the battle for control of her mind ceased. Instead, she felt the jewel's anger as agony stabbed at her temples.

I offer you everything, and you abuse me, put our life at risk! Take care, Mouse, your Mage-blood may be waking, but will not always win against me!

Whimpering in agony, she stumbled, sending herself crashing to the ground. As pain gripped her belly, Cullen landed on top of her. From a distance, she heard the sound of Kadron shrieking again.

"I'm burning up! Put it out! Put it out!"

"Get that damned beast off him first, you imbeciles!" Raithil roared. "It's not an adult, it's only a pup!"

"Mouse! Come on!" said Cullen, shaking her furiously. "We gotta get outta here! The place is on fire!"

Snarls turned to howls of rage, drowning out the voices. Smoke was beginning to fill the warehouse. Mouse lifted her head and peered at Cullen through the haze of pain the jewel was inflicting on her.

"Mouse, come on! They've chased the tarnach our way!"

"S'all right," she mumbled, trying to push herself up on her hands and knees. "Won't harm us." She fumbled around till her hand closed on her sword hilt. With an effort, she got to her feet, pulling Cullen upright beside her. Supporting him, doggedly, she began to stumble toward the door again.

You won't beat me, she said to the jewel. *Because*

I've had to fight all my life. It's all I know. And by the Gods, I'd die rather than give in to you!

"The tarnach, Mouse!" Cullen's voice was terrified as he clutched her forearm.

She could hear its rapid breathing as it drew level with her. "Forget it," she said, trying to ignore the pain that pulsed inside her head. "No danger." Damn the jewel! It was doing all it could to slow her down, as if it wanted Kadron's thugs to catch them! She began to cough as fumes started to sting her throat and make her eyes water.

"Faster, Lady!" urged Zaylar's voice from beside her. "They follow!"

Ahead of them, the warehouse door slammed open, sending a blast of cold night air eddying round them, driving back the smoke. Suddenly, the jewel and the pain in her head were gone.

The tarnach snarled as Cullen gave a gasp of surprise. Blinking furiously, Mouse peered at the shape silhouetted against the night and lifted her sword, ready to defend them as best she could.

"It's the Human," said Cullen, his voice full of relief. "The one I said was asking questions about you and Kolin."

She heard footsteps, could sense someone approaching as she dashed her sleeve across her eyes.

"Take it easy, kids," said a quiet male voice. "I'm on your side. Tell your snarling friend I'm here to help."

She could see him now. Tall, his long pale hair held back by a headband, he stood with his sword held ready, looking over her head at Kadron's men.

He reached out with one large hand, taking Cullen's weight from her. "Get yourself outside, lad," he said, pushing the boy behind him. "We've got a fight on our hands."

Mouse spun round, thrusting her free hand into her cloak pocket. "No, we haven't," she said quietly. "You help Cullen. I'll see to this."

He gave her curious glance, then nodded briefly before backing up to help the boy.

Kadron, his tawdry finery ripped to shreds and stained by smoke, was leaning on the arm of one of his men, hobbling toward them as fast as he could go. He was yelling at Raithil and his companions as, swords drawn, they advanced on her. Behind them, the fire had taken hold, sending smoke and flames billowing up to the ceiling. The roaring drowned out their words, but she could hear them in her mind. She, not the jewel, had used magic on him. Frightened, she looked at their feet, shutting out their thoughts.

"Look behind and tell me when they're clear," she hissed at the tarnach as she readied the three glass vials.

"Cullen and the Human are gone," said Zaylar, shifting restlessly on his four paws. "We leave *now*, Lady. Or tell me to kill them."

Mouse grunted and began to slowly back off. She was the one they wanted now, not Cullen.

"Better they die, Lady," insisted Zaylar. "I cannot kill unless you order. Not supposed to help unless you ask me."

She spared him a glance. So the demon had acted on his own, had he? "No. I'm a thief, not a killer," she said.

"They try kill you."

"No," she repeated, glancing behind her. She was

almost at the doorway now, and there was no sign of the Human and Cullen.

"Get her!" yelled Raithil, making a dash for her.

Spinning around, Mouse raced out the door into the yard, then stopped dead to turn and fling the vials into the doorway. The glass smashed on the cobblestones, filling the yard with clouds of thick, white billowing smoke. The wind caught it, whipping it into the warehouse and sending it swirling round Mouse herself.

Shouts and screams filled the night as the inhabitants of Balrayn realized the warehouse was on fire. Pain gripped her briefly again, making her almost double up as she clutched her belly. Confused and as blinded by the smoke as Kadron and his men, Mouse didn't know which way to turn. Panic flooded through her as a hand closed round her arm.

"Good going," said the Human's voice as he pulled her out of the smoke. "Let's leave now, while we can."

In the distance, they could hear the siren of the spaceport's fire service.

"I can manage," she said stiffly, pulling her arm free and running over to where Cullen leaned against the wall of the inn.

"Sure you can," he said, his voice a lazy drawl. "Not as if you'll be noticed, is it? Or that Kadron's thugs might follow you. One small girl and a cripple, accompanied by what looks like a young tarnach. Especially when tarnachs are so wild only the Port police can train them as guard dogs." He sheathed his sword and came over to pick Cullen up. "You need to get off the streets now. I can help you make far better time than you could alone." He began to head off down the alleyway.

Mouse stared after him, taken aback by his calm assumption of leadership.

"Lady," said Zaylar, pawing urgently at her foot. "Need to go now or Kadron's men will catch us."

"All right!" she snapped, sheathing her sword and beginning to run after them, cursing under her breath. He was right, but she didn't have to like it.

Kolin's house was on the edges of the old Market Quarter, last in a row of similar houses. The Human stopped outside the door, setting Cullen down gently on the ground before turning to face Mouse.

"Will you be safe in there alone?" he asked, a concerned look on his face.

"Yes," she said shortly. "We don't need you inside with us."

He grinned. "I wasn't going to offer. You have your strange little friend, after all," he said, pointing to the tarnach. "I suggest you get him to take on a different shape next time he goes out with you, though. A small tarnach isn't much of a deterrent. Or have him on a leash, it looks better. The guard tarnachs are leashed." He turned and began to walk off down the street.

"Thanks," Cullen called out after him.

Mouse turned to look down at the tarnach, blinking as Zaylar seemed to fade before her eyes, only to reappear in his usual demonic form.

Cullen yelped. "That's Zaylar!"

"I know," she said, irritated. Her belly still hurt and the Human's attitude had annoyed her. "He could see you," she said accusingly to the demon. "And you didn't tell me you could change shape!"

"Not Zaylar's fault, Lady," he said, looking up at her. "Human different. He see Zaylar without my help. Not allowed to help anyone unless Lady says so, you know that."

"And the shape changing?"

The little demon shrugged his bare shoulders and looked away from her, shuffling his hooves in the dirt. "I told you Kolin gave me small magics. That was one. Not hiding it from Lady, just you never asked Zaylar about it."

"Huh," she said, digging her key out of her pocket and stepping past him and Cullen to open the door. "Tonight's been just full of surprises," she said, thinking back to how the arrival of the Human had coincided with the jewel's abrupt departure and continued silence.

She turned to help Cullen into the house. "Tomorrow I've got to get you a new crutch," she said. "Tell me about this Human."

"I told you last night," said Cullen, as groaning, he hopped into the hallway. "He's living down in the Quarters. He's got a seal from Lord Tarolyn himself saying he's free to go anywhere he wants on Jalna. He asks lots of questions and writes it all down in this book he carries around with him."

Mouse shut the door behind them, locking and bolting it securely. "Not many off-worlders get that kind of permission from Tarolyn. What's he want to know about me?"

"Same as everyone else. What you did to Kolin. I was trying to find out more when Kadron's men caught me."

"Zaylar, set the wards," she said. "And fetch me Cullen's old crutch from his room."

"Is there," said Zaylar, pointing to the wooden crutch leaning against the doorway. "Got it already. Knew you wanted it."

She looked at him, hearing his thoughts as if he

spoke them aloud. He wasn't usually this helpful, but he knew that the jewel had tried to force her to kill him. "Why'd you come to help me?" she asked. "I know you can't act for yourself, you have to wait for me to order you, so how'd you manage it?"

Zaylar squirmed under her gaze. "Had to. If Lady die, then Zaylar sent to another Mage, not get talisman. If jewel take you over, then Zaylar still not get talisman."

"Doesn't explain how you managed to help me."

"Zaylar sense Lady want help," he said, looking up at her and spreading his arms wide, his face taking on a helpless look. "Zaylar cannot ignore that."

He was able to pick up her thoughts, just as the jewel was, she realized with an icy shock. She felt the heat of his hand touch hers.

"Zaylar thank Lady for not letting jewel kill him," he said. "Must get book. Must find demon talismans and teach you magics quickly so that you can protect yourself from jewel. You still in danger from Kadron. He mad you use your magic on him, mad at fire. He come after you again, this time to kill."

So he knew what she'd done, did he? "I thought I had to learn to use magic," she said, leaning against the hallway wall as the pain returned. "You know, spells and the like. And how come it's never happened before? I've no idea what I did."

"It come on its own this time and last. You Mage-born, magic in your blood. Must learn to control it. Need more magics to do this if you to stay alive, keep jewel from besting you, keep Mages from challenging you." His small face was creased in real concern.

Mouse wasn't fooled. She knew his concern was self-centered, but for now at least, their aims were the same. "What last time?" she asked sharply.

"Remember firedrake when we steal Living Jewel? Remember guards and 'drake died?"

"You said that was the jewel."

"Was you, not jewel."

She could only stare at him numbly. "But they were crisped—as if they'd been burned in a fire!"

He nodded. "You did. You why Mages not let girls with power live. Male childs can control magic when becoming men, not girls."

Suddenly his meaning became clear.

"He's right," said Cullen. "Kadron's got a real grudge against us now."

"I know. You're not going out alone again. Forget begging, we got enough to live on here for a long while." She pushed herself up off the wall and started down the hallway for her room.

"We need help, Mouse," said Cullen, following her slowly. "Someone with muscle living here. You got money now, you can hire someone."

"Sure, and just where we going to find someone honest enough not to sell us out to Kadron?" she asked sarcastically.

"Could do worse than him," said Cullen. "The Human. Kris."

Kris. So that was his name. She grunted derisively even as the image of him standing in the warehouse doorway, sword in hand, came to her mind.

"He did help us tonight," Cullen pointed out as he stopped at the study door. "And Kadron ain't going to be the last man to want you," he added quietly, giving her an oblique look.

"What's that supposed to mean?" she demanded, coming to a halt. "You think I can't look after us?"

"No," he said hurriedly. "Knows you can. You rescued me, got us out of there without a fight. I just meant it was odd him turning up like that, 'specially when he'd been asking about you."

And that, along with the fact that she hadn't been able to sense Kris's thoughts at all, was just another of the night's surprises.

THE THRONESPELL
by *Diana L. Paxson*

Diana L. Paxson's novels include her *Chronicles of Westria* series and her more recent *Wodan's Children* series. Her short fiction can be found in many anthologies, including *Zodiac Fantastic, Grails: Quests of the Dawn, Return to Avalon,* and *The Book of Kings.* Her Arthurian novel *Hallowed Isle* was published in four volumes last year, and will be out in two paperbacks this year.

"A sixth spell I ken, if a thane wounds me with risted runes on root . . ." Grípir's voice creaked like the wagons that were bringing the new king's gear up from the landing, thought Kon, his truant gaze drawn from his foster-father's face to the road below them.

"Complete the verse!" snapped Grípir.

Kon blinked, striving to focus thoughts that soared like the gulls above the fjord. The day was fair and clear. It was all very well for an old man like Grípir to sit in the sun, but Kon was eighteen years old, his muscles strong from carving the rune-inscribed monuments that were their trade, and his body cried out for activity.

"On his head . . ." he mumbled, "shall heap the ills . . ." He stopped. Around the bend came warriors, and behind them several men mounted on sturdy ponies. He recognized the graying head of Sigurd of Lade, the most powerful man in the Norse lands. Beside him, just as tall, though not so broad, rode a youth as fair as Baldr in the springtime of the world.

"The rest, Kon!" Grípir's voice seemed to come from a great distance, "if you ever want to learn the remainder of the spells!"

". . . the ills of the curse he called on mine," the young man responded unthinking, his gaze still on the riders.

It was Hacon—it had to be—the last of Harald Hairfair's many children, whom men said was his father made young again. Hacon, who would be Norway's king . . . if his brother Eric Blood-Axe let him live.

"Trolls take you!" exclaimed Grípir. "It was not enough for you to learn the names of the runes and their meanings. You wanted their secrets, and now, when I lay the High One's wisdom at your feet, you listen with no more attention than a love-struck girl!"

"Grípir, it is the king!" Kon pointed, and the old man snorted.

". . . a woman's bed-talk, a broken blade, the play of bears, the child of a king . . . trust never so much as to trust in these!" he muttered, shaking his head. "I see I'll get no sense out of you until the excitement is over. Very well. Let us put on our good tunics and see if Sigurd Jarl can still find a seat for us in his hall!"

Between the king's household and the influx of other folk who had thronged in to see or petition or serve him, it would not have been surprising if Kon and his master had found themselves portionless. But Grípir was a craftsman of some standing. From their bench at the back they could see little of what the great ones were doing where Hacon sat in his carven high seat at the other end of the hall, but they were fed.

But if they could not see, they heard a great deal. It was said that Sigurd Jarl had been escorting Hacon's mother on her way to King Harald when her time came upon her. Thus, it was Sigurd who sprinkled the boy with water and gave him a name from his own family. 'Twas no wonder, observed one of the women, that the Jarl was Hacon's greatest supporter now.

His counsel was good anyway, answered one of the landowners who had come in to swear his oaths to the king. To give the smallholders their lands as an inalienable inheritance, rather than the gift of the king, was a sure way to win their loyalty.

"But what will Hacon do for money if the holders do not pay him a fee for the use of the land?" asked Kon, "And how will he reward new men who come to serve him?"

"By raiding the Danes, no doubt," replied Grípir, "like his father before him—"

"Or by confiscating the lands of those who still hold to his brother . . ." said the man who sat beside them.

"It seems to me that Eric Blood-Axe may have a thing or two to say about that," muttered his neighbor.

"Eric, or Gunnhild . . ." added another man, more softly still.

Even whispered, the name of the woman King Eric had rescued from Finnish sorcerers and made his wife was enough to bring silence. Eric had burned his own brother in his hall for doing magic, but his queen was said to know not only *seidh,* but the *galdor* chants by which one worked with the runes. Kon shivered and silently vowed that the next time Grípir tried to teach him spellcraft, he would pay more attention.

A serving-maid came toward them, carrying a

pitcher. The man who had spoken cleared his throat
and held out his beaker for more ale.

Hacon's arrival brought prosperity to more than the
farmers, for while men waited to speak with the king,
they had time to talk to Grípir, and he had collected
half a dozen orders for memorial stones before a week
had passed. The old rune master went about grinning,
but in Jarl Sigurd's hall, Kon began to notice worried frowns.

Suddenly, things were not going well. Jarl Sigurd
fell ill of a fever that kept him in his bed, and without
his guidance, the fifteen-year-old king had not the skill
to keep the men who stood before his high seat from
quarreling. Two duels were fought on the island in the
center of the fjord, and the son of a holder from the
Vik died. After that the other highborn folk began to
murmur, and men marked that the faces around the
king were not so friendly as before. Hacon himself
had lost some of his fresh color, and the laugh that
had seemed so blithe before now seemed the feckless
titter of a child.

Grípir grew sullen, seeing his new gold beginning
to vanish before he had even grasped it, and snarled
when Kon asked when they would resume his lessons.
Kon's fist clenched. For a moment he stared at it,
unable to understand why he felt such fury, then he
snatched up his bag of tools and strode from the hall.

It was better outside. He no longer had that sense
that an insect was whining just beyond his hearing,
but he still felt twitchy. The steel tools clanked in his
bag, and he sighed. It had been over a week since he
had used them—soon he would begin to lose his
strength, hanging about here.

But granite poked through the hillside above the

hall, good stone for carving. Hoisting the toolbag over his shoulder, Kon started toward it.

"What are you doing?"

Kon dropped the chisel and started to swear, then realized that the dark shape that stood between him and the sun was their young king.

"I am sorry—" said Hacon as Kon mastered himself. "I did not realize you could not hear me coming up the hill."

Kon shook his head, more unsettled by the apology than he had been by the interruption. "I carve runestones . . ." he mumbled finally. "I have to practice to maintain my skill." Scattered stone chips crunched as he sat back on his heels.

The young king looked from Kon to the serpentine line carved across the face of the boulder and then back again.

"Are you Norse?" Hacon asked curiously. "I have never seen such sooty hair."

Kon flushed, though he had heard that question put in terms much less polite, far too many times before.

"My mother was a woman of Bjarmaland," he muttered.

"Were you born a thrall?"

Kon jumped to his feet, glaring. Poor feeding in childhood had stunted his growth. His arms and torso were powerful, but Hacon was still a head taller.

"If I was, I am free now—" he growled, for though Grípir had bought him along with a sack of meal for a handful of silver, he had proved his worth, standing with the old man against a nightwalker, and now the old man called him son. For a moment the young king looked down at him, blue eyes grave above his high-bridged nose, fair hair stirring a little in the wind.

"They called my mother 'the king's serving maid,' " Hacon said then, having apparently decided that he could afford an apology. "When Harald tricked the English king into taking me to foster, Aethelstan thought it an insult, but he got to like me afterward." He smiled. "He gave me this sword—" he added, stroking the gold inlay of the pommel. "Would you like to see?"

Fascinated, Kon nodded. He had no doubt King Aethelstan had come to love his fosterling. Why could Hacon not employ this charm when he sat in his high seat in the hall?

Steel hissed from the sheath. "It's called *Kvernbit,* 'Quern-biter,' " said the young king, turning it back and forth to catch the light, "because I cut through a millstone with it all the way to the center hole!"

It was a boy's tone, and a boy's pride, thought Kon, feeling suddenly immeasurably older. But Hacon would not be allowed to stay a child for long. Kon wondered if he would be allowed to remain a king.

"Don't you believe me?" Hacon asked. His gaze lit suddenly, "Let us see if I can cleave this stone!"

"This is granite, harder than a troll's head-piece!" exclaimed Kon. "You must not risk your steel."

"Your chisel cut it—" objected the king, glancing scornfully down at Kon's tools.

"Its shape is different, and I sharpen—" But even as Kon spoke, Hacon shifted to a two-handed grip and brought the bright blade up and around in a wheel of light.

As if he could see into its structure, Kon knew it would shatter, unless there was some flaw in the stone—at the thought, his own hand moved, all the force of his need channeling through his rigid fingers,

up and across in the shape of the rune as he cried out
its name—

"Naud!"

The sword struck, but the stone was already break-
ing into two pieces with a crack that echoed across
the fjord.

"You dared!" hissed Hacon, the arrogance of seven
generations of Norse kings blazing in his eyes.

Kon stood his ground. "I saved your sword."

Hacon looked at the pale surfaces of the split stone,
where bits of crystal glinted in the sun, and slowly his
expression changed. "The millstone was a different
kind of rock," he said, and then, "How did you *do*
that?"

"The rune *Naud* has the shape of a sword," Kon
said tactfully. "I added its might to yours."

Carefully, the young king set the tip of the sword
into the mouth of its sheath and slid it hissing home.

"You are a runemaster . . ." said Hacon.

"I am learning to be—" answered Kon, wondering
when Grípir would relent and start teaching him again.

"I am a Christian, and there are things it is not
lawful for me to know."

"Then let others know them for you, my lord, for
the sake of the land," Kon said quietly.

Hacon sighed. There was a shout from below. Colored tunics showed bright against the green grass and
Kon recognized some of the young men who had
come with their fathers to wait upon the king.

"You had better go—your friends are calling you."

Hacon gave him an odd, unsmiling look. "Kings
have no friends—only followers, or enemies . . ." he
said, and then his long limbs bore him down the hill
and Kon was left alone.

*   *   *

In the days that followed, Kon watched the young king with new attention. They could not speak, but sometimes Hacon would catch his eye, and it seemed to the older boy that there was something—not friendship—but an odd sense of comradeship, in his gaze. If that gave the king some kind of comfort, Kon was glad, for matters were growing steadily worse in the hall.

Tensions ran high among the men who surrounded the king; even to be near them made Kon uneasy. He pitied the boy who had to sit still on his high seat, listening to their quarreling. Sigurd Jarl had hoped to bring all Norway to his protégé's hand before snowfall, but as the hay ripened, the holders were leaving, rather than coming in. They said they were needed at home to get in the harvest, but Kon did not think that was all. There was an indefinable air of ill-luck about this place, and he wondered how long before Grípir decided to take up the first of the contracts he had made and they, too, would be away.

On a night when men had been especially quarrelsome, Kon roused from an uneasy rest, eased from the blanket where he lay next to Grípir beside the long hearth, and made his way out of the hall. From the feel of the air he guessed it to be midway through the out-tide, the still hour between midnight and the early summer dawn.

By the time he returned from the privies, he was wide awake. His steps slowed as he crossed the yard. It was a fine night. A haze of mist from the sea blurred the western horizon, but overhead the stars shone clear and bright. Gazing upward at their beauty, it was hearing rather than sight that told him he was not alone.

Responses honed by a vulnerable childhood brought

him around in a feral crouch, but the figure by the horse-trough did not move, and in another moment Kon recognized the straight shoulders and the gleam of starshine on fair hair and knew it was the king.

"I couldn't sleep—" Hacon said unnecessarily. "I know it sounds foolish, but suddenly I could not stay another moment in that hall."

"No more could I," Kon answered him.

Hacon let out his breath in a long sigh and leaned back against the trough.

"The kingdom of the English is a soft land of rich fields and tangled woodland and long meadows sloping down to the sea. Not like here."

"But this land bred you—" said Kon into the silence that followed.

"Many things are still strange to me. I cannot tell an omen of disaster from the ordinary way of the land." There was another silence, then the king pointed upward. "What is that, that looks like a cloud of angels' wings?"

His voice trembled only a little, Kon noted. He tipped his head back, searching the sky until he, too, saw in the southeast a luminous, opalescent cloud.

"Some believe that is Gimle, the heaven that lies beyond Asgard where the high gods dwell. To see it should be an omen of good fortune, not bad."

"You know a great deal," said the king. His voice did not alter, but some of the tension in his stance had eased.

"My foster-father is rune-wise, a follower of Odin."

"The lord of all devils, they call him in the Christian lands. I need someone who can master demons," muttered Hacon, "I think they are haunting Jarl Sigurd's hall . . ."

Kon shrugged. It was as good an explanation as any.

"Everything was going so well for us," the king continued, "but as soon as I sat down in that high seat something began to trouble me."

Kon straightened, frowning. "Something . . . like a sound you cannot quite hear?"

Hacon nodded eagerly. "It sets my teeth on edge. Men who sounded wise and reasonable before snarl like bad-tempered bears, and I hear myself whining back at them like a child."

"A spell—" Kon exclaimed softly. "That would explain it—a spell set upon the high seat to bend men's minds and warp their wills."

Hacon spat in disgust. "Can you counter it?"

"Can *I?*" Kon stared at him. "I am still learning the Heruli craft—it is Grípir, my master—"

"No!" the king stopped him. "It is bad enough that a Christian should have to speak of such things. I do not wish the world to know my shame! We will go now, while the world still sleeps, and see."

Kon took a step backward, hearing, as once before he had seen, the authority of all Hacon's royal forebears in those words. He turned the involuntary flinch into a bow.

"As my lord commands—"

Surely in a moment someone would wake and challenge them, thought Kon as they felt their way through the darkness of the hall. The dim glow of the coals showed them the humped shapes of sleeping men and the row of wooden pillars rising like the ghosts of trees. At the head of the hearth he could just make out the four posts that supported the high seat, carved with a serpentine interlace of branches and god-faces whose staring eyes seemed to follow them as they crept through the hall.

Men stirred as they passed, snorting as they changed position, but it was the hour when folk sleep most deeply, and no one challenged them. Kon stared up at the high seat, suddenly at a loss. He could hear Hacon breathing at his shoulder, waiting for him to do something. He reached under the cushion, knowing already he would find nothing.

"If the spell is carved into the wood, we will have to wait for daylight—" he muttered.

Hacon shook his head. "I can *feel* it, buzzing like a wasp in my ear. Look underneath!"

Young the king might be, but even his whisper could command, and with the words of objection unvoiced on his lips, Kon found himself reaching under the slats at the side, feeling for some gap. Any ill-wisher would encounter the same difficulty he was having, for there was scarcely an hour in the day when the hall was empty. If anything had been added, it must be small enough to slip through an opening.

Kon's breath caught as one of the boards moved. As he tried to reach past it, the wood sprang back, almost trapping his hand. He stifled an oath and tried again, but he needed his other hand for balance.

"Hold this!" he hissed, forgetting, in that moment, that one does not give orders to a king. Without a word, Hacon reached past him and gripped the board. His big hands would never have fit through the opening, but he had the strength to keep the pieces of wood apart as Kon strained, grinding his shoulder against the pillar, to touch the object he knew must lie within.

Then his fingers brushed something that stung like nettle. Kon flinched, then reached again, gripped what felt like a piece of twisted wood and pulled it through the opening. The board snapped back with a snick

that seemed to echo through the hall as Hacon let go.
The two young men froze as one of the warriors sat
up with a grunt, staring sleepily around him.

It seemed an age of the world before the fellow lay
back down and they could breathe again.

"You have it?" murmured Hacon.

Kon nodded: He did not need to see what he held.
If venom had a texture, it would be like this, simulta-
neously sharp and slimy.

"Then take it out and destroy it—" Even in a whisper, the loathing in Hacon's voice was clear. "Men
will be waking, and I must be where they expect to
find me."

As the king moved toward his boxbed at the end
of the hall, Kon wrapped the bit of wood in a corner
of his cloak and retraced his steps toward the door. It
was none too soon, for outside the pallor of dawn was
dimming the stars, and already the thralls who tended
the fires were beginning to stir.

Kon eased through the door behind a man with a
load of wood and started up the hill. The spellstave
ought to be burned, he knew, or cast into the cleansing
sea, but a wise man knows his enemy, and it seemed
to him that there might be something to be learned.
He had grown too accustomed to thinking of himself
as an apprentice, forgetting that moving forward alone
is the first step to mastery.

He settled himself beside the shattered pieces of the
boulder the king had split just as the young sun lifted
above the eastern hills.

"Hail to thee Day, hail, Day's sons—" he murmured as he unwrapped the piece of wood. "Lady
Sunna, purify this place of all ill with thy holy light!"

His fingers brushed the wood and he jerked as if he
had touched a wasp. It was a piece of tree root, hard

and polished. In the growing light he could see that the surface had been incised all over with runes. He made out words for bane and bale, and with them an odd rectangular sigil crossed at the corners and leading into angled lines at whose meaning he could only guess. In a serpentine border he identified a succession of twice-crossed hail runes, and the simpler single slashed upright of Need. The scratched signs showed rusty red against the pale wood. Whose blood, he wondered, had been used to color them?

Kon took the waterskin that hung from his belt and dribbled water over the spellstave, watching as the brownish liquid dripped to the ground.

"I wash away from the king the hate of his foes and the malice of ill-working women and cunning men. As the sweet rain of heaven dissolves this blood," he whispered, "may the power of this spell be diluted and drain away . . ."

Within a few feet of the boulder he found enough sticks to make a little fire. When it was burning steadily, he took out his knife and picked up the spellstave once more. The washing had taken some of the sting from it, but it still felt slimy in his hand. Carefully he pared a portion of the serpentine border away and let it fall into the fire.

> "Hailstones melt in fiery flame!
> Need unbind, in Odhinn's name!
> As these runestaves char and burn,
> Magic to maker shall return!"

Curl by curl, the wood on which the runes had been carved went into the fire. Now the energies that border had contained buzzed around him like bees. Swiftly the sharp knife stripped each line and gave it to the flames, and as he banished each bit, Kon called upon the gods to turn the evil back upon the one who had set it there.

When he was finished, he held a much smaller piece of wood, hacked and haggled, stripped of its malice, though it still held an impression of unease. Grimly, he continued to whittle until the last curl caught fire.

After that things seemed to get better. Jarl Sigurd was recovering from his fever, and men no longer needed to go armed to meals. And yet, if the active evil was absent, the spellstave had left an atmosphere behind it like the aftertaste of spoiled ale. When he sat on the high seat, even Hacon's determined cheerfulness faltered, and men who in the springtime had been full of ambition sat glum and silent as the season turned toward fall.

When this had gone on for a while, Kon began to look for a chance to speak with the king alone. For a time he thought he would have to lie in wait by the door in the darkness, but on a morning about a week after Kon had removed the spellstave, Hacon commanded his presence, saying he wanted to discuss a memorial stone for his father.

"Master Grípir has gone up the valley for a few days," said Kon. "You must take that up with him on his return."

"By then I may be occupied once more," Hacon said loftily, and Kon realized that he had known very well that Grípir was away. "Walk with me, and I will tell you what I desire."

Some of the aristocratic youngsters who were trying to attach themselves to the royal household frowned as Hacon motioned to Kon to follow him. He suppressed a smile as he followed the king up the hill.

"Is it destroyed?" asked Hacon as soon as they were out of earshot of the others.

"Every bit—burned to ash and scattered on the wind. Gunnhild, or someone, must be having an uncomfortable time by now, for I sent as much of the power back to its maker as I could."

"Then why is there still a shadow on my soul?"

"Have you never had to clean up after a puppy?" Kon replied. "The stink of a turd still lingers, even when the mess is gone. The spellstave lay hidden in your high seat for some weeks. Let me take the thing apart and purify it."

"No! I will not have it said that I dealt with heathen powers!"

Kon blinked. "How can you avoid it? This is a heathen land. No one will think the less of you for this compromise."

Once more, Hacon shook his head. "I know that no man, even a king, can command another's soul. But I promised King Aethelstan that I would not forsake the faith in which he raised me and I hold to the oath I swore!"

"Then let it be," Kon answered. "I suppose the stink will wear off in time. Tell Jarl Sigurd to take you to another hall."

Hacon sighed. "Word has come that Trygvi and Gudrod are on their way to me here. They are sons of my brothers that Eric killed—at least he killed Gudrod's father. Some say that Trygvi's father was poisoned by Gunnhild. I cannot leave till they have come, and when they do, they must accept my lordship."

"I see why you are concerned, but if you will not let me take action in the only way I know, I can give you no other answer," Kon said then.

"You are as stubborn as one of your stones!" exclaimed Hacon.

As if the words had been a physical blow, Kon flinched backward. Men said that King Harald had been like that, when rage took him. Christian this boy might be, but he was his father's son. How was Kon, who did not even know who his father had been, to withstand him? *I am the child of Ríg,* he told himself, *and good enough to stand with any man.*

"My lord, if I am stubborn, then you are a match for me!" For a long moment his dark gaze held that of the king, until the steel went out of the blue eyes and Hacon sighed.

"Then Christ pity us both!"

And may Odin aid us— observed Kon. But he did so silently, for he had learned already that a king, even one who is—almost—a friend, likes to have the last word.

That night Kon slept restlessly. In the still hour before dawn he fell into a deeper slumber, and found himself walking a white road through a dark forest, and knew he had seen this place before. Presently he came to a clearing, in whose center he made out the dim bulk of a standing stone. Its power drew him; slowly he approached and laid his hands upon the gritty surface, tracing the shapes of carven runes.

That kank at átta . . . "An eighth I ken, that all can sing—" He tensed in excitement, for this was one of the spells that Grípir had not yet shared with him. But as his eager fingers probed more deeply, he felt the granite turning to rough wool, and the body beneath it radiated heat like a fire.

Kon leaped back with an oath, staring at the tall

shape that leaned on the spear, the hood of his cloak drawn forward so that it hid one eye.

"I know you . . ." he whispered.

"Perhaps," came the answer. "But do you know what you need to know?"

"How to turn Hacon heathen?"

"Do you think that matters to me? He will be a good king. You must help him."

"How can I do that, when he will not listen to me?"

The god sighed, and began to chant softly:

> *"An eighth spell I ken that all can sing*
> *for weal if well they learn;*
> *where hate waxes amid heroes' sons,*
> *I calm it with that song . . ."*

"You do not care if he honors you?" asked Kon, and then, as the silence deepened, "you want me to help him, even against his will? What must I do?"

"Touch the stone . . ." came the answer, and even as Kon reached out to him, the shape of the god was changing, solidifying, becoming granite once more.

Kon's clutching fingers caught on stone, grooved and indented with lines that hummed as he touched them. Back and forth moved his hands, independent of his will, memorizing the runes.

His fingers were still twitching when the morning bustle of the hall awakened him, and his throat still vibrated with the tones of the spell.

He felt for his bag of tools and stumbled out of the hall, eyes half-closed for fear that the sight of the world would drive out the fading memories of his dream. Laughing, the serving maids asked how much he had drunk the night before, but Kon was listening to the song in his head and did not answer them. He remembered the shape of the spell in his blood and bones. He had only to retain it until he could transfer it to some more enduring material.

Instinctively he sought the hillside where Hacon had split the boulder, and fell to his knees, sweeping the ground clear before him, and feeling about him for a pointed stone with which he could draw.

For this spell, it was the old runes of the Heruli that he must use. Swiftly he drew in a large Mannaz, the rune of human kind, retracing its two halves to double Wunjo, the rune for joy. By emphasizing the lines that crossed between the staves, he added Gebo, the rune of exchange. That was a good start, he felt, considering them. There was a saying in the lore that Grípir had been teaching him, "Man is the joy of man," that should bode well for a king.

Kon thought for a few moments more, trying to remember what else he had seen, then drew the two angles of Jera to bracket the bind-rune with good seasons, and for protection, a circle of Elhaz runes all around.

That should be sufficient, he thought, surveying the marks on the ground. It had the same feel as the design in the dream, and in any case, it was all he could remember. He sorted through the pieces of stone until he found one that would fit through the gap in the back of Hacon's high seat, and braced it securely. Then, taking up his smallest graving tool, he began to tap out the first rune.

As he worked, he softly chanted the rune names, and inch by inch the bind-rune grew, the tapping of his hammer giving rhythmic accompaniment to his song. When the design was complete, he slashed the edge of his chisel across the inside of his arm, catching the dark blood on the edge of his risting tool and laying it into the grooves in the stone. As he did so, he began to sing once more, running the rune names together in a wordless croon—

"Jera . . . mann . . . gebo . . . wun . . ."

The syllables were repeated again and again until the work was done. Kon took a deep breath, dizzied by the outrush of power.

"By blood and will, this spell be bound,
Elk rune ward the circle round!"

One thing was still lacking. Below the bind-rune, he chiseled the name of the young king.

Kon returned to the hall through a side door, as concerned now to avoid Hacon's eye as he had earlier been to catch the king's attention. But the party escorting Hacon's young nephews had been sighted on the eastern road, and everyone else had gone out to welcome them.

It was the work of a moment to pry back the board, and slip the piece of stone through the gap. Kon could barely hear the thud it made as it hit the planks of the flooring, but inner senses told him that its power was reverberating through all the worlds. That was only to be expected, he thought as he moved away again, since the spell had been given to him by a god.

He pulled off his tunic and went out to plunge head and shoulders into the horsetrough, and was waiting, dressed in his good tunic with his damp hair tied back with a thong, when Hacon and the others returned to the hall.

He saw the flicker of anxiety in the king's eyes as

he took his seat, and the frown and flush as Hacon
sensed the change. The king's keen gaze swept the
hall. Kon stood a little straighter when it found him,
meeting Hacon's eye with a defiant grin.

You will not remove the spellstone, my lord, he
thought, *nor will you give that task to another, for to
do so would be to admit belief in my magic.*

Of course the king might still find some way to pun-
ish him, but as he heard Hacon's speech grow in certainty, and watched men's faces light with hope as
they listened to his judgments, it seemed to Kon that
he would suffer Hacon's disfavor willingly, knowing
that he had helped to keep him king.

A moon passed, and Gudrod and Trygvi departed,
content to rule Vestfold and Ranrik under Hacon's
lordship. The season was turning, and the storehouses
here were nearly empty. Wild geese flew southward,
sketching their wavering runes across the pale sky. It
was time for the royal household to move down to
the island of Stord where they would spend the winter.

Grípir was still at the farmstead up the valley. He
had a cough, his messenger had said, and would stay
there until spring. Kon packed up their things, but
found himself making one excuse after another to put
off joining him. Although Hacon had not sought him
out, Kon had the sense of something still uncompleted
in their dealings.

I will wait until he sails down the fjord, he told himself, *and then I will go.*

"You did something to the high seat, didn't you?"

Kon, who had been watching the men load the
king's longship, turned so quickly he nearly fell. He

searched that familiar, high-boned face, and wondered if he should be afraid.

"My king," he said carefully. "Do you truly wish to know?"

Hacon shook his head with a sigh. There was a long silence, as the two gazed out at the sparkling sea. That denial had been all the answer the king could give, thought Kon, and all the thanks he was likely to get as well.

"You will have a good day for sailing—" Kon said at last.

"Come with me—"

Once more, Kon was startled. "In what capacity, my lord?"

"As my friend," said the king.

"What about all those noble youths I see glaring at us from the shore?"

A hint of smile flickered in Hacon's eyes. "I can trust them to serve themselves and their families. I trust you to serve the Norse land—whether or not I will it."

And by saying so, the king *had* willed it. The god must have known Hacon's heart, whatever his conscience might say. With that thought, Kon's last anxiety regarding the lawfulness of his deed faded away. *It needed no spells of mine to make this one a king!*

"Then I will come—" he said aloud.

The glint in Hacon's eye brightened, and in the next moment both of them were laughing.

AND KING HEREAFTER
(a Boscobel League story)
by Rosemary Edghill

Rosemary Edghill is the author of over two dozen books, including *Speak Daggers to Her, The Book of Moons,* and *Hellflower.* Her short fiction has appeared in such anthologies as *Return to Avalon, Chicks in Chainmail,* and *Tarot Fantastic.* She is a full-time author who lives in the mid-Hudson Valley.

Silver Stick in Waiting was worried. Since the death of the old king—his mind kept treacherously wanting to insert "the *true* king"—almost a year ago, both Palace and Realm had been unsettled. The Young King was unmarried, and even at forty-two was long past the age when royal princes had married and begun families. The succession must be preserved at all costs: so Silver Stick in Waiting had always accepted unthinkingly.

But the Young King did not seem to agree.

The trouble had begun just after the war that had nearly destroyed human civilization. The Young King had served with distinction, stepping out from beneath the looming shadow of his father to become a leader of men in his own right. And on his return home, he had expected to receive a hero's reward: the right to marry the woman he loved.

For the first time in centuries it was possible—the shadow of the war had caused the King-Emperor to

decree that henceforward the members of the royal
family would find their brides among the aristocracy
of their own land, rather than contributing to the tan-
gle of marital alliances that had pulled down a dozen
thrones and nearly driven Mankind back to barbarism.
The Young King had reason to believe his father
would approve his choice: for months he pursued the
Duke's daughter who had captivated him when they
were both under arms, and in the very year of the
Peace he presented his choice to his father.

But the King-Emperor refused him. Madness tainted
the girl's family, and the King-Emperor feared to add
its taint to his own inbred line. Within the year, she
had married the Young King's best friend, and within
a decade she was dead. The Young King never spoke
of her again.

Had he known what was to come of his refusal,
Silver Stick thought, surely the King-Emperor would
have welcomed a thousand madwomen into his son's
life. Infuriated by the callous dismissal of his hopes,
the Young King threw himself into a round of frivo-
lous dissipation, mounting a number of mistresses and
never again casting his eyes upon a suitable bride.
For the next decade, as his siblings—Gloucester, Kent,
York—married and set up their households, the King
in Waiting idled away his responsibilities.

And the kingdom slid irresistibly toward another
war, a war that bore all the signs of being more devastating than the first.

But even that was not the worst. *She* was the worst:
disastrous the day that the Viscountess had introduced
her into the Young King's Fort Belvedere set seven
years before, and to Silver Stick in Waiting's everlast-
ing grief, his friend and master, the King-Emperor,
had lived to see all but the worst of it.

At first it had seemed safe enough—the woman was married, after all, and on her second husband. She was neither pretty nor splendid, nor English, nor over-young . . . but despite those handicaps, her brash Colonial hold over the Prince grew, until the courtiers were murmuring uneasily, remembering the Royal Astrologer's prediction. Cherio had said that Prince Edward Albert Christian George Andrew Patrick David would someday throw over all he possessed to pursue a grand passion. Perhaps Bessiewallis of Baltimore was to be that passion.

By the summer of '34, the Baltimore socialite was the reigning queen at the Prince's grace and favor residence in Windsor Great Park; David had broken with his brother the Duke of York over it and ruthlessly discarded the mistresses he had been devoted to since the disastrous end of his romance with Lady Rosemary. The Old King's death was two years in the future, but there were already signs of an open break between King George and his heir. Mrs. Simpson appeared at public events—including King George's Silver Jubilee Ball—dripping with jewelry paid for from Civil List funds, and David did not seem to care who was hurt by his flaunting of his lowborn concubine.

Then the King-Emperor died.

The household held its breath, praying that the new King Edward would awaken to his responsibilities, put aside his rebellious passions, and seek out a young woman who was suitable in every way for the exacting job of Royal Consort. Instead, by the day of the royal funeral, the American whore was installed in the Palace itself, and her complaisant husband was arranging to do the accepted thing by getting himself discovered in an adulterous connection in a Continental hotel.

Less than a month after the funeral, David was back

at Fort Belvedere, and Mrs. Simpson was its acknowledged ruler. State papers of the utmost delicacy were
scattered unread through its rooms for anyone to see,
and the ambassadors of foreign powers even now pre-
paring for war shamelessly courted the woman who
might be Queen. There were whispers of marriage,
though no one dared to speak of it openly. The Coronation was set for May 12, 1937, and the Young King
swore he meant to be married before that.

At least his romance had kept him out of Munich
that summer. The Olympics this year were a showcase
for the German Chancellor's imperialist ambitions,
and the King had never made any secret of his admira-
tion of the decisive strong men who ruled Turkey,
Italy, and the new Germany. But this summer, the
King was more occupied with his humiliating gutter
affaire.

In July the Court came out of mourning. By August
"Wallis" photo was on the front page of every paper
in the world, her name linked publicly with the
King's—his impersonation of the "Duke of Lancaster"
had fooled none of the journalists who had followed
him and his lady on their Balkan tour—and less than
six weeks after the King's return to England with his
leman, the hearing of her divorce petition from her
English husband was announced. Prime Minster Bald-
win begged the King to intercede.

Reflexively, Silver Stick in Waiting touched his
breast pocket, where the brief note he had received
that morning from Number Ten rested. As insiders
had expected, the King had refused to stop the suit
from going forward. In seven days the Simpsons would
come before Sir John Hawke at Ipswitch: there was
little doubt that the decree *nisi* would be granted, and
by next April Mrs. Simpson would be free to marry—

and an Empire poised upon the brink of war would face the prospect of a twice-divorced, barren, American queen with the manners and morals of a gutter prostitute and the wits of a mental defective.

The thought was unbearable. And, unfortunately, Silver Stick was in a position to do something about it. The draconian housecleaning that had followed the King's return—dozens of loyal retainers and lifelong couriers dismissed without reason—had not yet reached the London complement, and for now, Silver Stick still had his post and its contacts . . . and a duty to the King. For Silver Stick in Waiting was not only the King's chief equerry, but one of the King's secret guardians.

He drew the signet ring from his finger. Automatically his fingers worked the secret catch, and he stared sightlessly down at the revealed device, symbol of his bondage. Against a silver field an oak tree in summer foliage stood. At its foot a white unicorn slept with head upon the ground, and in the branches, a crown in glory burned: Boscobel, the King's Oak. The sign of the Boscobel League.

For over three hundred years, since the Glorious Restoration of 1660, the Boscobel League had existed, the more effective successor of The Sealed Knot: a tiny band of men and women drawn from the highest and lowest in the land, loyal to King—or Queen— before Country. It was by the decree of their royal founder, Charles II, that their numbers should never exceed twelve, and that each Monarch, upon his accession, should be given one chance, and one chance only, to disband them. Ten kings and one queen had not.

The Young King had not been given the chance.

That omission had been a source of great friction

within the League. Since even His Majesty's government was withholding State papers from Edward, the League had agreed to postpone revealing itself to the Young King until the Coronation. But after that, who knew what might happen?

Silver Stick tried to pretend to himself that it didn't matter. He could resign his post in the Royal Household, return to his Mayfair townhouse, his collection of incunabula, his music, and his study of sorcery, and still serve the King's person should he be summoned. Silver Stick in Waiting knew his *haut magie:* this world was only one of many, each branching from the next like tributaries from a stream. In another world, perhaps the Young King did not sit upon the throne. Perhaps he had never even met the American divorcée. Or perhaps he had never been born at all—or died in the war—and his younger brother George and the Lady Elizabeth reigned, their two beautiful daughters, Elizabeth and Margaret Rose, ensuring the continuity of the monarchy.

Somewhere. But not here. Silver Stick in Waiting ran his hand through his flaxen-pale hair. There was no use in daydreaming. Things were as they were, and in this world, Silver Stick's oath of fealty still held, and the King must be protected . . . even from his own foolish heart.

Silver Stick had known in his heart it must come to this, but he had put off the decision as long as he could, hoping he would not need to make it. But with the king's refusal to act, the last hope was gone. Silver Stick sighed, and shook his head, and headed toward the Royal Mews, where his private car was kept garaged.

He must act, and only History would be able to say

if he had acted as the Young King's friend, or his direst enemy.

Behind the wheel of the black Daimler, his black mood lifted for a time, but Silver Stick knew it was only a temporary reprieve. Though he drove like Jehu, he could not outrun what he must do.

He had been to the little cottage at the edge of the New Forest only a few times before. Its inhabitant was a journalist and author . . . and witch.

Dame Sybil Leek greeted him graciously, her pet jackdaw perched on her shoulder.

"I knew you would come, Peter," she said.

"Then you know what I have come for," Silver Stick in Waiting answered.

"What you propose is a grave matter indeed," Dame Sybil told him a few minutes later. Once he had told her why he had come, Dame Sybil had offered him tea. Silver Stick had accepted, knowing that she wished to read the leaves for guidance.

"I had hoped that matters would mend themselves," he admitted reluctantly. "But he is set on marriage, and once this marriage is made, it can never be dissolved." The King was the head of the English Church. Divorce was impossible for the sovereign. It would destroy the kingdom more effectively than civil war.

"Why come to me?" Dame Sybil asked pointedly.

Silver Stick in Waiting stared down into his teacup. "My own skill is not sufficient to do what must be done."

"You mean to summon the Woman of the Wood," Dame Sybil said, using one of the nonce-names the Wiccakin had for their Goddess. She was England's

Goddess as well: Brigantia, Lady of Albion, who had given Her name and Her threefold gift to the land She had ruled as Her own uncounted thousands of years ago. She ruled the hidden paths and byways of the land still, granting knowledge and power to those who knew to seek Her.

"Yes," Silver Stick in Waiting said. "I will ask Her to take this choice from him, so that he can rule us as Destiny intended."

"You know that there is always a price?" Dame Sybil asked steadily. "In blood, in peace, in years— always a price."

"I am prepared to pay," Silver Stick in Waiting said. "Black Rod can take over my duties; Chipsie is a good fellow. Assuming any of us survives His Majesty's economy campaign," he added gloomily.

"I will not help you unless I agree with you that it is necessary," the witch warned, "and I have not yet made up my mind. Drink up."

The tea was well-made, though after the stress of the morning Silver Stick would have much preferred a stiff whiskey and soda, and he soon drained the small porcelain cup. There was a small accretion of tea leaves at the bottom, suspended in the last few drops of tea. Knowing what was to come, Silver Stick passed the cup on its saucer across the table to his hostess.

She swirled the dregs of the tea around three times, then abruptly upended the cup into its saucer. When the last drops of liquid had trickled out, she turned the cup right side up once more and peered down into its depths, reading the patterns the tea-leaves had made.

Silver Stick sat very still, watching her scry. He wasn't sure which he dreaded more: hearing that she agreed with him on the need for action, or discovering that she would not help him.

At last Dame Sybil took a deep breath and sat back in her chair. She set the cup back on its saucer and absently crumbled a piece of scone for the jackdaw before she spoke.

"I see great tragedy in the King's future should he make this marriage. The future of England . . ."

"Is the future of the King—so we must change it," Silver Stick in Waiting said.

Dame Sybil nodded slowly. "I will do what you ask."

He had brought with him all that was necessary to make the spell: a photo of Mrs. Simpson, one of many that had been taken on the disastrous Balkan cruise, and a lock of her hair, obtained years before. Perhaps silver Stick in Waiting had always known it would come to this, deep in his soul, that he must fulfil his oath of loyalty and service by striking a devastating blow to the heart of the man he had sworn to serve. And so, on an October midnight, in a circle of broken stone in the heart of the New Forest, Dame Sybil summoned up the great power to Silver Stick in Waiting's call.

The fire of nine sacred woods burned brightly within the copper cauldron. Handfuls of particular sacred herbs, moistened with oils and powdered with aromatic resins, made a bright column of smoke that coiled heavenward, only to be torn to scraps by the autumn wind.

Silver Stick stood beside the fire, bundled into his cashmere greatcoat and shivering with cold in spite of its protection. Dame Sybil was swathed in her ornate ritual robes and looked warmer than he, though her

head and her arms were bare. Firelight glinted from
the silver crown and cuff she wore, and from the clear
glowing horse-corals of her amber necklace. In a
husky firm voice she chanted the ancient summonses
and petitions, reminding her Hidden Queen of the
pacts and promises sworn between them many life-
times before.

Perhaps nothing will happen, Silver Stick thought to
himself. He could feel the prickle of the Wild Magic
across his skin, but he knew from his studies that many
times a spell or ritual had no visible effect. And if
Dame Sybil could not summon the Lady of the Wood
into manifestation, then Silver Stick in Waiting could
not beg his fatal boon.

"I don't think—" he began.

"Who summons me?"

The sound of that inhuman voice filled him with
atavistic terror, but Silver Stick held his ground. At
the edge of the trees, he could see a shadowy figure.
He had no doubt who it was—and knew, further, that
if he gave in to the terror She inspired within him,
he would become easy prey for Her red-eared, white-
coated hounds; the stag to Her Hunt.

She was far taller than any mortal woman, wearing
a long gray cloak that billowed about Her body like
the smoke from the cauldron. Beneath the cloak he
could see the glint of armor. Her long blonde hair
cascaded down over Her shoulders, and in one hand
She held a spear, its shaft black with blood. Her lips
were red as the rowan, Her skin was leprous pale, and
Her eyes were blue as death: this was Brigantia,
Queen of Britain, Mistress of the Wild Hunt.

"Who summons me?" She asked again.

"I do." Silver Stick's voice shook only slightly. He
stepped forward. Behind him, there was a flare and

sizzle from the flames. Dame Sybil had flung the picture and the lock of hair into them.

"I summon you to right a great wrong, to save our land and our King from a great misfortune. There is a woman who has bewitched him—"

"I see into your heart—and beyond," the goddess observed. "Do you know what you ask of Me?"

"I do," Silver Stick answered, forcing his voice to be firm. "And I know the cost." He was conniving at murder, no matter how lofty the justification, and in doing so he had destroyed something pure and fine within his own heart. But the price, though high, was one he would pay gladly, if only the King could rule the land!

Abruptly the goddess smiled, and Her smile was more frightening than Her severity. "No," She answered. "You do not yet know the cost, Lord Peter. But you will. Before you die, mortal man, you shall know the cost in full. Watch well, and see what you have chosen come to pass."

Between one moment and the next She was gone, and the tension that had filled the air snapped like a faulty bowstring. Silver Stick drew a deep shuddering breath and staggered unsteadily backward. Despite the chill of the autumn night, he was drenched in sweat and trembling, and in that moment the echo of phantom guns filled his ears, and he was back in the trenches, in the blackest days of the War, surrounded by the screams of the maimed and dying. He covered his face with his hands, panting harshly, and at last the shades of the past withdrew. One did not lightly confront those elemental beings whose lives underlay one's own reality. Even to speak with them was harrowing, as he had discovered to his cost.

Dame Sybil poured water into the cauldron, dousing

the flames. The water hissed over the embers, producing a thick puff of herb-scented steam as it quenched them. Afterward, stave in hand, she walked to the edge of the trees.

"Here," Dame Sybil said, lifting up something small and round and black from the ground, "She's left you something."

"What is it?" Silver Stick asked, despite himself. At the moment, he wanted nothing more than to be behind the wheel of his Daimler racing for home. This one night had convinced him that the Great Forces were far better left to go their ways than to be summoned to attend upon their mortal kindred. In that moment he wished he had simply gone and shot the woman himself, but an assassination would have done nearly as much damage as a wedding. But though he would see shadows in every corner for as long as he lived, this night's work would be worth it, did it only accomplish what he prayed that it would.

Dame Sybil inspected the object critically and then held it out to him. "I think it's a mirror. . . ."

At 2:17 on a Tuesday afternoon in late October, Silver Stick in Waiting stared down into the black glass mirror that had been the gift of a goddess, watching as Mrs. Simpson strode down the steps of the courthouse in Ipswitch beside Theodore Goddard, her solicitor. The divorce had been granted. She turned to address some remark to Goddard, and Silver Stick saw her rouged lips stretch into a smile. She was still smiling as she stepped into the street.

The runaway carriage—driverless and empty—came out of nowhere. The foam-flecked white horses which drew it careened blindly forward, pulling the black-suited woman beneath their silver-shod hooves. In a moment it was over. There would be no abdication, no American queen. The King would ascend to the throne in solitude. Silver Stick in Waiting turned away from the glass, drawing a deep breath of relief.

And so he did not see the image that next formed within the glass, of the balcony of Buckingham Palace draped in the red, white, and black banner of a foreign empire, of the slender blond king in a glistening black uniform, saluting a captive populace beneath the sign of the broken cross.

Author's Afterword:

The Boscobel League first appeared in *The Shadow of Albion* (1999), written with Andre Norton. It is set in 1805, and deals with an England that never was, one in which the Stuart line retained the throne after the death of Charles II. "King Hereafter" is set in another, similar, alternate world, where the League and magic exist but history has not yet deviated from the course we know it to have taken. It is 1936, and the House of Hanover—which has lately renamed it-self Windsor—reigns unchallenged over Great Britain and its empire. But the tree of history has many branches. . . .

THE MIDAS SPELL
by *Julie E. Czerneda*

Canadian author and John W. Campbell award finalist Julie E. Czerneda lives in a country cottage with her family. Her novels include *A Thousand Words for Stranger, Beholder's Eye,* and *Ties of Power.* A former biologist, she has written and edited several textbooks, including *No Limits: Developing Scientific Literacy Using Science Fiction.* A hockey and football fan, Julie wrote "The Midas Spell" in tribute to those athletes whose moment of glory is not necessarily in a game.

NO RELIEF IN SIGHT

It was the time of year when floodwaters lapped up trailer parks and spat out dead cows, when rivers shouldered trees, muddy silt, and cars toward the ocean with equal disdain. It was the time in a pro athlete's career when everything was supposed to be easy, irresistible success flowing to a triumphant finale, a confident, assured last season of glory.

The marsh was desert dry.

And the career of all-star running back, Leonard Paul Wiggins, Jr., had turned to dust.

Leonard P., the initial irrevocably tagged to his name by some long-forgotten high school coach, swatted the twenty-or-so mosquitoes enjoying his wide neck, and wondered why the pests hadn't noticed the drought.

He also wondered how the tires of his Porsche could find mud on this excuse for a road, when the tips of the reed grass stretching to the horizon on either side looked dead and scorched, as if the wildfires leading the news had already passed this way. Leonard P. kept a wary eye on a heavy line of cloud to the west, judging it unlikely to be dust, definitely not rain.

The gas gauge snickered again. *Damn car.* "The same to you, Aunt Trish," Leonard P. said cordially, more than ready to head back and confess failure to his wizened and iron-willed relative—if there'd been room to turn around. Over the past hour, the road had dwindled into this one-lane beaten track, humped in the center, its edges descending into the reed grass with a suspicious lack of ditching. *Fine place to look for toads and 'gator eggs,* he told himself, but a lousy one to test the ability of this car to dig itself out of the mire, dry or otherwise. He should have brought the four-wheel, but that would have raised Sheena's eyebrows for sure. His wife of eleven years knew he hated driving the unresponsive brute.

"Sorry, Auntie," Leonard P. continued aloud, preferring the sound of his voice to the slide of withered grass under the almost soundless purr of the engine. No radio stations out here; he'd never cluttered the car with discs. "It's not your fault I'm on this ridiculous quest into the boonies."

The fault lay in him.

Oh, they all knew; they all could see. But they didn't care. So what if his wind was less than it had been? his moves ordinary? his edge gone? Leonard P. was in top shape for his age, the team doctors boasted, as though his finely-tuned body represented their victory over time, not his grueling work ethic, day-after-day, off-season or on. His pain was their gain.

So what if his hand bore no heavy ring? Management decisions, economics, the astrological cycle, pick your broadcaster and get your answer for why his team—*his team*—had gone twice to the Super Bowl and never won. No one doubted he'd done his best, earning MVP in the last attempt; he'd tossed the trophy into a closet, convinced he could have done more.

Leonard P. had tried every remedy known to medicine, then those shunned by medicine; as long as it wouldn't harm him, he'd give it a whirl, or taste, or strap himself into some infernal machine. Nothing had made any difference.

So what if he owned every possible record for his position? Time didn't care any more than the media did. They said he should have retired last year after failing to set a new yards rushing mark. It didn't seem to matter that the record was his to break. They'd grudgingly acknowledged he'd single-handedly kept his team in last week's game until the final seconds, when a missed field goal drove a stake through all their hearts.

How could he retire then?

Leonard P. had lived his dream as a player. He wanted the rest of it, to be on a winning team. If he'd been willing to be dealt—even so, who would want him? Contenders didn't need him; he didn't need anyone else. Leonard P. had already beaten the odds and the calendar, playing his best at an age when most players had been out to pasture long enough to grow a gut and lose their hair. It was beyond imagining he had another MVP season in him. But this was the year—his last chance. This team could still do it, if he could.

"All the hoops," Leonard P. announced morosely

to the world of wasted brown and harsh blue. "You'd think something would have worked."

There was something ahead. *At last.* Involuntarily, Leonard P. lifted his foot from its feather touch on the accelerator, feeling the car slow to a bumpy, slippery crawl. Instead of feeling overjoyed at finally finding a sign of humanity in this sleeping lifelessness, he stared at the road's end and shivered. *Where had Aunt Trish sent him?*

She'd patted his face, her gnarled hands cool and dry where their twists let them contact his skin. Her pale, rheumy eyes were as sharp as they'd ever been— cutting into his soul as easily as they had twenty-five years ago, when he'd come, cocksure and full of himself, to board with her during his first time away from home. The tiny old lady had been more than a match for him, despite his giant frame and equally inflated ego. Aunt Trish set him straight, taught him to accept his gifts for what they were and be grateful, to put back into the school and community that raised him, every bit of his time and soul he could. She'd never guided him wrong.

"Until now," Leonard P. grumbled out loud, letting the car sigh to a dead stop. Triumphant battalions of mosquitoes whined in through the open windows— he'd shut off the air conditioning once the gas tank held more air than fuel. Heat never bothered him anyway. Aunt Trish had grudgingly given him this address—*a joke, no way the postal service came out here*—her very reluctance a sign this might be his only chance. He'd refused her stern advice: to be satisfied, to do his best for the remainder of the season, then retire. She'd assumed he'd accept the assistant coaching job at his old alma mater, understanding what Leonard P. hadn't admitted to himself. Yet the moment she'd spoken, he'd known he would never sit in front of a camera with former rivals, talking about the work of other players until his own place in the game sank into oblivion.

He'd dropped to his knees then, still towering over her, and engulfed those butterfly hands in his, able to show this woman the anguish he'd hidden so successfully from everyone else, including his own wife and daughter. *The playoffs. Wild card. A team victory.* He'd sobbed helplessly about things he knew Aunt Trish considered meaningless, unable to stop.

And because she did believe his torment to be real, if incomprehensible, and took pity on him, Leonard P. sat in his Porsche and stared at a perfectly charming English cottage, in the midst of a dying swamp.

EXPERTS PUZZLED; SUSPECT SUNSPOTS

Blood-red geraniums guarded spikes of foxglove; dark-eyed daisies watched the thyme as it swallowed his footsteps in fragrance. Even the air of the walkway to the front door felt—wary. Normally, Leonard P. was a man devoid of fantasy, contending with enough real demons on the playing field. Here, having finally climbed out of his car to approach the cottage, he found himself ready to believe almost anything.

It didn't help his imagination that the hungry mosquitoes abandoned their pursuit when his foot touched the edge of the garden or that the air Leonard P. drew into his lungs more deeply than usual was suddenly not only perfumed, but cool and moist.

"Anybody home?" he called, stopping short of making a fist to knock on the door—this was no time to demonstrate the power of a hand that could swallow a football. Mind you, it was a sturdy-looking door—

solid oak, perhaps, nothing like that hollow sham of a thing he'd put his shoulder through quite by accident at his mother-in-law's last party. He'd never live that one down, not when Sheena's brother persisted in cautioning everyone to take cover whenever Leonard P. came looking for a beer.

A beer would be great. Leonard P. ran his tongue over cracked, dry lips, proof he'd been in the drought, despite the mist weaving phantom tendrils around his knees. *Six might be better, given he could avoid tomorrow's practice.*

The door opened, then stuck fast until a grumble and jerk from inside convinced it to move. Leonard P. blinked, unsure what he'd expected and quite certain it wasn't this stoop-shouldered man with blood-shot brown eyes squinting up from behind thick lenses, wearing a worn yet elegant velvet jacket. Burgundy, with gold trim. The man's legs protruded like fuzz-coated twigs beneath a yellow-green kilt complete with rabbit-hide pouch. Instead of thick socks, the kilt-wearer's legs were bare. His feet were encased in very large, pink, pig-nosed slippers.

Any other day, any other place, Leonard P. would have dismissed the man as a nutcase, like the grotesquely-outfitted fans who somehow could afford those great center field seats. But he met the magnified gaze within the lenses with the disturbing conviction this man dressed as he chose because the opinion of humanity was simply irrelevant.

"Well? What did you come for? What do you need?" The man's questions were sharp but not discouraging; rather, they were businesslike, as if merely finding this place meant any visitor here had sufficient purpose to be interesting.

"My great-aunt—Mrs. Patricia Wiggins—told me

you could help—" The improbable condensation on
the leaves nodding above the doorway was encouragement to speak the bitter truth. "I need my edge back,"
he said flatly. "I need my team to win."

"That's two," the man harrumphed. "It doesn't
work that way. There can be only one need."

Leonard P. put his well-muscled shoulder to the
closing door, surprised when this had no effect whatso-
ever. "I have only one," he shouted in desperation
through the diminishing crack. "I need my edge back.
The team will win if I've got it!"

The door stopped moving, slowly opened wider.
The man peered over the top of his glasses, as if really
looking at Leonard P. for the first time. "You're that
good?" he asked mildly.

"I was," Leonard P. said, feeling as though every
dew-drenched plant around him leaned forward to listen, as though he had just opened up his soul to something truly able to judge it. "I need to be again."

SPARTANS FACE ELIMINATION

The man introduced himself only as the Proprietor, as
though he'd abandoned the rest—names, titles, what
they represented in family and alliances—long ago. He
led Leonard P. through an umbrella-filled foyer into
a room that appeared to fill the entire first floor of
the cottage. Windows looked out on every side, as if
spying on the flowerbeds surrounding the building like
a moat of bruised purple and tiger's eye gold. The
mist slithered against the thick panes, pressing into
droplets here and there. Leonard P. didn't know why
he felt safer indoors than out, but he breathed a sigh
of relief as he settled his bulk with habitual caution
onto a piece of tapestried furniture his great-aunt

would call a divan and he viewed as unlikely to survive any fidgeting on his part.

The Proprietor moved across the floor, his slippers making a soft scuffing sound on the wood planking. The sound reminded Leonard P. of his mother, up at the crack of dawn to be sure her boys had a hot breakfast. For no reason, he shivered. His host sat himself behind a large carved desk, flattening his long-fingered hands on its surface; that surface was bare of any objects, yet stained and charred as if, for some reason, the Proprietor routinely barbecued indoors.

"You need this edge of yours back," the odd man said, with a faintly impatient air. "Who can give it to you?"

Leonard P. frowned. "I thought you—"

The Proprietor silenced him with one raised finger. "Answer my questions or don't waste my time, Mr. Wiggins. When you play this sport of yours—what inspires that extra effort, this edge you so desire?"

Inspiration? Leonard P., experienced with humoring charlatans of many kinds, gave this some thought. Intuitively, he avoided the glib answers, the sports' sap he'd learned satisfied the craving for quotable sound bites. "A good crowd," he said slowly. "The kind who believes I can do anything, that hangs on my every move out there as though any moment might be special. I could always dig a little deeper for them." *The kind of crowd,* he added truthfully to himself, *I rarely deserve these days.*

A glint of light off the lenses, or deep within the eyes distorted through them. "Excellent. Excellent. A large diffuse source is always best. I hate working in particulars. It's a recipe for failure. Absolutely. The bigger the better—well . . ." For some reason, the proprietor looked over his shoulder at his lush garden, leaves now bent under an impossible rain. "Well, usually."

"So, the Midas Spell it is—" he continued in a satisfied voice, attention back on Leonard P. and a confident smile on his lean face. Most of his teeth were crooked, *which was,* Leonard P. thought distractedly as he ran a tongue over the smoothness of his own, *one advantage of having your own knocked out and replaced.*

"Spell," Leonard P. repeated, the bizarre hope he'd begun to feel turning to ash. "As in magic? You've got to be kidding—"

A scornful flash from the glasses as the Proprietor straightened proudly. "Spells are the only thing I do, young man. Patricia Wiggins sent you; what else did you expect? There is no 'kidding' involved. If I accept you as a client, you must take the consequences personally. I don't supply any type of coverage."

In disgust, Leonard P. tallied up the wasted afternoon he could have spent at his daughter's baseball game, the bites and taste of dust, the condition of his beautiful car. Then he matched it against the ending of his dream and shrugged.

The light in his eyes was that of final, ultimate desperation.

Fourth down and long. No time on the clock.

"Cast your spell."

FAITHFUL WONDER: IS THERE ANY HOPE?

"Where have you been? Don't try telling me it was at Tracy's game," Charlie hissed, hurrying Leonard P. down the slanting corridor to the dressing room. The concrete floor rang with the urgent staccato of his cleats. The rest of the team must be out on the field, warming up. "Man, the coach will go ballistic."

What else was new? Leonard P. thought, bone weary and definitely in no shape for a practice. He'd been up half the night with that lunatic. As if that weren't enough, he'd had to walk out of the marsh, finally hitching a ride to the stadium—his Porsche having been the Proprietor's fee. Leonard P. hadn't argued, overwhelmingly grateful to be away from that place and knowing the gas tank was empty.

What had happened? The details were oddly vague. He remembered a flame impressively, if hazardously, produced on top of the Proprietor's desk. Funny how he hadn't seen any matches. Or smoke, for that matter. He'd been told to cup his hands above it—feeling sufficient heat to prove the fire's existence, if not explain it—then found himself accepting a damp chill handful of torn leaves and ruined petals. Then, foggiest of all, an image of the Proprietor's face coming unpleasantly close to his own, and the feel of ice-cold fingers wrapping around his like clamps. There had been a flash of light . . . guttural words . . .

. . . *Nothing but some tricks,* Leonard P. decided, following Charlie toward the team dressing room. *What was he going to tell Sheena about the car?* He'd missed supper and breakfast; his stomach had caved in to his spine from the feel of it. The trainers kept rocket juice on ice; that would have to do. Leonard P.'s mouth was so dry the mere thought helped push his heavy legs faster. *Spells and magic.* As well expect an accurate weather forecast, for hadn't the mist and rain he'd found so uncanny at the cottage extended right to the stadium—was state-wide, in fact, ending the drought with a suddenness the forecasters scrambled to explain and the trucker who'd given him a lift called a miracle.

"Hey, clear out!" Charlie moved in front of him, called sternly to the teens milling in front of the locker room door. "You kids know you aren't allowed down here—"

"It's okay, Charlie," Leonard P. found energy somewhere, surprising himself, and smiled at the fans. Needing no more encouragement, they surged forward, waving pens and autograph books at him, careful to edge past an obviously disapproving Charles "The Ripper" Dodge with a polite duck of their heads. In spite of Charlie's impatience, Leonard P. knew this was as much what the team asked of him as any athletics on the field. And unlike some, he never tired of answering the same shy questions again and again, never let exhaustion or mood hinder the warm smile he knew had become as famous as his records. Aunt Trish had made sure he understood these things.

At the end, he shook their hands, mindful as always not to squeeze the small fingers or to accept the challenge of a young man's too-tight grip. The group walked slowly to the exit, heads together as they compared treasures.

"I'd like to make some of the practice, Mr. All Star," Charlie said without rancor, but with a slightly desperate look in his eye. Leonard P. being late would be forgiven; his own standing with the coach was much less secure. "It could be the last one, y'know. Not that I'm say'n—"

"Go ahead," Leonard P. told his friend, feeling better by the moment. The glow of meeting his fans like this acted like a tonic, cheering him immensely even if it couldn't improve anything else about his life. "Tell the coach I had car trouble. I'll be out in a few minutes."

Maybe a decent workout could burn away the frustrated memory of being taken for a fool on top of everything else.

WHAT'S UP WITH WIGGINS?

What Leonard P. hadn't expected, making him quietly thoughtful during supper and into the night, was how he'd performed during that practice. Given what he'd done to himself the preceding day and night, he should have been sluggish at best. Instead, he'd found his mind and body back in exquisite harmony, feet moving with the agile speed he remembered from years past. Every play they'd run with him had been just that—play. Had any of the defense so much as touched him? They might have been standing still. There'd been the surprising slap on the shoulder pad from the coach, the lately unfamiliar but cheery profanity of the trainers as they rewarded his body with massage and towel. It was like the old days. The glory days.

What was different?

For an instant, the thought crossed his mind: *Had the old fraud's spell actually worked?*

A whisper in his ear: "Penny for them."

Leonard P. started, dismissing the errant thought immediately as though it could utter itself and really land him in trouble. "What?"

"You've been a bit—preoccupied?" Sheena's arms slipped cool and soft around his neck as she nestled her cheek against her ear. It gave her voice a pleasant gravelly buzz. "Is it about last night?"

Since "last night" had included Leonard P.'s first

substantial lie to his wife—mainly from the conviction
he wouldn't want to be the Proprietor when Sheena
descended on him to retrieve Leonard P.'s car, doubtless tearing strips from the peculiar recluse in the process, spells or no spells—he could only nod.

"Did they say how long the repairs might take?"

Leonard P. closed his eyes and shook his head.
"Weeks," he ventured, hoping to postpone the inevitable until the end of the season, when the prospect
of time together usually outweighed any of his faults.

For quite suddenly—and for no reason he dared
name—Leonard P. was convinced there would be
more than one game in his future.

WIGGINS RAINMAKER AS SPARTANS BREAK DROUGHT

The headlines said it all. The reaction of the fans to
the Spartans' Monday night wild card victory had been
as heartfelt and passionate as any by farmers watching
their crops come back to life as the overdue rain continued. Leonard P.'s agent, Stan Malone, kept a copy
of the *Daily Tribune*'s front page in the pocket of his
suit, ready to flash in an instant if any one doubted
his boy's return to form.

The coaching staff, knowing a miracle when they
saw one, insisted on the team moving into a hotel to
keep both delighted family and salivating media at
bay. There was a curious electricity to that night's
team briefing, an unusual brightness in the eyes which
flickered between Leonard P. and the coach.

Leonard P. listened and obeyed without comment.
He rubbed one wrist thoughtfully, expecting soreness
from the most spectacular of the many mid-field colli-
sions from the game and not finding it. His body felt—

perfect. Somehow he knew he could jump up, here and now, and play another half. The rest of the team sagged in their chairs, leaning this way or that as they favored their damaged parts and sore muscles.

Not sure what to make of that, or his own performance, Leonard P. focused grimly on what he did understand. Coach said it and he unconsciously nodded with each word. Three more wins to reach the Super Bowl.

No one asked what had to be on all their minds.

Could he do it again?

DOWNPOUR DOESN'T DAMPEN SPARTAN FANS

"So?" Charlie began breathlessly, face full of anticipation.

"So?" Leonard P. repeated, when this appeared to be the only word coming.

Charlie had knocked softly at his door an hour after curfew—a rookie play the big nose tackle usually knew better than to try, especially the night before a big game. But he'd insisted Leonard P. let him in, that it was important.

"So," Charlie went on, "what are you using, Leonard P.? Must be something special, if the drug tests aren't finding any. They were at you after both wins."

Leonard P. scowled, an expression lesser, or wiser men knew better than to discount. The extra tests were sore points in an otherwise splendid two weeks. "You know I'm not a user. Coach knows. I've told you, Charlie. My edge's back. That's all."

It was heartbreaking watching the excitement fade from Charlie's face, to be replaced with something older and darker. "Man, don't you lie to me. We've been friends too long."

Leonard P. swallowed the angry words rushing up his throat. Charlie was almost his age; playing at the top of his game took an extra fifteen hours a week and painkillers before each workout. "If I knew what was happening, Charlie—if I thought it was something I could pass around to help you, to help the rest of the team—don't you believe I would?"

There was doubt in Charlie's eyes, then it faded to honest embarrassment. "M'sorry," he mumbled, heading for the door. "You can see how it looks, Leonard P. It's strange. You've been playing like magic."

"What did you say?"

Charlie looked puzzled, "I said it's been strange—"

"Not that."

Charlie's teeth showed in a sudden grin. "I said you've been playing like magic. Maybe that's it, right, Leonard P.? You've found yourself a magic spell to bring back your edge, is that it?" He began laughing, then cupped his hands over his mouth in mock-alarm. Shoulders heaving with the effort to keep safely quiet, Charlie let himself out the door and closed it ever-so-softly behind him.

Was it possible?

Leonard P. stood up, walked over to the door, and flipped the night lock closed. He found himself staring at his hand, the back of it still bearing a line of glue from the bandages hastily applied over a cut during this afternoon's practice. There was no mark on his skin. "If this is magic," Leonard P. whispered to himself, tasting the idea, "then how does it work? What is it doing?" He'd loved tales of witchcraft and magic as a child, still devoured high fantasy novels during the long road trips. None of it had encouraged him to believe in magic. Now, however, what he read came back to chill his heart. "What does it cost?" he breathed, raising his hand closer to his eyes as though it held some dreadful answer.

The Proprietor had said he wasn't responsible for the consequences. He had demanded to know Leonard P.'s one true need. He had cast a spell.

"The Midas Spell," Leonard P. reminded himself, shivering despite the warmth of the hotel room. He forced himself to climb back into bed, turning out the bedside lamp he'd put on when Charlie had awakened him. The ability to fall asleep quickly in strange surroundings was one of many side effects of his career.

At the moment, sleep was the farthest thing from Leonard P.'s mind. During the past weeks he'd done his best to forget that humiliating night and the loss of his car. Now he fought to remember every detail, every word. *If it was possible . . . what had he done?*

Midas. The king who bargained for the magical ability to turn objects into gold at a touch.

Lying in the dark, Leonard P. could almost smell the burning wood, the damp wet fragrance as the leaves in his hand warmed, then smoked. The words . . . they floated through his thoughts, incomprehensible.

His hand. That was important. Leonard P. turned the light back on, sat up, and stared at his hands. They looked unchanged. Feeling a fool, he reached out and touched the bedside table, the lamp, even put a finger to the bulb that he snatched back and put into his mouth to ease the pain.

Nothing magical here. Leonard P. fluffed his pillows and threw himself back down, stretching his legs out until remembering at the last minute that a king-sized bed was not his custom-made one and he'd better not stretch all the way if he wanted tucked-in sheets. *There's no such thing as magic,* he comforted himself, curling in a lonely ball. But, just in case, he was going to call Aunt Trish after tomorrow's game.

SPARTAN DREAM LOOKING SOLID

"Sell-out crowd," Charlie shouted, reaching out to tug Leonard P.'s shoulder pad into place. The clatter of the players' cleats in the tunnel was drowned by the oceanlike roaring of the crowd ahead. Beer and popcorn competed with the heady smell of wet grass.

"Semifinals usually are," Leonard P. observed dryly. They'd been here before; he, for one, wasn't going to let the crowd's anticipation or his own get in the way of the job. He gave Charlie a warning shot in the arm. "Get a grip. It's going to be a long afternoon."

The other man bounced lightly away, a substantial feat for someone who had about a hundred pounds on Leonard P. "It's going to be a great afternoon, Leonard P. You're the magic man, remember?"

The offensive line, ready to head out before him, overheard. Leonard P. gritted his teeth and forced a smile at the predictable chant: "Magic Man . . . Magic Man."

They were in sight of the rain-drenched field, waiting in the shadows for the official team introductions. His nostrils flared as he felt the inevitable and welcome rush of adrenaline flooding through his body like some beast stirring within. *Would it be enough?* he doubted abruptly. *Were the last two games flukes?*

"Leonard P.! Leonard P.!" This chant was higher-pitched than most, and nearer, carrying easily through the din. He felt his smile soften and warm, unsure until now if they'd allow this request of his—the organizers of playoff games made their own rules, it seemed, and tradition didn't always count.

But here they were, lined up alongside the runway into the field, a group of umbrella-laden kids who had only one claim to fame: they played football for fun. Leonard P. headed up to the first, starry-eyed child, likely about his daughter's age, and accepted the offered handshake as the honor it was.

He went along the row, taking care to touch each hand, whether a high-five or a tight grip. The crowd screamed its approval; Leonard P. could care less. He had been one of these young players in their well-patched jerseys; this meeting was only fitting. At the end, just as the loudspeaker rang with his name, he paused and turned to wave one last time.

It wasn't unusual for an overwhelmed fan to faint. It wasn't even unusual, given the heat and humidity, to have two or three grow dizzy or weak.

He'd never seen thirty healthy kids suddenly reduced to leaning on one another. He started back.

"C'mon, Leonard P.!" Charlie had one of his arms. Tom Smithers had the other. Both made it look as though they were all good buddies, while gripping tightly enough to ensure Leonard P. did move where they urged him.

Leonard P. shook them off easily, too easily. Shocked, he felt the restive power surging up inside him, waiting to explode on the field. It was like—magic.

"Those kids—"

"They'll be fine," Tom said. "Must have been a hell of a bus trip down. Look, they're all smiling—get moving before they think something's wrong, will you?"

He craned his head for another worried glance at

his small fans. Several waved at him as they were helped from the field.

"Yeah, c'mon, Magic Man. We've got a game to win."

Magic Man. The words settled like rain-slicked stones around his heart as Leonard P. stared down at his now-trembling hands. *Was this the Midas Spell at work? Had it made him—steal—what he needed from those children?* Bile rose in his throat and he retched.

Sympathetic, if heavy, hands clapped him on the back. This much was familiar stuff to the others on the team. Many of them had the dry heaves before career games like this—and all knew the pressure on Leonard P.'s broad shoulders.

"Let's play some football," said the one voice able to penetrate Leonard P.'s misery. He looked up at his coach and nodded, mute.

WIGGINS A WONDER! SPARTANS CAN CLINCH RIDE TO SUPER BOWL!

Leonard P. rocked back and forth, glaring at the phone, willing it to ring. He'd already torn off the tensor bandages the trainers had wrapped around his ankle, tossing them to droop uselessly over the TV. *He felt,* he told himself savagely, *fine.*

His need must have grown like some over-watered and -manured garden. The more he'd wanted to play his best, the more he'd unconsciously reached out to those who cared, to touch—and take.

Oh, he'd played his best, all right. The Spartans won the game. He'd broken his rushing record. And only he knew at what cost. Was the children's exhaustion easier to bear with the gift of the signed game-winning ball for their team? Would they forgive him if they knew?

Leonard P. was afraid they would. "Call me back, Aunt Trish," he pleaded to the silent phone. "Hurry."

Would Sheena?

He buried his head in his hands, endlessly replaying what had happened after the game. Confident of victory, the coach had surprised the team by flying in close family and hiding them in the dressing room to share the players' joy. Sheena had hurried to his side, so proud, so happy. He'd cupped her dear face gently in his hands, overcome by his own emotion, only to watch helplessly as she collapsed in front of him.

In the confusion, voices had overlapped: "It's okay, Leonard P." "Put her by the door, where it's cool." "Likely the heat—in her condition—"

No one had been surprised he didn't know Sheena was pregnant. It was perfectly reasonable for a player's wife to save distracting news for the post-season. Other, worse, things had waited: his parents' divorce, news of his brother's cancer—sometimes it felt as though the world waited with bated breath until the team disbanded. Some years, Leonard P. had been afraid to walk out of the stadium at season's end.

Even though Sheena had instantly recovered, blushing prettily about her now-revealed secret, he'd done his best to keep away from all the well-wishers in the room, refusing any touch—even that of the trainers, who put it down to nerves. The Magic Man could be forgiven anything.

Ring, damn it.

Leonard P. could feel his edge slipping away, a normal exhaustion settling deep within his bones. He shuddered with relief, tears squeezing out from beneath his tightly shut eyes.

Behind his lids lay the darkest vision of all: the Midas Spell at work. A cheerful cry had startled him:

"Daddy!" His daughter had leaped into his arms before he could avoid her. In utter horror, Leonard P. had watched the glow of her smile dim, the luster of her eyes fade, all as the cursed vitality came flooding through his body.

He had thrust Tracy into Charlie's arms, turned and fled through the crowded room as if recovering a broken play on the field. He hadn't stopped until he'd locked himself in his hotel room.

Waiting for the only help he could imagine.

SUPER BOWL LOOMS: ARE SPARTANS SET?

Leonard P. wore thick gloves, though he suspected it would make no difference. The rain was a light drizzle, not much, but the constantly dull skies were beginning to elicit comments. Flood risk had supplanted fire warnings on the radio, as broadcasters enthusiastically looked for the doom in any weather change.

Leonard P. knew his great-aunt's habits and found her, as expected, dozing in the main hall outside the cafeteria. There was no trouble with the nursing home. His great-aunt had the staff thoroughly cowed; more importantly, the staff knew and trusted Leonard P.'s devotion to her. No one even questioned his asking for help lifting her into the passenger seat, though he usually whisked her up in his arms.

"I knew you'd bring the truck," Aunt Trish said with distinct satisfaction; she was very fond of big machines, especially gaudy ones like Sheena's beast.

He climbed in his side and started to drive. "Your friend took my Porsche."

"In payment," she corrected, her hands fluttering in her lap as though the joy of a ride out was too much for the reason to quell it. "And he's no friend of mine, Leonard, merely an acquaintance."

"What did your acquaintance do to me?" Leonard P. said in a low voice, gripping the steering wheel so firmly the material began to flex.

"He sold you what you thought you needed most."

Leonard P. couldn't help glancing at her, then quickly looked back as a car cut in front and he had to adjust his speed. "That's not true. He turned me into some kind of monster."

"I had expected a bit more—finesse—in the matter," she said, which Leonard P. took for tacit agreement. There was a hum as Aunt Trish adjusted the seat hydraulics, moving herself up and forward, then down and back. She considered this the most civil technology to come along since the remote control, and found the choices endlessly fascinating. It drove Sheena crazy to have her in the truck. "Don't worry," Aunt Trish continued in her dry, firm voice.

"Don't—" Leonard P.'s voice strangled on the word.

"Now, dear. Can we take the Interstate? I do so enjoy the view from this baby when we go over the skyway."

WIGGINS BREAKS CURFEW; COACH NO COMMENT

The reed grass was verdant again, vigorously intent on reclaiming what little road remained. In places, its tips bent together overhead, catching in the roof rack and snapping off with a juicy sound. The muscles on Leonard P.'s arms stood out as he fought the wheel. He had to maintain a good speed to keep the tires from settling into the mud, making for a rough ride despite the four-wheel drive. He would have worried about his passenger if Aunt Trish hadn't been laughing at every jar and slide, insisting on keeping the windows open so the flying mud was now decorating the back seat. *It was,* he admitted, *rather fun.*

Until the truck bounced up once, seeming to burst through some invisible barrier, before landing with a harder-than-usual thud.

Leonard P. braked, then shut off the now-pointless windshield wipers before they smeared bug guts and mud into an impenetrable film.

He turned off the engine, got out, and walked around the front of the truck to help his aunt, careful to offer only his elbow.

The cottage still stood. The flagstones meandered their way from their feet to the door as before. His Porsche sat forlornly to one side, as if he'd just parked it for the night.

Everything else had changed.

The sky was as gray as anywhere they'd traveled today, but the air was searingly hot and dry. Leonard P. found himself sweating, but the sweat didn't evaporate to cool his skin, instead collecting in runnels to soak into his shirt. The ground beneath their feet was cracked and hard as stone. Ahead, the gardens looked deceptively alive, bands of colour encircling the cottage as though holding it under siege. But when Leonard P. reached down to brush his fingers against the nearest bloom, it toppled from its stem. The leaves below were coated in dust and withered along their edges.

"Nincompoop," Aunt Trish pronounced with a dignified snort. "The man's a nincompoop. I regret recommending his services, Leonard."

She wrapped both arms around Leonard P.'s and

they walked slowly to the door. There was no scent to the air; only a burned grass taste. *No mosquitoes,* he noticed.

The door opened the moment they approached, the Proprietor leaning out with every appearance of surprised delight. "Madame Wiggins! It's an honor, ma'am. I—"

"Stow it, Oscar," Aunt Trish said in her feathery voice. "Get out of our way and brew some tea. Now. You've got some work to do."

Leonard P. felt a smile coming and tactfully tucked it within a cough.

The Proprietor blustered and fussed, but hurried to make the tea. Leonard P. looked down at the top of Aunt Trish's scantily-haired head and shook his own. *I'm not going to ask,* he decided, although her familiarity with spells and their casters could explain how her boarding house had withstood the antics of dozens of football players over the decades.

In record time, his aunt was enthroned on the divan, a delicate three-legged table within easy reach supporting a china teacup and saucer. There was also a fluorescent green tray of otherwise elegant cucumber sandwiches. Leonard P. loomed beside his aunt, attempting not to glower at the Proprietor since the man was obviously anxious enough. The view through the windows might be one reason. If ever a garden was reproaching its owner for neglect, that garden rustled angrily outside.

"So, Madame Wiggins," the Proprietor began, looking slightly more at ease once he'd sat behind his imposing desk. "What brings you here?"

"Take your spell off me," Leonard P. growled. "Now!"

Before the man could respond, Aunt Trish tsked-

tsked, "Leonard. Let me handle this, dear." Her gnarled hands fumbled a bit as they handled the cup. Leonard P. ached to help, but knew better. She managed.

"We had an arrangement, ma'am. Hasn't he told you? I'm not responsible—"

"Competence was expected," Aunt Trish said very calmly.

A spark of light from the thick lenses as the Proprietor winced slightly. "The Midas Spell doesn't get taken off," he protested in a faint voice, looking at Leonard P. as if for support. "It has to be used. That's its nature."

"I don't want to use it." Leonard P.'s nostrils flared. "I won't use it!" he had a sudden inspiration: "If it has to be used by someone, then I'll give it to you, Aunt."

"Whatever for, Leonard?"

He sensed disapproval, but went down on one knee beside the table so he could look into her face. "Couldn't this spell give you health, maybe your youth back? This will give it to her, won't it?" this last to the Proprietor, who nodded warily.

"Why?" she asked, her hand stroking his cheek, her pale eyes shining a bit more than usual. "What would I want with this old me in a young body?"

"I don't want to lose you. I want you here when Tracy goes to high school. I want you to see the new baby—"

"And whose life should I rob to stay?" she answered gently. "No, Leonard. There are good reasons why this spell, poor as it is, belongs to those who can't act on their own." Her lips pursed in a smile, the soft wrinkles of her face curving into pure mischief. "Anyway, all this rain has been murder on my arthritis."

Leonard P. blinked, surprised by this last.

The Proprietor raised his long hands in alarm. "But, Madame Wiggins—"

"This is your fault, Oscar Stedman. You're the one who conjured the damn thing in the first place—all so you could have a garden that would tend itself, that could take what it needed. Look where that got you!"

"I'm working on an alternative. There are mentions in Gilford's text—"

"Once a spell is cast, it can't be undone. Not while the caster continues to exist, that is—" There was something so completely implacable in the look Aunt Trish gave the Proprietor it sent a flash of cold down Leonard P.'s spine. Not for the first time, he was glad he'd decided to love the tiny old woman rather than fight with her.

The Proprietor saw it, too.

"Stand over there," he ordered Leonard P., with a defeated little sigh.

"If it makes you feel any better, Oscar," Aunt Trish said primly, "I'm sure Leonard will let you keep that horrible excuse for an automobile. He has a much nicer one outside."

After that, the details were vague again, as though something about the summoning and moving of things magical cloaked themselves in mystery by their nature. Leonard P. tried to focus, but all he truly took with him in memory was the sound of a teacup against its saucer and the smell of chamomile tea. And one last, very satisfying image of the Proprietor staring worriedly out his windows as mist patted the panes with greedy interest.

"Since you've given away my Porsche, Aunt Trish," he ventured afterward, as he lifted her into the passenger seat of the truck, hurrying to avoid what promised to be a sudden downpour, "any suggestions on how to explain that to Sheena—or the insurance company?"

"You are always signing things for fans," she offered, pausing as he clipped her seatbelt closed. "Thank you, dear. Tell her you gave the silly car to one."

He shook his head ruefully. Still, looking like an idiot was coming out lightly from this. "Think we'll win without the spell?" he asked, climbing in to the driver's seat and turning on the engine. The wipers struggled to clear the baked-on soil and bug bits.

Aunt Trish reached over and put her hand on his. "I think you did, Leonard," she said, the pride in her voice worth more to him at that moment than all the hardware in the world.

When Leonard P. looked back, the flowers were nodding under the first heavy drops of rain, dried petals falling to the ground in echo, dust running in brown channels from every leaf.

CAMP OPENS; HOPEFULS READY

"Man, he's tough."

"Sure he is," Wilmont Tucker Jones answered in a whisper. There wasn't supposed to be any chat during the post-practice, but the two rookies were taking advantage of the dressing down being given to the now-humbled defensive core. They'd not only failed to execute their last play— they'd failed to stop the assistant coach from running right through them with the ball. An old man, no less! "He's tough. That's why I'm here—to learn from the best."

"Let's hope you don't get cut in the next round, then, hot shot," his teammate shot back. "Or you'll be learning how to pump gas back home."

"Hey, you!"

Wilmont quivered. The assistant coach was talking to him. He tried to look attentive and fresh, not about to drop from a workout ten times harder than anything from high school. This was his dream, suddenly in the hands of a man who had lived it.

"What's your name?"

"W-wilmont Tucker Jones, Coach Wiggins."

That smile was as famous as the records. "Welcome to the team, Wilmont. Report tomorrow." The assistant coach began walking away, then turned to gaze back where Wilmont stood, paralyzed with joy. "Mind if I call you Willy T.?"

FORECASTERS STYMIED BY FAIR WEATHER

It was the time of year when marshes seethed with life and rivers carried secrets in their murmuring depths. It was the time in a pro athlete's career when achievements sorted themselves into crystal-shards of memory, to be shared or hoarded; decisions made to give back or simply fade away.

The marsh was lush and green.

And the career of all-star running back, Leonard Paul Wiggins, Jr., had gently turned to gold.

EMBRACING THE MYSTERY
by *Charles de Lint*

Charles de Lint is a full-time writer and musician who presently makes his home in Ottawa, Ontario, Canada, with his wife MaryAnn Harris, an artist and musician. His most recent books are *Somewhere to Be Flying*, *Jack of Kinrowan*, and his single author collection entitled *Moonlight and Vines*. For more information on his work, visit his Web site at <www.cyberus.ca/~cdl>.

I heard a dog speak once.

It was Christmas Eve, 1993. His name was Fritzie, a gangly, wirehaired, long-legged mutt that I inherited when my best friend Gina drowned herself. There's a legend that for one hour after midnight on Christmas Eve, animals were given voices so that they could praise the baby Jesus. But Fritzie wasn't praising anybody that night. Instead, we talked about how much we missed Gina.

This isn't something I imagined, though I can understand your thinking so. Truth is, I'm the last person to believe anything improbable, even given such an experience. I don't care what anyone says. One miracle doesn't make fairy tales and that weird world you can only find in supermarket tabloids suddenly real, though you wouldn't know it from some of my friends.

But I'm getting ahead of myself.

While I heard a dog speak, it was only that one time. Fritzie never spoke to me again. Not all through that year, not the next Christmas Eve when the bells struck midnight, nor on any Christmas Eve after that. Though it's funny. Right now he's looking at me as I write this—with that big, sad-eyed gaze dogs do so well—and it's like he knows I'm writing about him. Still, that's only my anthropomorphizing him.

It's not that I don't think he has feelings. I know he does. He just doesn't talk, except for that one time, and I don't know what that was. A miracle, I suppose. Or a dream that I want to have been real because right then, that night, I really needed to talk to someone who'd been as close to Gina as I'd been, and there was no one else except for Fritzie.

I don't know.

What I do know is that animals don't talk. Hey-diddle-diddle, dishes and spoons can't run. Neither Elvis nor Kurt Cobain will be gigging again any time soon. Sorry.

"Okay," Jilly says, holding up a finger to get everyone's attention. "Question: If you were the eighth dwarf, what would your name be?"

"Lazy," Sophie says.

Wendy smiles. "As if. I'd be Willy," she adds to a general round of laughter.

"What, what?" she asks.

"You don't even have one," Sophie says. "Not unless you've been keeping the operation from us."

"Oh, please. I was referring to Shakespeare, as in poet, writer—you know, your general, all-purpose scribe."

"What about you, Sue?" Jilly asks.

"Tired," I say.

Jilly shakes her head. "Too close to Sleepy. Try again."

"What would yours be?" I ask instead.

"Oh, that's easy," Wendy puts in before Jilly can answer. "She'd be Silly."

Jilly attempts a stern expression while muttering, "Bloody poets," but she can't hold it.

"I think I'd have preferred Saucy," she says.

"Or Spacy," Sophie offers.

"Would it work the same for Spice Girls?" Wendy asks.

"Then I'd definitely want to be Saucy Spice," Jilly tells us.

We're sitting in The Yo-Man club, waiting for the band to come on stage, two artists, a poet, and a city architect who spends more time in meetings than at her drawing board: Jilly and Sophie, Wendy, and me. They're the ones who draw inspiration out of thin air to make their art, but I think of them as the three muses, *my* three muses, because they remind me of the world I'm not a part of. They ground me, connect me to the art I can't seem to release from the end of my own pencils and brushes anymore.

Sometimes they're like fairy tale presences in my life, moving to a hickory-dickory-dock soundtrack, three blind mice that can see more clearly than I ever can. They're the wise women who live in those cottages deep in fairy woods with herbs drying from the rafters and dark-eyed birds perched in the corners. Three small, tangle-haired women with the knowledge of some otherworld in their eyes and enchantment in their fingers. It's all so real for them. Wendy collects fairy tales. Jilly believes in fairy tales. And Sophie . . . well, Sophie pretty much *is* a fairy tale.

Like I said, I don't really believe in fairy tales or the magical things that can happen in them, except for that one time, when Fritzie spoke. But I find my-

self thinking about Gina more and more these days,
and now I really want to hear Fritzie's voice again. I
want him to remind me of things I might have forgotten, because while I can't let go of Gina, I'm losing
her all the same. I'm losing the details of who she
was. I'm shedding them like snake skins until one day
all I'm going to have left of her is the fact that she
drowned herself.

Fritzie almost died after that Christmas Eve when
he talked to me. It was as though, without Gina, there
was no point in his living, and he just started to pine
away. I brought him back. I don't know how, exactly.
Lots of loving, I guess. But even now, five years later,
he still carries an air of melancholy. I know he hasn't
stopped missing her any more than I do. I know he
needs to talk about her, too. And maybe he does, only
I'm not able to hear him anymore.

"How long do dogs live?" I ask.

The question pops out of me during a lull in our
conversation, out of the blue, with no connection to
what's gone before. But that doesn't faze this group.
They can jump from topic to topic, helter-skelter, as
though all words are part of this one large ongoing
conversation in which no subject is inappropriate.

"I think it would depend on the breed," Jilly says.
"Holly would know."

Holly Rue has a used book store on the edge of
town. Because of this Internet-based information stor-
age program called the Wordwood that she helped to
develop, all of her friends have taken to thinking of
her almost as an oracle: if you have a question, Holly
can find the answer. Anyone with a computer and a
modem can access the Wordwood themselves, which
is where Holly gets her answers, but most of this
crowd don't own either. I've logged onto it a couple

of times, but something about the site bothers me, and I haven't pointed my web browser in its direction for a long time now.

"I think I heard somewhere," Wendy puts in, "that little ones live longer than big ones."

"Are you worried about Fritzie?" Sophie asks. "How old is he now?"

"I'm not sure. Ten or eleven, at least."

"Dogs can live a long time," Jilly assures me.

Wendy nods. "I've heard of them living until they're eighteen, or even older."

Except the clock's running out, I think. It's ticking for all of us, but it moves much faster for animals. I take a breath, put aside the practical, commonsensical Susan Ashworth these women know, and say what's really on my mind.

"I'd like to hear him talk again," I say.

This is the only group to whom I could come out with something like that and not have them laugh at me.

Jilly and Sophie exchanged glances.

"You really need to ask Holly," Sophie says.

"Or visit the Wordwood yourself," Jilly says. "You're on line, aren't you?"

I nod, unsure how to explain that something about that place spooks me. In the end I don't say anything at all.

But when I get home, I log on to my server, download my e-mail, then activate the bookmark that will take me to the Wordwood. When the home page comes up, I sit there and look for a long time at the image of a deep, old English oak forest that probably doesn't even exist in Britain anymore. Finally I type my question in the little box provided.

How can you make a dog speak?

And hit return. My cursor turns into an hourglass, and I wait for a few moments. The Wordwood works a bit like this search engine called Ask Jeeves, except instead of bringing up a page of links to other sites, it brings up links to various books and discussions that might exist on its own voluminous site. Or it asks you to clarify your question.

That's the thing that I find so eerie. No matter what the time of day or night, the Wordwood responds as though there's a person manning a keyboard, somewhere out there in its pixilated kingdom, and we're in chat mode. The words even appear on my screen as though they're being typed, the letters dropping neatly into the somewhat larger white box that has replaced the one that was first waiting for me when I arrived at the site.

>>When you say 'speak' are you referring to an actual, interactive conversation?<<

I hesitate for a moment, then type in "Yes."

>>This might take a moment.<<

I stare at the trees behind the box. They're like a video, rather than a static image—real smooth streaming, too. I swear I can see leaves moving and there's nothing jerky about their shivering movement. A sound like a breeze comes up out of my computer's speakers. I leave the site when I think I see a little figure moving in the shadows behind an enormous branch just beside the white reply box—a small shape, the size of a squirrel, or a monkey, but human. Wearing clothes.

I'm not stupid. I know it's not real. I know they can do pretty much anything with special effects these days, and the Internet's always been cutting edge. But it spooks me all the same. I can't shake the feeling that the image of that forest is a real-time video of some forest that only exists out there in whatever space it is that the World Wide Web occupies. Not the hard drives that house all those hundreds of thousands of Internet sites, but some other place that can't be measured, or weighed, or touched. A place that should be impossible to access, like the other music that lies in the silences between the notes we hear in a song. The invisible words that lie between the lines of a story or a poem.

Between, between . . .

That's where Jilly says all magic begins. In the hidden places that lie between things.

I turn off my computer and take Fritzie for a walk. That night I dream of Gina in a wood. An old oak wood like the one that was on my computer screen before I went to bed. She's no bigger than the size of my hand, sitting there on a branch, looking down at me, and she's about to tell me something very important, but my alarm goes off and I wake up.

When I get off work that day, I go home and change, stick a few dog biscuits in my pocket, and take Fritzie for a walk. He seems a little confused because we're not out as long as we normally are, but he perks right up when I take him to the car instead of back inside. I wish it was that easy for me.

I wasn't joking when I said if I was the eighth dwarf I'd be called Tired. I'm forever tired these days, it doesn't matter how much sleep I get. There's always too much to do at the office, where downsizing only means that people keep getting laid off and their workload is divided up between those of us still left, like we weren't already overworked. It's impossible to get any sense of accomplishment because nothing ever seems to actually get completed.

Jilly keeps saying I should simply quit and go back to doing fine art like I did when we first met— "You were *so* good," she'd say. But even then, it was a hobby for me, not a vocation. She doesn't really understand that while I might have retained my motor skills as an artist—I still do some hands-on art at work, for all the endless meetings my department head insists upon—I don't seem to have the heart of an artist anymore. I can appreciate. But I can't create. At least not anything outside the realm of architectural drawings.

Fritzie doesn't have to think about those kinds of things.

"Do you know where we're going?" I ask him as I open the passenger door for him. "To visit Snippet."

He gives me a grin, tongue lolling. Maybe he recognizes the name of Holly's little Jack Russell, maybe it's just because we're together and going for a drive. Life's simple for a dog.

I don't really know Holly that well myself. She has a used bookstore up in the north end of the city. It's not an area where I normally go on my own, but I'm forever giving rides to Christy and Jilly and the others, so I guess we've become something more than acquaintances over the years. And Fritzie and Snippet took to each other straight away. Often when I'm chauffeuring someone up to the store, I leave them with Holly and just take the dogs out for a ramble in the fields behind the store.

I'm not a book person the way she and Christy are. I'm just as happy reading whatever's new and in paperback as I am some rare old classic that hasn't been in print for thirty years. Though I do have to admit that I was quite taken with a Robert Nathan novel that Holly lent me once; so much so, in fact, that when I realized none of his books were still in print—and how could that even be, he was so amazing—I went and borrowed them from the library, one by one, until I'd read them all.

I'm thinking of Nathan's books as I pull into the small parking lot by Holly's store. Maybe I should ask her to recommend someone else to me. But first things first.

I let Fritzie out of the car. He runs to a nearby telephone pole to check his pee-mail and leave a new message of his own, then rejoins me at the front of the store. We can see Snippet in the window, muzzle pressed against the glass just under the modest store sign that reads:

HOLLY RUE, USED BOOKS

When Fritzie notices her, the two of them dance and try to touch noses through the window. I can see Holly inside, laughing at the pair of them, and I wave to her.

The store is its usual jumble. I have to admit that I find something just a little disconcerting about a retail establishment that offers up its goods in such a haphazard manner. It feels like you have to be part packrat, part spelunker, just to make your way through it all. I give Snippet and Fritzie each one of the biscuits I stuck in my pocket earlier, than make my way by a circuitous route to where Holly's sitting.

She looks the way she always does, red hair held back from her face with bobby pins, hazel eyes bright and welcoming, the same fashion sense as Jilly: all baggy clothes on a small trim figure.

"This must be a first," Holly says. "I don't think I've ever seen you up here on your own."

I take a few books from a chair and put them on one of what seems like twenty cardboard boxes full of books that are clustered around Holly's desk like livestock at a feeder.

"It's possible I've gone all literary on my own, isn't it?" I say as I sit down.

"Eminently so," she assures me.

"But not true," I tell her. "I've just come to pick your brain instead."

Holly's eyebrows rise in a question. I have to gather my courage—this isn't Jilly or the others I'm talking to now.

"I was wondering," I say, talking quickly to get it all out before I lose my nerve, "if you could check in the Wordwood to see if there's a way to make a dog talk."

"You mean bark?"

I shake my head. "No. I mean to really be able to communicate with them. Share a conversation."

Holly smiles.

"I'm serious," I say.

"I wasn't making fun of you," she tells me. "Or if I was, I was making fun of both of us, because I've already looked it up for myself."

It takes a moment for that to register.

"What did you find?" I finally ask.

Holly shrugs. "Nothing terribly useful. The most effective method seems to be to get the Welsh goddess Cerridwen to let you stir her cauldron and then sneak a few drops of the magical brew when she's not looking."

I just look at her.

"Well, apparently it worked for Taliesin," she says.

"He was able to immediately understand the language of birds and animals after one taste."

"A Welsh goddess . . ."

"I know. You won't exactly find one setting up shop at the local mall . . . or even in the Market. One of my own favorite bits of animal lore comes from *The Book of Bright Secrets* by A.S. Ison. She says that if you look between a dog or cat's ears, you can see what they're seeing—not just what's in front of them, but those mysterious things that only they can see."

I know what she means. Fritzie can sometimes spend a half hour or longer, simply staring at a corner of the room, like there's a window to a whole other world hidden there.

"And then there's Christy," Holly goes on. "In one of his books he talks about this idea that if you put your forehead against that of a cat or a dog and lock gazes with them, you can see what they've seen."

"Have you ever tried any of these things?" I find myself asking.

Holly smiles. "I haven't run into Cerridwen yet, but yes on both counts to the other two. All I got for my trouble was one very happy dog and a face full of licks."

"So they didn't work."

"They didn't work for me," Holly says. "Maybe I'm just not magical enough."

If you have to have magic to make them work, then I'm really out of luck.

"There was a whole bunch of other stuff in the Wordwood," Holly goes on, "none of which struck me as having any more practical application than the ones we've already talked about. But you could look them up. Are you online? I can give you the Wordwood's URL if you like."

"I've already got it bookmarked."

Holly waits for a long moment, then says, "But visiting the site makes you uncomfortable."

"How did you know that?"

She shrugs. "People either fall in love with it, or get spooked—though most of the ones who do get spooked would probably never admit that, even to themselves. They'll just convince themselves it's too boring to revisit."

"So there *is* something weird about it."

"There's something weird about everything," Holly says, sounding like Jilly.

"Do you believe in magic?" I have to ask.

"I think so. I believe in something. There's too much anecdotal evidence to discount the idea that there's more to the world than what we can see. I believe that there's *always* been more, but each generation categorizes it a little differently."

"How so?"

"I correspond with this fellow in Arizona named Richard Kunz," Holly says, "and he has a really interesting take on all of this. He thinks that the detonation of the first atom bomb forever changed the way that magic would appear in the world. That the spirits live in the wires now instead of the trees. They live and travel through phone and modem lines, take up residence in computers and appliances, and live on electricity and lord knows what else. How else do you explain the spooky ways computers act sometimes?"

"So the Wordwood . . .?"

My question trails off because I'm not even sure what it is that I want to ask.

"We started the Wordwood simply as a digital storehouse of knowledge," Holly says. "An electronic library of all the world's books. But then we started noticing texts appearing in it that none of us had entered and its URL no longer led to a hard drive with a physical address. The spirits got into it and now it's something else again, something we can no longer control and can't explain." There's an odd look in her eyes when she adds, "And some of those spirits have even crossed back over into our world again."

"What do you mean?" I ask.

"Do you know Christy's girlfriend, Saskia?"

I nod.

"I think she was born in the Wordwood."

"But that . . . that's impossible."

Holly nods. "So's magic."

We sit for a while, Holly with Snippet on her lap, me with Fritzie's head on mine. I think about Saskia Madding. I've only met her a few times, but there is something . . . well, luminous about her. Like a Madonna or one of the saints in a Botticelli painting. She just glows. I would never have thought magic. Charisma, yes. But maybe that's a part of magic. A glamour . . .

"You know what I'd do?" Holly says.

I pull myself up out of my thoughts to look at her and shake my head.

"I'd make my own ritual," she says.

"What do you mean?"

She straightens a couple of books on her desk, before lifting her gaze up to meet mine.

"It's just what Christy and Jilly say," she tells me. "The magic's already there. Here. All around us. To tap into it you have to really be able to focus on it— it's like what mystics do when they meditate. It's all intent and concentration. That's the whole idea behind spells and rituals. They force you to focus completely on what you're doing."

"So they don't really work," I say.

Holly shakes her head. "No, they do. But not for the reason we think they do. They work because they make us concentrate so completely that the magic has to pay attention to us. It's like communion and singing hymns in church. People really do get closer to God because they're focusing on these rituals and no longer listening to that constant dialogue that goes on inside their heads."

"I wouldn't know how to make up a ritual," I tell her.

She smiles. "Me, neither. But it sounds good in theory, doesn't it?"

That night I give it a try, making it up as I go. Fritzie follows me from room to room as I gather up candles and herbs and whatever else I can think of and bring them all into the dining room. I turn off all the lights and sit in the dark for a few moments before I light the candles. I burn some piñon incense. I paint symbols on a clay platter from a mixture I've made up of red wine, spit, and flower pollen. I have an old Tangerine Dream album playing at low volume on the stereo. I write the words, "I want to hear Fritzie talk," on a slip of rose-colored paper, then cut it up into tiny pieces and burn it on the platter with pinches of herbs. Anise. Thyme. Cilantro. Mint.

The odd thing is, the more I get into it, the more I feel it's actually going to work. I can feel something, like the charge in the air before a big storm.

Be patient, I tell myself. Focus. Believe.

I sit there for a long time, taking in the acrid smell of burning paper and dried herbs as it mixes with the piñon.

Then I have to laugh at myself.

"So what do you think, boy?" I ask Fritzie. "Is any of this making you feel talkative?"

He comes over and licks my hand.

"Yeah, I thought about as much."

I turn on the overhead and put everything away. I don't know why I thought it would work in the first place. It's weird the things we'll do for hope.

Before I go to bed, I check my e-mail. I delete the messages as I read them, reply to a couple. Then I find this one:

```
Date: Wed, 08 Jun 1999 17:55:42-0700
From: Webmaster@TheWordwood.com
To: SueAsh@cybercare.com
Subject: Your question

Why do you want to speak to your dog?


The Wordwood
http://www.TheWordwood.com/
```

I stare at it, my cursor arrow hovering on the link to the site, but I don't click my mouse to take me there. After a long moment I remember to breathe. I close my e-mail reader and turn off the computer.

It's late and I should get to bed. Instead I go out and sit on the balcony, Fritzie lying at my feet. I stare out at the darkened city and have no idea what I'm thinking about. I just sit there, waiting for morning.

Remember when I said that Sophie is a fairy tale? It's this theory that Jilly has. She says Sophie has fairy blood, but Sophie only smiles when the topic comes up, so who knows what she really thinks. But Sophie does have these fascinating serial dreams that, if you were given to believing in parallel worlds and the like, would certainly lend credence to the theory. She has this whole other life, apparently, over there in her dream world, but the strange thing is that she says she's met people here, in what Christy calls the World As It Is, that know her from her dreams.

It's not a traditional fairy tale, but then, Jilly says, it's not supposed to be. And we're still in the middle of it, so it's hard to say how it will all turn out.

Do I believe it's true? Of course not. But when I've had a glass or two of wine, and Jilly's there pumping Sophie for the latest installment of her dream serial, and Sophie's describing these wonderful things, all so matter-of-factly, like how her boyfriend there is this guy named Jeck who can turn into a crow, or this wonderful shop where you can buy all the books and paintings that never got made in our world, somehow it all does make a certain kind of lopsided sense. And I realize that whether or not it's true isn't what's important; what's important is that we have the story.

Because, getting back to Robert Nathan's books for a moment, there's this bit in *The Elixir* where he says that the difference between man and animals isn't that we have thumbs, but that we have fairy tales. Everything has a history, even the rocks and trees. But we have legends and dreams that weave into one another. We're part of them, and they're part of us. The trees have history, but they have no legends.

I think of it all as a metaphor for imagination, but I want it to be real. I want the reason that mechanical objects don't work properly around Sophie—her wristwatch running backwards, Christy's computer crashing when she tries to use it, her radio bringing in signals from Australia when it's tuned to a local

frequency—to have a magical rather than a biochemi-
cal explanation.

So the next morning, as soon as the hour's decent,
I take Fritzie out for his morning constitutional and
follow a meandering path that leads us to the door of
Sophie's building. Because what I need now is for one
of my muses to lend me some of her imagination.

Sophie sits us out on the old sofa on her balcony
for tea and biscuits. She seems a little amused when
I tell her why we've come—not amused at me; more
amused at the idea of her fairy blood, the way she
always is, but not denying it either.

"I can't do anything here," she says after a long
pause. "But maybe in Mabon you can find someone
who can help you." She smiles. "Since it exists because of magic, somebody there should know how to
make an enchantment work."

Mabon is the name of her dream city. Fritzie seems
to pick up his ears when she mentions it.

"Can you take us there?" I ask, but then I think of
how often Jilly's asked the same question.

Sophie shakes her head. "People seem to have to
find their own way," she says. "I don't think it's a rule
so much as just the way it works."

"Find my own way," I repeat.

"Have you ever tried lucid dreaming?" she asks.

"I wouldn't know where to start."

"You have to picture the place you want to be when
you start to dream," she says.

I sigh. More of this focus/centering oneself business.

"But I've never been there before," I tell her.

How could I? The place doesn't exist except in Sophie's dreams.

But she smiles and gets up. When she returns
from inside, she's carrying a small ink drawing of

an old-fashioned storefront. The leaded windows are crammed full of books and above the door a sign reads:

MR. TRUEPENNY'S BOOK
EMPORIUM AND GALLERY

"Try using this," she says as she gives it to me. "That's where it all started for me."

When I get home I put the drawing beside my bed. I called in sick before I went out this morning, but I'm feeling too guilty to take the whole day off. There are so many projects on the go at the moment and if I'm not there it just means everybody else has to work that much harder. So I change into my office clothes, send this e-mail:

```
Date: Wed, 09 Jun 1999 11:49:34-0400
From: SueAsh@cybercare.com
To: Webmaster@TheWordwood.com
Subject: Re: Your question

>Why do you want to speak to your dog?

Because he used to live with my best friend before
she died and I want to talk to him about her.
```

And go to work.

There's no reply from the Wordwood when I return to the apartment that evening. Fritzie and I go for a long walk after supper. I do a little work on some files I brought home from the office, then try to watch some TV, but I can't concentrate. I keep thinking of the drawing that Sophie gave me, of lucid dreaming and the possibility that it might actually take me into Mabon—in the sense of my dreaming I'm there, of course. Finally I have a bath to try to get rid of some of the day's tension, but it doesn't really help. When I finally go to bed, Fritzie curled up on the end where he usually sleeps, I can't stop thinking.

I lie awake for hours until finally I get up and check my e-mail again. Still nothing from the Wordwood.

When I finally fall asleep, it's almost four in the morning and the next thing I know my alarm's going off. I drag myself out of bed, walk Fritzie, then hurry off to work. Getting home, I find this waiting for me:

Date: Wed, 10 Jun 1999 16:51:57-0400
From: Webmaster@TheWordwood.com
To: SueAsh@cybercare.com
Subject: Re: Your question

>I want to talk to him about her.

Perhaps he simply has nothing he wants to say.

The Wordwood
http://www.TheWordwood.com/

"Is that true?" I ask Fritzie.

It's not something I ever considered. That maybe he can talk; he just doesn't want to.

Fritzie cocks his head like a curious crow. He knows I'm asking him something, but since I'm not using his primary vocabulary—"Hungry," "Walk," "Get the ball"—he can't do anything except wag his tail and look at me. So scratch that theory, Mr. Webmaster.

I try the lucid dreaming again that night, fixing the

image from Sophie's drawing firmly in my mind before I go to bed, but I'm so tired that I drop off like I've been drugged. If I have any dreams, I don't remember them.

I think maybe the intense focus everybody's telling me about isn't the way to go with this. Maybe magic can only be approached from the side. Maybe it wants you to slip up on it like an image will appear in the corner of your eye.

I'm thinking this because I have no luck the next night either. On the fourth, I don't even think about it. Fritzie and I stay up to watch the news, then go to bed after Leno's monologue and the next thing I know we're standing on a cobblestoned street looking at the physical counterpart to the bookshop in Sophie's drawing. By the light, it seems to be late afternoon. There are people around us, window-shopping, or simply out walking. They're of all sorts—from Bohemians to those dressed for the office—and of all nationalities. No one pays any attention to the fact that I simply popped into existence here, though one little girl across the street gives me a happy wave with her free hand, the other held fast in her mother's.

I wave back, then study my surroundings a little more.

What surprises me the most isn't that it worked, that I've dreamed my way into Sophie's city, or at least my own version of it, but that Fritzie's here with me. he looks at me, grinning, tail slapping the cobblestones. I expect him to say something—after all, we're in a dream now; we're in this magical city—but he only gives me that "test the limits" look animals get, then gets up and casually walks over to the nearest lamppost to give it a sniff, checking over his shoulder to see if I'm going to call him back.

As he lifts his leg, I turn away and study the signs on the other shops that line the street. Halfway down the block, on the other side of the street, I spy a sign that reads:

KERRY'S CAULDRON
HOPES MET, DREAMS FULFILLED

I remember the story Holly told me about the Welsh goddess and her magical cauldron. Kerry is close enough to Cerridwen, so far as I'm concerned. And anyway, this is my dream, isn't it? If I want there to be a shop here with a magical solution waiting for me in it, then why shouldn't it simply be here as needed?

I call Fritzie, and he trots along at my side as I cross the street. The lack of motorized vehicles reminds me of the Market area back home, but I can hear traffic, cars and buses, one or two blocks away. A bell tinkles when I enter the shop, and my eyes have to adjust to the dim lighting. It's like an old-fashioned apothecary inside and has a bewildering smell: herbal, but like a garden, too, and underneath it all, something wild. There are shelves and shelves of bottles holding all sorts of powders and dried herbs, each neatly identified with small, handwritten labels. Bunches of herbs hang from the ceiling behind the long wooden counter with its glass top and sides. I spy boxes of candles, mortar and pestles, sacks and little boxes of oddly-named teas, innumerable packages and pouches with labels in no language I can recognize.

A lace curtain behind the counter is pulled aside and a tall, dark-haired woman steps out from behind it. She looks a bit like a Gypsy—or at least my roman-ticized image of one: dark complexion, white blouse, flower-print skirt, long black hair spilling in loose tan-gles from under a red kerchief. Her gaze goes to Fritzie who's sniffing a barrel by the window with great interest.

"Oh, I'm sorry," I say. "I never thought to ask if he could come in. Come here, Fritzie," I add, hoping he doesn't decide to pee on the barrel.

She smiles. "True dreamers are always welcome here."

I don't know what to say to that. Does she mean me or Fritzie?

"How can I help you?" she adds.

That I can answer. It's why I'm here, after all.

"Hmm," is all she says once I've explained.

Then she lifts a lovely paisley scarf off of what I realize is a notebook computer and starts it up.

"What are you doing?" I ask.

"I don't know that spell," she tells me, "so I need to look up the recipe in the Wordwood."

"You're kidding me, right?"

Bad enough a database is sending me e-mail. Why does it have to be in my dream as well?

She looks puzzled. "Why would you think that?"

"I don't want it here," I say.

"You don't—?"

I'm feeling like a petulant child, but I can't seem to stop myself.

"It's my dream," I tell her, "and I don't want that . . . that whatever it is in it with me."

She gives me a long look, and then that smile re-turns. "This is your first visit to Mabon, isn't it?"

I nod.

"I thought so," she goes on. "Did you get here by accident, or did someone show you the way?"

"Someone showed me. But—"

"Well, the first thing you need to know is that you're not dreaming. It's true that Mabon exists because Sophie Etoile first brought it into being, but it's taken on a life of its own since then."

"You know Sophie?"

"Do you know the founders of the country you come from?" She doesn't wait for my answer. "The point is, that Mabon and our life here in the city goes on, whether you're visiting us or not."

"But the Wordwood—how can you access it here?"

"How can we not? The site's stored in the computers that are housed in the basement of the university library."

I suppose, in some ways, that explains a lot, but I'm still not comfortable with the idea of the Wordwood being here as well. Before the woman can access its site, I tell her that I've changed my mind. I call to Fritzie, and he follows me back out onto the street— somewhat reluctantly, I think, until his ears suddenly prick up. I turn to see what's caught his attention and can't believe who I see coming down the street towards us.

"I was just thinking of you," Gina says as she draws closer.

She looks the same as always, thin features, tall, rangy frame. She's dressed in jeans and a T-shirt, a black cotton jacket overtop, wearing those crazy red-and-yellow cowboy boots that she always loved. Her dark curls spill out from under a wide-brimmed hat. Bending down, she accepts Fritzie's wet kisses and lifts her face to me, smiling under the brim of her hat. I see the difference then. That haunted look I remember always being in her eyes those last few years isn't present.

"Are you a . . . ghost?" I ask.

She laughs. "Are you?"

"No, but I'm not . . ."

"Dead," she finishes for me when my voice trails off.

She sits down on the curb, and Fritzie half crawls onto her lap, tail slapping the cobblestones. After a moment I sit down beside them.

"I guess it is confusing," Gina adds.

She turns to look at me, her eyes merry. I can't remember the last time I saw her genuinely happy. She was so sad, for so long.

"So . . . do you live here?" I ask her.

She has to think about that for a moment. "I think so. I think someone needed to see me so badly that they dreamed me into being here."

Me, I think. Only then I look at Fritzie, wriggling on her lap as she pats him. I remember what the woman in the store said when I asked if it was okay for him to be inside. Something about true dreamers always being welcome. I realize that I didn't bring Fritzie here with me; he brought me.

"Did Fritzie ever talk to you?" I ask her. There are a hundred things I want to ask her, but this is what comes out.

She smiles and shakes her head. "But he's a good listener. Aren't you, my brave little boy?"

"I don't understand any of this," I say.

"That's probably a step in the right direction," Gina tells me.

"What's that supposed to mean?"

"Well, you know how you like to make sure everything fits in its proper little box."

"I don't."

She ignores me because we both know it's true. "I think it's better to believe in what you don't know. What you don't know encompasses everything. Embrace it and you embrace the mystery of the world, of the whole universe. It brings you closer to the great spirit that made everything and to which everything returns when its time is done."

I guess being here in dreamland is why that actually seems to make sense.

"What's it like?" I ask her. "The place where we go when we die?"

She gives a slow shake of her head. "I don't really know. I think I'm there and here at the same time and the me that's here isn't privy to everything the me that's there knows."

"Fritzie brought you here," I say.

"I know."

After that we don't talk so much—or at least not about anything important. We go wandering through Sophie's dream city like children on a holiday, curious about everything, unconcerned with the world where things fit into a box and make sense. We're just being pals, the way we were before the world turned dark on Gina and I started figuring out what fit in which box and made sure it stayed that way.

When I finally wake up, I find that Fritzie has crawled from the end of the bed to lie with his head beside me on the pillow. The first thing I see when I open my eyes is the wall of my bedroom, over the top of his head, looking between his ears. I remember Mabon and Gina, like being there with her really happened. The dream seems so vivid that I have trouble focusing on where I am. This world has the dreamlike quality, not simply at this moment, when I wake, but throughout the day.

I almost quit work that day, I hate being there so much, though of course I don't. I can't. I could never leave everybody hanging like that. But I find myself doodling during the morning meeting, and later on the phone, too. Sketches of what I remember of some of the places I saw in my dream. The funny café where we had lunch—all the umbrellas had the same red and yellow pattern as Gina's boots. This odd street we followed that dwindled until it was only the narrowest of footpaths squeezed between two buildings. Fritzie having a staring contest with a cat, the old tom lying in the display window of an antique shop between a stuffed rooster and a stack of old books. And Gina, of course. The way the wind caught her hair, the crinkle of her smile, the laughter in her eyes.

They're simple sketches, but they're good, too. I can tell. The lines have character as I put them down.

That evening our walk takes Fritzie and me to Jilly's studio where she and Wendy are sitting on the sofa, taking turns reading to each other from a new fairy tale picture book loosely based on *A Midsummer Night's Dream* that's going to be published in the fall. It's something Wendy's supposed to review for *In the City,* which is why they have this advance copy of it. Wendy's particularly chuffed since she and the book's illustrator share the same first name.

Fritzie immediately makes himself comfortable on the Murphy bed which I don't think I've ever seen folded back into the wall. I pull a chair over by the sofa.

"I'm so jealous," Jilly says when I tell them my story and pull out my sketches.

I blink in surprise.

"Oh, not of these," she says, tapping the sketches

with a paint-stained nail. "Which are wonderful. I told you that you still had it, didn't I just?"

"So you're jealous because . . .?"

"That you got to go to Mabon. I've been wanting to go there for simply forever. . . ."

Wendy nods in agreement.

"But we're glad you got to go," Jilly adds.

"And at least I've got a great new story for my tree," Wendy says.

Wendy has an oak tree that she secretly planted in Fitzhenry Park and feeds with stories. I told you they were like fairy tale people. Who else would accept my story at face value?

"What was it like seeing Gina again?" Jilly asks.

"Weird," I tell her. "It's hard to explain. Mostly it was like we were just taking up from before—as though her death had never come in between. But then every once in a while I'd get this sudden, sharp ache in my heart and I'd remember. But before it could really take root, Gina would sweep it away with something outrageous or sweet or simply thoughtful."

"You're going back, right?" Wendy says.

"I'm certainly going to try."

But whatever magic let me slip up on it sideways and take me away doesn't come back. At least not for me. But I know Fritzie's making regular trips to Mabon. I guess it's not hard for him, being a true dreamer.

I finally log back on to the Wordwood site and get it to drop down a list of links on how to make a dog speak. There are well over three hundred entries, from the cauldron business that Holly told me about to this really convoluted process that wakes up the diluted animal blood many of us are supposed to have running through our veins, none of them really practical, or workable. Most of them are the kind of thing that you have to slip up on from the side, which isn't very easy for a put-things-in-their-box person like me.

Holly doesn't really seem surprised when I tell her where the Wordwood's URL leads.

"But don't you think it's amazing?" I ask her.

She grins. "Of course it's amazing. But then everything about the Wordwood is pretty much unbelievable and amazing."

"Can a person be jaded by that sort of thing?"

"I suppose," she says. "But wouldn't that be sad?"

I nod in agreement.

I don't expect Sophie to be able to help me get back to Mabon, and she can't, though it's not from a lack of desire on her part.

"I'd love to have all my friends there," she says, "but I don't make the rules." Then she laughs. "I don't even know if there are rules. I mean, why do some people see ghosts and fairies, while other people don't? Or can't?"

"Maybe some people are just gifted," I say. "Or more observant."

She grins. "I suppose. Or maybe they're crazier."

But I know what I'll do if I do get back. I'll find a travel agent and see if I can pick up the Mabon version of a rail pass, something that'll let me travel back and forth at will, the way a rail pass lets you take any train you want. I mention this to whatever the entity is that talks to me from the Wordwood. We've struck up an e-mail correspondence. The reply I get reads:

Date: Tue, 29 Jun 1999 08:10:20-0400
From: Webmaster@TheWordwood.com
To: SueAsh@cybercare.com
Subject: Re: Rail passes and boxes

Why not? It seems worth a try. And boxes and
magic aren't mutually exclusive. After all, look
at me.

The Wordwood
http://www.TheWordwood.com/

I suppose that's true. Anything can be categorized.
But then I think of what Gina told me, about embracing one's ignorance of the universe, and I think maybe
that's true as well. We can categorize what we know,
put everything into its box as it fits. But we also have
to leave our minds open to embrace the great mystery
of the world—all those things we know nothing about.
Because if we do that with an open and generous
enough heart, we might find the mystery embracing
us back.

I still miss Gina.

I heard a dog speak once.

I've been to the magical dream city of Mabon.

I'm drawing more, and that's sharpening my obser-
vational skills because when I pay attention to the
detail I can see, it reminds me about all the other
detail that I can't. At least not yet.

I think Robert Nathan was wrong about one thing.
Trees and rocks *do* have their own fairy tales and
legends. Everything does. The trouble is, we only ever
understand our own. And so long as that's all we do,
we're putting ourselves in a box that doesn't simply

categorize what we know, but also shuts us away from all we don't.

Fritzie dreams well—I can tell by the way his tail beats against the comforter when he's sleeping. Maybe tonight I'll lie down beside him. We'll be like a couple of spoons and my dreaming eyes will see how the world looks when viewed from between his ears.

THE CATFANTASTIC ANTHOLOGIES
Edited by Andre Norton and Martin H. Greenberg

FANTASY ANTHOLOGIES

Don't Miss These Exciting DAW Anthologies

Irene Radford
Merlin's Descendants